THE ADVENTURE OF THE MURDERED MIDWIFE

The Early Case Files of Sherlock Holmes
Case One

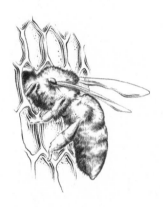

Liese Sherwood-Fabre

978-0-9984112-9-3

EARLY PRAISE FOR "THE ADVENTURE OF THE MURDERED MIDWIFE"

The Adventure of the Murdered Midwife is a great nod to classic Sherlock Holmes. Liese Sherwood-Fabre paints a vivid picture and transports you back in time, in what I'm sure will become a bestseller. Fans of Sherlock Holmes will love this new take and appreciate [Liese's] attention to detail.

A classic in the making!

—Gemma Halliday, *New York Times* and *USA Today*
Bestselling Author

[Dr.] Sherwood-Fabre's attention to detail and vivid prose are on full display in this delightful look at the evolution of a young Sherlock Holmes.

—Book Life Prize

To Angelo and Izabella

CHAPTER ONE

They told me the Battle of Waterloo was won on the playing fields of Eton, and I knew I should have been honored to be at the institution; but at age thirteen, I hated it. The whole bloody place. I remained only because my parents' disappointment would have been too great a disgrace to bear.

My aversion culminated about a month after my arrival when I was forced into a boxing match on the school's verdant side lawn. I had just landed a blow to Charles Fitzsimmons's nose, causing blood to pour from both nostrils, when the boys crowding around us parted. One of the six-form prefects joined us in the circle's center.

After glancing first at Fitzsimmons, he said to me, "Sherlock Holmes, you're wanted in the Head Master's office. Come along."

Even though I'd been at the school only a few weeks, I knew no one was called to the director's office unless something was terribly wrong. I hesitated, blinking at the young man in his stiff collar and black suit. He flapped his arms to mark his impatience at my delay and spun about on his heel, marching toward the college's main building. I gulped, gathered my things, and followed him at a pace that left me puffing to keep up.

I had no idea what caused such a summons. If it had been the fight, surely Charles would have accompanied me. I hadn't experienced any controversies in any of my classes, even with my mathematics instructor. True, earlier in the day I'd corrected him, but surely it made sense to point out his mistake? For the most part, the masters seemed pleased with my answers when they called on me.

I did have problems, however, with most of my classmates—Charles Fitzsimmons was just one example. Except he was the one who'd called me out. Surely, *that* couldn't be the basis of this summons?

Once inside, my sight adjusted slowly to the dark, cool interior, and I could distinguish the stern-faced portraits of past college administrators, masters, and students lining the hallway. As I passed them, I could feel their judgmental stares bearing down on me, and so I focused on the prefect's back, glancing neither right nor left at these long-dead critics. A cold sweat beaded on my upper lip as I felt certain something very grave had occurred, with me at the center of the catastrophe. Reaching the Head Master's office, I found myself unable to work the door's latch, and with an exasperated sigh, the prefect opened it for me and left me to enter on a pair of rather shaky knees.

My agitation deepened when I entered and found the director examining a letter with my father's seal clearly visible. He glanced up from the paper with the same severe expression I'd observed in his predecessors' portraits. Dismissing his appraisal, I concentrated on the details I gathered from the missive in his hand.

Taking a position on an expansive oriental carpet in front of his massive wooden desk, I drew in my breath and asked, "What happened to my mother?"

"How did you know this involves your mother?" he asked, pulling back his chin.

"The letter. That's my father's seal." My words gathered speed as I continued. "It doesn't bear a black border, which means at least at this point no death is involved. My father's hand is steady enough to write, so he must be well, that leaves only some problem with my mother."

The man raised his eyebrows at my response, then glanced at the letter in his hand before tossing it onto the desk's polished surface. "As you have surmised, a problem at home requires your return. Your father has requested that we arrange for you and your things to be sent to the rail station. Your brother will be arriving from Oxford to accompany you the rest of the way."

My heart squeezed in my chest, dread rushing through my body. Home. Underbyrne, the family estate. And not just for a short visit. Packing all my things meant I was leaving for the remainder of the term. Something terribly wrong had happened. Grievous enough to pull Mycroft out of his third year of studies at Oxford. Blood *whooshed* in my ears, and I barely heard what followed.

"I've already requested Mrs. Whittlespoon to assist you in your packing." Head Master turned his attention to the rest of the mail on his desk. He glanced up to add, "She'll be in your room already."

"Thank you, sir. Good day, sir." I recovered enough to respond to his statement, but not to ask the reason behind Father's directive.

With a wave of his hand, I was dismissed before I could inquire. As I closed the door behind me, I heard him mutter, "As much a prig as his brother."

For a moment, I considered opening the door and requesting more information about his assessment as well as what else my father had provided in his letter, but social convention restrained me from questioning an elder—and the Head Master at that. I was left to ponder my unspoken concerns as I returned to my chamber.

By the time I arrived at my room, my trunk had already been brought down from storage, and Mrs. Whittlespoon, the house dame, was placing my belongings in it.

"There you are, dearie." She pointed to a set of clothing on my bed. "You go change into your traveling clothes while I finish this up."

I paused, considering for a moment to ask her what she

knew of the events surrounding my departure, but she had turned her attention to the drawer with my undergarments. Having lost the opportunity for the moment, I retrieved the clothes and carried them to the bathing facilities.

Since the Head Master was not forthcoming, and Mrs. Whittlespoon might have only limited knowledge, my best hope for additional information as to what had occurred with Mother would be Mycroft—if he was in the mood to share. Knowing my brother, he might not be inclined to discuss this or any other matter on the journey home. He'd been overjoyed to return to university after the summer's break and pulling him out would definitely sour his mood.

Mrs. Whittlespoon turned to me when I re-entered the room and placed both her hands on my shoulders for a moment to scrutinize my appearance.

"You look a right proper young gentleman." She smoothed out the sleeves of my coat. "You go on down to the carriage, now. I'll finish up here and have Jarvis take the trunk down to the carriage. I assume you'll want to carry *that* yourself."

She waved her hand at my violin case lying on the bed. A wave of guilt swept over me. At my mother's insistence, I'd begun lessons two years before and developed some skill on the instrument. Since entering Eton I hadn't found the time to practice as promised. How could I report such a failure to her? I swallowed as my next thought rose, unbidden. Assuming, of course, she was in a position to ask—or understand—my answer.

No sooner had I taken a seat in the awaiting carriage, resting the violin case on my lap, than a loud clomping at the dormitory door announced the arrival of my trunk. The handyman's back bent low, and he knees splayed outward. The driver helped him take it the final yards to the rear of the carriage with Mrs. Whittlespoon following behind, shouting orders all the way.

"Mind how you secure it. I didn't spend all that time laying things neatly just so—here now, watch that strap."

The vehicle rocked as the trunk was fastened on. When the movement ceased, Mrs. Whittlespoon stuck her head in the window and passed me a small basket. "Something in case you get hungry on the way."

I bobbed my head. "Thank you. It's quite kind of you."

Before either of us could say more, the driver gave a shout, and the house dame stepped back only a second prior to the carriage jerking forward.

Throughout the trip to the station, I turned over in my mind what little I had gleaned from my exchange with the Head Master. I had assumed the issue lay with her health— although I knew her to be quite hale for a woman of forty-six. What other situation would cause my father to pull both his sons out of school? Scandal possibly. Although, she came from a good family with a stalwart reputation, and my mother was by nature a moral upright person. The most shocking character on either side of her parentage was my grandmother, the sister of Horace Vernet, the artist. Being French and having the patronage of Napoleon III certainly raised eyebrows in some corners, but that would hardly create a scandal worthy of removing Mycroft and myself from school.

The basket Mrs. Whittlespoon had given me bumped my elbow. To distract myself from the thoughts swirling about my head, I took the opportunity to check its contents. A small apple, two thick slices of bread, and a medium wedge of cheese. I found the thought of food unsettling and closed the basket.

Soon after the driver deposited me and my trunk on the station platform, a train pulled in spewing a cloud of smoke and dust. I spotted my brother leaning from the window of a first-class compartment at the rear of the train. He pointed to a man pushing a cart toward me, and once free of my baggage, I joined him.

My brother and father were "cut from the same cloth"—as they say—with thick waists and high foreheads. One had only to examine my father to know how Mycroft would appear thirty years hence. The exception being the eyes. Not in color, but in sharpness. My father's lacked the keen intellect apparent in my brother's. While Father was quite an accomplished man—as a squire he served as a justice of the peace and was versed in many subjects, especially entomology—Mycroft's intensity marked him as our progenitor's intellectual superior.

That keenness also gave him little patience with others.

LIESE SHERWOOD-FABRE

Despite being my only sibling, I was never truly comfortable around him. With rare exceptions, I guarded my words and actions carefully in his presence, knowing they would be weighed, and mostly likely found lacking in some aspect. For that reason, when he indicated I should sit in the tufted, blue seat opposite him in the compartment, I didn't argue. He had taken the backward-facing middle seat because it was less prone to the smoke and dust blown in through the window.

I plopped down on the cushion, and a small cloud of ash rose from my action, sending me into a brief coughing fit. When a small smile graced his lips, I ignored it and settled Mrs. Whittlespoon's basket next to me.

Mycroft jutted his chin at it. "What's that?"

"Mrs. Whittlespoon gave it to me. For the trip."

"What'd she give you?"

"You want it? I can't—I'm not hungry."

He took the proffered basket and studied the contents. Putting the cheese between the two slices of bread, he took a bite and caused my stomach to flip yet again. It hadn't quite settled when the train lurched forward and another wave of nausea swept over me.

To distract myself, I stared out the window at the passing countryside and summoned the nerve to ask him what had occupied me for the past several hours. "What exactly happened to Mother? I know she's not dead, but I have no information beyond that. Is she sick? Dying?"

"She's fine."

"Someone's not, or we wouldn't be called home."

No reply.

"I'm going to find out. Wouldn't it be better for me to learn it from you now, than when we arrive at Underbyrne?"

Through his cheese sandwich, he said, "You want to know, you little twit? Here it is. Mother's in gaol, accused of murder."

The force with which this pronouncement hit me was the same as if he'd given me a blow to the stomach. The queasiness I'd battled since my fight with Fitzsimmons returned with a vengeance. Bile surged into my throat. The compartment closed around me, and my deepest desire was to flee. I stood, realized there was truly nowhere to go, and dropped back down into my seat.

"Put your head between your legs."

I glanced at Mycroft, but his words sounded as if I were under water.

"Put your head between your legs."

When I remained immobile, he grabbed me by the hair and bent me over.

"Breathe," he said.

After several gulps of air, my hearing improved, and my heartbeat slowed. "You can let go now."

He sat back, and I raised my head. "Mother? Wha— How?"

"I don't know all the particulars. I gleaned it from my own analysis of the information in the papers."

He pulled part of a newspaper out of his breast pocket and passed it to me. Despite the train's movement, my original agitation subsided enough for me to read the dispatch concerning Mrs. Emma Brown having been found dead on our estate.

"Mrs. Brown, the midwife?"

Mycroft nodded. The whole village knew the thin, older woman. She'd been at the delivery of at least half the town. The other half had been seen either by Dr. Farnsworth, the village doctor, or Mr. Harvingsham, the village surgeon. As far as I knew, Mother had little contact with Mrs. Brown. Dr. Farnsworth or Mr. Harvingsham tended us during certain severe illnesses, but my mother relied mostly on her own knowledge of herbs and medicine to treat our ailments.

He then handed me another newspaper sheaf. This one was from a larger paper and included an editorial decrying the bias in some county judicial systems. In point, the author noted a recent incident of a justice of the peace's wife whom a local businessman had accused of his wife's murder and yet the woman still resided at home.

"You believe that this refers to Father?"

"How many dead bodies do you think crop up on the property of justices of the peace? Of course, it's referring to our parents, idiot. And after that editorial appeared, the constable was forced to arrest Mother and put her in gaol."

Calmed by the supplied information instead of my own dire speculations, I returned the two papers to him and contemplated this new turn of events. One didn't argue with

Mycroft or his ability to deduce specifics from the barest of details. He had exercised his ability to knit together bits of intelligence from various sources into a whole truth for as long as I'd known him. And he was seldom, if ever, proved wrong.

All the same, one glaring omission remained.

"She's innocent," I said.

"I lack enough information to make that assertion." Mycroft pulled the apple out of the basket. "You sure you don't want this?"

When I shook my head, he bit into it and then spit out what he had in his mouth. I could see the apple's brown inside from across the compartment. Had the circumstances been different, I might have found this comeuppance amusing. Instead, I found no satisfaction in the event, not being able to shift my focus from the idea of Mother as a murderess. Unable to conceive of her in those terms, I returned to my original contention that she had been unjustly accused. And I had to find out what had truly happened—which only Mother could supply.

At that moment, I resolved to find a way to visit her.

I knew where the gaol was. The old, square building sat on a corner near the edge of the village center. Did one simply knock on the door and ask to see a prisoner, as when calling upon a neighbor?

While I wanted to ask Mycroft about the process, he'd already rested his head back against his seat, his eyes closed. I tried to follow my brother's example but found myself unable to rest. I kept imagining my mother locked in a dank cell and found the only way to keep the vision away was to watch the green countryside pass by my window until dusk fell and all that remained was my own reflection staring back.

FATHER STOOD on the station platform when we arrived. He said little in greeting other than, "Simpson's waiting with the cart and the footman. Have them bring your trunks out."

Before either of us could respond, he spun about on his heel and left us to follow him.

Once on the road to Underbyrne, I considered raising the issue of visiting Mother, but knew better than to bring up the discussion in front of a servant. Even one as trusted as our steward, Mr. Simpson. The tall, thin man had been with the Holmes family since before my parents married. Given the lack of safe, conventionally acceptable topics to discuss (somehow the weather and the train ride seemed too mundane in the present situation), we rode the hour to the manor house in silence.

When we pulled up to the front door, the familiarity and *sameness* of Underbyrne held me in my seat for a moment. I saw no change in the red-brick structure with its white-framed gabled dormers on the third floor. Nothing suggested anything out of the ordinary had occurred within. Even the sight of Mrs. Simpson in her usual coffee-brown dress standing stiff-backed under the entrance's covered porch appeared normal.

Only when Father said, "Get a move on," did I stir and retrieve my violin case from beside me on the seat and follow the others inside.

"Welcome home, boys," Mrs. Simpson said. Her strained voice was the first indication of the pall over the house. "Your rooms are ready. Mr. Simpson will bring up your trunks directly. Are you hungry? I had Cook prepare plates of cold meat for you."

I shifted my feet, somehow unable to move farther into the entryway. I glanced about at the all-too-familiar surroundings, seeking some solace in them. In the candle-light, everything had a sort of gilded edge to it, giving off a sense of normalness otherwise lacking in everyone's mood. The entry hall, open to the second floor and lined with three generations of Vernet paintings and the stairway on the right leading to our bedrooms, hadn't changed. Neither had the doors leading to Father's library and office on the right or the parlor and sitting room to the left. The grandfather clock between the two rooms on the left marked the time as it always had.

I glanced at the time. That late was it?

Even the scents of wax and lemon oil said, "home," but I found myself as ill-at-ease as in a stranger's residence.

Ignoring—or perhaps unaware—of my discomfort, Father spoke to me over his shoulder as he passed on to the dining room. "Leave your case in the library before joining us."

Once I was alone with Mrs. Simpson, she held out her hand. "Pass that to me, Master Sherlock. I'll take it up to your room if you wish."

"Is my uncle about?" I asked, handing over the violin.

Her mouth turned down. "He's terribly upset about your mother, you know. He's been keeping to himself for the most part, taking his meals in his workshop. If you like, after you eat, you can take a plate to him. I'm sure he would enjoy a visit from you. Go on now and have a bit of supper. Your moth—" She stopped herself and swallowed hard. "God bless her. She'd want you to keep up your strength, so you could put on the brave face needed at a time like this."

I shifted the weight on my feet. Nothing in the many lessons my father had imparted provided me with the appropriate response for "a time like this." I knew which piece of silver to use with which course, the polite greeting for the different classes of people, and proper dinner conversation; but how did one comport oneself when one's parent faced the possibility of hanging?

Both men were already at the dining table deep in silent contemplation over their meal of cold roast beef and potatoes. I slid into my chair and stared at the thinly sliced meat and potatoes, both with a slight sheen of fat covering them. My earlier repulsion toward food returned, and a lump formed in my throat. Knowing nothing solid would make it past, I sipped the glass of milk beside it.

"Aren't you hungry?" Mycroft asked.

Father lifted his head and studied me for a moment before saying, "You need to keep up your strength, son."

I poked the meat with a fork. Bile threatened my throat again. "What do you suppose Mother is eating?"

He shook his head. "Outside of what we've provided, I suppose whatever they serve her."

"And what's that? Has she told you?"

"I haven't seen her." That statement drew stares from both me and Mycroft. He placed his fork and knife onto his plate before speaking. "It's not that I don't want to. She's forbidden it. The only one she's allowed to see her is Ernest."

"Why our uncle?" Mycroft asked.

I, too, was surprised with her choice. While her younger brother was terribly devoted to her, for all the time I'd known him, he'd actually been more reliant on her than the other way around.

My father merely shrugged. "Her instructions were explicit. I was not to try and visit her, but to send Ernest instead."

"Did she say anything about us?" I asked. "Might I visit her?"

Barely were the words out of my mouth before he responded with a sharp, "No. She said only Ernest."

I wanted to argue, but the firm set of his jaw told me not to pursue the matter further. With a final glance at my uneaten food followed by a churning in my stomach informing me to not even consider sending any of it down, I finished the glass of milk and asked, "May I be excused?"

"You're not going to eat that?" Mycroft asked.

When I shook my head, he pulled my food to his place.

I rose to head to the kitchen.

"Where are you off to?" my father asked.

"Mrs. Simpson asked me to take a plate to Uncle Ernest."

Another shift in the seat. "Very well, but don't stay too long and overtire the man."

In the kitchen, I could see Cook was already preparing a basket for me to carry to my uncle. More of the cold roast beef and potatoes, some bread and butter, and a crock that I was certain contained more milk. Ernest didn't believe in imbibing spirits.

"Finished already?" Cook asked. I nodded. "Good, then. Take this on over to your uncle. I'm sure he'd like to see you."

Another bob of the head, and I headed out the back door to the converted barn behind the house. Uncle Ernest had come to live at Underbyrne before I was born. He'd served with the military in Afghanistan, and, as Mother put it, the experience changed him. Tending to keep to himself, he tinkered there on different inventions. For the most part, his devices involved gunpowder and other explosives and new ways of using them to project items toward walls and other objects. More than once, I'd been involved in testing a prototype. Despite several attempts to interest the military in his contraptions, they had never responded to any of his correspondence.

Loud clanging greeted me about halfway through the yard. Whatever he was fashioning involved metal.

The noise masked the arrival of a woman, who startled me as she stepped from the shadows and into my path. Only because her reflexes were quicker than mine did Uncle Ernest's dinner basket not drop to the ground.

"Master Sherlock," she said in a low whisper as she handed it back to me, "I didn't mean to scare you."

"I wasn't frightened. You merely took me by surprise." Now that she was out of the shadows, I recognized her as one of the women who bought my mother's herbs. "Rachel Winston, isn't it?"

A shy smile spread across her face. "How kind of you to remember me."

How could I not? The woman, a maid at Lord Devony's estate, had been married for just over three years and had been coming to see my mother for almost as long. Always for the same thing.

"My mother's not here. Sh-she's——"

"I know. But don't you worry. I don't believe for a minute she had anything to do with Emma Brown's death. Your mother is the kindest, most generous woman I've ever met. The whole village thinks so—at least, them's who know her."

"Did you want to see my father, then?"

"No, sir. Actually, I was hoping to see you. Do you know what your mother gives me? I'm almost out and…"

Her voice trailed off and both of us glanced toward the greenhouse—my mother's refuge—at the other end of the house.

"I…uh…" How did I explain that while I helped my mother with her plants, the exact nature of their various preparations was not known to me? She had taught me the plants' properties, but I was not privy to the exact proportions or extractions for the concoctions she prepared for "the ladies," as she referred to the village women. "I'm sorry. I don't—"

Her hand flew to her mouth. "Oh, please, sir. I need those seeds. I-I can't have a baby yet." She squeezed her eyes shut and gave a stifled sob behind her hand. "Now with Mrs. Brown gone, the only one left is Mr. Harvingsham, and he won't—"

A sob cut off the rest of her thought. I glanced toward my uncle's workshop and shifted my weight from one foot to the other. Once again, my father's etiquette lessons were failing me. What did one say to a practically hysterical female?

"Please don't cry, Mrs. Winston. I'm hoping to see my mother shortly, and I'll ask her about them. Come back tomorrow night, and I'll let you know if I could determine what she gives you."

She grasped my free hand. "Thank you, sir. Thank you." After turning away from me, she stepped back into the shadows with a whispered, "I'll see you after I get off tomorrow night."

Once she had disappeared, I continued on to my uncle's workshop and knocked on the door. When he didn't respond, I let myself in.

As I stepped inside, Uncle Ernest's shout echoed through the cavernous old barn. "Duck, boy, duck!"

CHAPTER TWO

Something flew over my head and embedded itself in the doorframe as I dropped to the floor.

My uncle hurried toward me, lifting a pair of goggles to his forehead as he did so. "Good lord, my boy, are you hurt?"

I shook my head, still slightly shaken by the close call I'd had with a...I studied the object that had nearly taken off my ear. It was star-shaped with the points honed razor-sharp. Ernest reached over with a work-gloved hand and tugged at the projectile to remove it from the frame. "You should've knocked first."

"I did. You couldn't hear me over the noise," I said, finally finding my voice. "What is that exactly?"

"The Japanese call it a *hira shuriken* or 'sword in hand.' Of course I made some improvements upon it."

The *hira shuriken* finally gave to my uncle's wrenching, and he placed it flat on his palm so that I might examine it. My first observation was that it appeared even more dangerous when the whole item could be seen. "What sorts of improvements did you make?"

"Its propulsion." Ernest beamed. "Samurai warriors consider them a minor weapon to be used in conjunction with the sword. They would be thrown by hand toward the eye or hand to further injure an opponent. But I have developed a device to throw these in swift succession and greater force, making them a possible weapon of first resort."

I followed him to one of the workbenches dotting the place. Each displayed a project in some stage of assembly. His current project appeared to be a modified crossbow. Several of the star-shaped objects were lined up in a slot along the bow's central arm. He swiveled the weapon to face it away from the door.

"I'm having some trouble, however, with the trigger," he said. "The *hira shuriken* have to be propelled along the launching arm with enough force for them to travel a great enough distance. At the moment, the slightest touch on the trigger will send them off."

"What was all the banging I heard? Were you working on the trigger?"

"I was straightening the *hira shuriken*. If they were flat enough for them to fit more perfectly into the launching groove, perhaps the spring mechanism wouldn't have to be so strong and the trigger less prone to release unexpectedly.

Of course, that's not the only issue. Look at how this one bent. They can't be reused at the moment without a great deal of readjustment. I have to work that out before I can share it with my military contacts."

He dropped it onto his bench and pounded it with a mallet.

I held up the basket Mrs. Simpson had given me and shouted over the noise. "I brought you supper."

Stopping in mid-swing over the star, he contemplated the bit of information I'd provided. Accustomed to his lapses into deep thought, I waited as my mother had taught me. A moment later he let the mallet fall onto the table and turned to me. "Why, yes. I'm famished, actually. Thank you for being so kind as to bring it. Shall we have a seat and a talk?"

After he dropped his tools onto the table, we moved to his sitting area at the back of the building. Separated by a folding screen, the space was furnished with some of my parents' discarded chairs, a low table, and a cot. Ernest removed the food from the basket and arranged it on the table. After settling into one of the armchairs, he rubbed his work-blackened hands together and studied the items. "Care to join me, Sherlock?"

"No, thank you. I've already had my supper."

"You can tell me about school while I eat."

I shifted on the edge of the other armchair. I had no interest in sharing about my first few weeks at Eton, but I'd learned from our long association I had to find the right moment to broach the subject of my mother's incarceration.

Resigned, I asked, "What do you want to know?"

"Let's start with the basics," he said around a bite of roast beef. "What classes are you taking?"

"The usual, I guess. Latin, mathematics, science—"

"Science? What sort of science?"

"Biology at the moment. Plant life."

He slapped his knee. "You're probably ahead of all the others in that area. Thanks to Violette." At the mention of my mother, he quit chewing and stared at me for a moment. "She's in gaol, you know."

"Father says she's forbidden him to visit."

"It's a bit more complicated than that, I suppose. As you know, he's a justice of the peace. They've dismissed him from his duties for the moment. She's trying to avoid him having his reputation as an impartial court official being questioned. If he doesn't see her, there can be no talk of him interfering in the case. Besides, she truly worries about him seeing her in that place." Ernest nibbled on a potato he'd speared on a fork. He swallowed. "I'm her solicitor, you know."

"Have you ever practiced?"

"Not really, but Violette specifically requested me. They only allow visitors once a month, but legal counsel can come and go as often as required." He leveled his gaze at me. "And they often bring young assistants along to carry their papers. Your mother suggested I have you do just that."

My heart skipped a beat.

"I could visit Mother with you?" Another thought immediately occurred, and I frowned. "Father's said I can't see her."

He dropped the fork onto the plate and reached over to take both my hands. "My dear, dear, boy. Your mother gave me specific instructions to bring you along. She wants to see you straight away."

"What about Father?"

He screwed his mouth to one side, as if trying to remember something. "I'm afraid she didn't anticipate your father being opposed to your visiting her. But there are ways around that. In the meantime, you should just let him know you are assisting me. We simply won't mention with what."

The plan made perfect sense to me. I often assisted my uncle in his workshop. We both enjoyed tinkering, and I had learned as much about engineering and practical science from him as anything my tutors had presented.

"Besides carrying your valise, how else will I help you?"

"I guess we'll have to ask your mother. She has something in mind, I'm sure."

Something in mind.

My uncle's statement pointed out that my mother already had some design developed. To have her brother be her legal representative and me assist him meant she wanted the two of us to work together, but on what?

"If I'm going to be your aide, perhaps I should know

more about the case. Father didn't provide much information. I do know Mother found Mrs. Brown in our garden."

He nodded and shifted in his seat. "She'd gone out in the morning to pull some onions for some concoction, and there was the Brown woman, lying face-down in the dirt, the pitchfork in her back. Violette ran back to the house and called for your father. By the time he arrived, she'd removed the pitchfork and was leaning over the woman to see if she could minister to her in any way."

"Was she"—I took a deep breath before I finished my question—"dead?"

"Your mother said she was both stiff and cold," he said with a nod. "That she'd been there for a while. Your father sent Mr. Simpson into town for the coroner. He came, studied the garden, and had them take away Mrs. Brown and the pitchfork."

"She wasn't arrested right away?"

Another glance away from me. "The constable came later and asked her about an argument she and Mrs. Brown had had the day before. Her husband had reported it and insisted Violette be arrested for the murder."

"Mr. Brown is behind it all?"

He nodded. With a father who served as a justice of the peace, I had observed the workings of the parish legal system from a young age. While a constable arrested criminals, the decision to do so often depended upon the victim's or victim's family's investigation and persistence to ensure the arrest and prosecution of the accused. I'd heard of victims hiring an itinerate lawyer in some cases, but for the most part, the aggrieved party had to pursue the charges, even to the examination of witnesses in court.

"That's why your father has pushed for a special coroner's inquest."

"There's to be an inquest now? Shouldn't that have been held at the beginning?"

He shrugged. "Brown insisted the constable arrest Violette. Said it was obvious who killed his wife and wanted her put in gaol—coroner or no coroner."

"When's this special inquest?"

"Shortly. Your father saw this as the most expedient way to get her released. This quarter's assizes have already passed, and he didn't want her waiting until the next time a judge can pass through."

I stilled, considering all the information he'd shared. As a justice of the peace, Father judged less serious crimes quite regularly, but ones involving capital punishment had to wait for a visiting judge during the quarter assizes. And the next one would be *months* from now. While I contemplated the upcoming inquest, my uncle focused on his food. He speared the last bit of potato, ran it around the plate to pick up any crumbs, and popped it in his mouth.

"When are you going to see her next?" I asked as he chewed.

"I do have a lot to do...." His gaze strayed to the crossbow on the table.

I bit my tongue to squelch the angry retort rising within

me. What could be more important than my mother's arrest? I'd learned long ago, however, forcing my uncle into another direction never ended well. His concentration would still be on whatever endeavor he'd been pulled from, and his distracted nature became a hindrance rather than a help. The only way to prevent this was to return my mother's case into his main focus by involving his ability to tinker with a problem.

"You do have a sticky problem with the trigger," I said finally. "Anyway, it's too dark to see anything in the garden, but tomorrow I do want to see where they found Mrs. Brown. Do you have a magnifying glass by any chance?"

A smile spread across his face. "Of course. What size? I have quite a collection, you know."

"Can you gather them for me?" Having nudged my uncle's attention toward the true problem at hand, I allowed myself a smile as well. "They could prove handy."

Shortly after, I left my uncle at the task of collecting the magnifying glasses scattered about the workshop. He already carried at least five of various sizes in his hands and seemed to be on the hunt for more. I wasn't sure what I'd find at the site or even that I'd need the glasses, but I felt compelled to visit it. Something inside me told me it would be important—just not how.

A single candle burned on the kitchen table when I entered through the back door. Cook had obviously left it for me. I placed Ernest's now-empty basket on the table and picked up the candle to light my way. In the hallway I saw a light shining under the door of the library. After a moment's hesitation, I turned my steps to that room instead of the stairs.

Pushing open the door, I found my father sitting in his favorite armchair, his feet upon an ottoman. The scent of old cigars and lingering smoke of a new one filled my nostrils, and a wave of nostalgia swept over me. How many times had I spent time here with Mother searching for a book stored among the shelves? I shuddered at the memory and turned my focus to my father.

The light I'd seen through the doorway had been a dying fire in the grate. His head lolled to one side and rested on one of the chair's wings. A book lay opened in his lap. I picked it up and recognized it as one of his favorite illustrated tomes on insects. I marked the place and put it on the table. He rustled slightly in the chair and opened his eyes a crack.

He blinked at me as if he were trying to place me. "Sherlock, son. What are you doing up so late?"

"I was visiting with Uncle Ernest. He was telling me about Mother's case."

"Your mother…." He sighed and glanced away. In the firelight I caught the glistening in his eyes and the empty wine glass on the floor beside him. He asked the glowing embers, "Why doesn't she want to see me?"

"Maybe—" I paused. How much should I tell him of my visit with Ernest? "Maybe she doesn't want you to see her in…th-that place?"

"Perhaps. Perhaps," he said with a sigh.

"I'm going upstairs. Come up with me."

His eyes slid under his half-opened lids in my direction, and he studied me for moment. "I'm fine right here," he said finally.

"Wouldn't you prefer—?"

"I-I...can't. I'll stay here."

He closed his eyes again, and I stared at him, considering his refusal to go upstairs to bed—the one he shared with....

I understood at that moment he was avoiding sleeping alone there.

I turned to leave.

Before I could take a step, he called my name and gestured for me to come closer. As I did so, I was struck by how neat his clothes remained despite what I considered a state of inebriation. Of course, he had always impressed upon my brother and me the importance of remaining a proper gentleman regardless of the situation, which only made his statement even more disconcerting. Not so much the words as his tone and the emotion it displayed.

"I've missed you, son. Are you...are you...*good* at Eton?"

I glanced about me, selecting my words before I replied. "Things are...all right."

"It's important, you know. To go there. The contacts. *That's* what you are making at school. You'll find them essential later."

As much as I longed to share with him that the contacts

I'd made with the other boys up to this point had been primarily in the form of punches, I simply responded, "Yes, sir."

"I do hope we'll be able to send you back shortly. As soon as this mess with your mother is over." He fixed his gaze on me. "You do think Ernest will be able to help her?"

"Mother has faith in him."

"I've never known her intuition to be wrong," he said with a sigh. "*I* was the one to push for the special inquest on Friday. That Brown man. He insisted your mother's a murderess and got the constable involved. Then he got me dismissed from my duties." Another sigh. "I just want her home."

I tightened and loosened my fists.

"Yes, sir."

"You best get to bed, son," he said and patted my arm.

On the way up the stairs, I stopped as the full import of the conversation hit me. Once Mother was found innocent and released from gaol, no reason existed to keep me from returning to Eton. My heart raced at my next thought. If, however, she stayed imprisoned, I could continue at Underbyrne. I shook my head to dislodge even the contemplation of such an outcome. My mother's future was more important than any torment I might experience at Eton. I would certainly undergo even worse for her freedom.

My focus had to remain on absolving my mother.

I finished my ascent but paused at the second-floor landing to glance in the direction of my parents' room.

Once again, an awkward pain filled me—similar to a toothache that may abate only to return with a vengeance. I swallowed hard and continued in the opposite direction to my room.

Mrs. Simpson had seen to the unpacking of my school things and one of the maids had turned down my bed. I set the candle on the nightstand and changed into my bedclothes. No sooner had I crawled into bed than Mycroft appeared in my doorway. "Been with Uncle Ernest all this time? What did he have to say?"

"I'm to be his assistant and help him in preparing for the hearing," I said, having decided not to share my conversation with Father. "But mostly he talked about his new invention. A cross-bow that shoots *hira shuriken.*"

"Ah, the Japanese 'sword in hand.'" That Mycroft knew of the weapon didn't surprise me. His knowledge was quite encompassing.

"I plan to visit the garden in the morning. Why don't you come with me?"

The silhouette in the doorway shook its head. "Too many extraneous bits of information. Simply report back to me what you find that seems pertinent."

"All right." I yawned, suddenly exhausted from all that had happened that day. "Good night, Mycroft."

"Good night." He turned and shut the door again.

I pulled the covers close and lay back in the bed, staring at the shadows on the ceiling and contemplating my brief conversation with Mycroft. For most of my life, he'd ignored me. When he did direct his attention to me, it was usually to criticize me—either for my lack of knowledge or naiveté.

For the first time, I realized I now served a purpose—to bring him information, similar to what he would glean from the papers. An interesting turn in our relationship. I held the upper hand, and a desire to capitalize on it tempted me to dress and head to the garden immediately. Only the reasonable half of my brain told me to wait until morning when the light would allow proper examination.

My attention was directed to the other side of the room when moonlight broke through the clouds and spotlighted my violin case. My fingers itched to pull the instrument out and practice the last piece I'd been working on with my mother. Accomplished on the pianoforte, Mother had worked with me on a duet, and one of my last promises to her when I'd left for Eton was that I would have it perfected by the Christmas holidays. My roommates had not appreciated my efforts and so after the first week, I'd dropped my practicing. I now vowed I would rehearse at least an hour a day so that when my mother was released from gaol, I would be able to complete my promise.

I fell asleep reviewing the musical score and my fingering.

It seemed I had barely gone to sleep when someone shook

me. I opened my eyes a crack to find Uncle Ernest leaning over me.

"Time to dress and be on our way," he said in a low whisper.

"To where?" I checked out the window. The sky might be brightening slightly, but it was still very early—even in comparison to morning rising in Eton. "It's still too dark to examine the garden."

"The gar— Didn't I tell you we are going to visit your mother this morning? I promised her I would bring you as soon as I could after your arrival."

"Why so early?"

"The best time to see her alone. Besides, that way I can bring her and the staff breakfast. Bringing food to all of them allows us a little time alone. Your mother's idea. Get dressed and come down to the kitchen. Cook should have it all prepared."

With that instruction, he left me to complete my toilette, and I joined him in the kitchen where Cook was putting the finishing touches on another basket when I entered. The aroma of spice and tea caused my stomach to growl. Ernest treated the prison staff well if he was providing them with Cook's cinnamon buns. I must have appeared hungry, because the moment she saw me, she pointed to a plate on the table. "Don't you worry, Master Sherlock. I saved one for you."

Before the sentence was even completed, I was at the table and lifting the still-warm bun to my lips.

I was licking my fingers by the time she pounded a cork into a crock.

"The tea should still be warm by the time you get to the gaol," she told Uncle Ernest and then turned to me. She passed me a slice of bread. "Save this for later."

Ernest barely gave me time to stuff the slice into my coat pocket before he ran his arms through the basket's handles and lifted it from the table. Cocking his head to an item on the floor, he said, "Time to be my assistant. Carry my valise to the carriage."

I grabbed the case's handles and followed him out the door to Mr. Simpson and a waiting carriage.

Once inside, Ernest leaned his head back onto the seat and pulled his hat over his eyes. "Let me know when we get to town."

His snoring commenced shortly after we turned onto the main road. I tried to follow his example but was too tightly wound to sleep, despite the early hour. My mind kept shifting from elation to dread. I was on my way to see my mother. In gaol.

The carriage jerked to a halt an hour later, and Ernest roused himself in mid-snore. Eyeing me, he asked, "There already? Come along then."

When we stepped up the stairs into the square brick building housing the county's criminals, a guard opened the main door and waved us in.

"Quite a brisk morning, eh, Mr. Parker? Who's this with you?"

"My assistant."

The guard eyed me for a moment before turning his attention back to my uncle. I had learned a long time ago because of my age, no one paid much attention to me, and it was the same in this situation. A moment, later, however, I understood his true interest in my uncle.

"The weather's turning. I can feel it in my bones. Mornings like this, a man could use a bit of a nip to keep off the chill."

"Quite right, quite right," Ernest replied and slipped a small bottle out of his coat pocket and into that of the guard's. "For medicinal purposes."

The man placed a finger on the side of his nose with a nod. "Let's step inside so's I can inspect what you're carrying."

With a deep breath, I hefted my uncle's valise a little higher and entered a gaol for the first time. In later years, I had many an occasion to visit any number of prisons to interview criminals and the accused, but as with most major events, the first one is generally the most memorable. To this day, the right brew of odors—sweat, dust, urine, and mold—will draw me back to that tiny antechamber where Ernest set his basket on a rickety rectangle of a table and motioned me to do the same. With the first whiff, I can still see the green mold in the intersection between the room's brick walls and stone floor and hear the distant plink of dripping water and far-off moans of the prison's inhabitants. Immediately, my palms dampen and the same despair and melancholy settles about me as on that day.

Ernest, for whatever reason, appeared not to be affected at all by the surroundings, perhaps because he had already experienced them and grown used to them. He and the guard joked and chuckled while they pulled some sliced ham, thick bread, and butter from the basket as his share of the breakfast offering. The man even produced a tin cup from somewhere for his portion of the still-warm tea in the carefully wrapped crock and added a dollop of something from a flask he pulled from his pocket.

Once provisioned, the guard opened a door at the other side of the room and shouted down the hallway. "Mr. Parker's here to see his client."

"Have him wait in the visitor's room," a woman responded with a similar shout.

We followed the man down the hall to a wooden door he unlocked. Benches lined the walls, and three wobbly tables, each with four spindly stools, occupied the center of the room. While designed to accommodate a much larger crowd, at the moment Uncle Ernest and I were its only occupants.

The approach of more than one set of footsteps knotted my stomach. A second door opened, and Mother stepped into the room, followed closely by a heavy woman in a blue uniform. When my gaze met my mother's, I drew in my breath and quickly averted my eyes. My first impulse was to run to her and bury my head in the rough, grey cloth of what obviously was some sort of prison apron over her dress. I was held in place, however, by my uncle's hand on my shoulder. Whether he placed it there to restrain me or warn me, I wasn't sure, but the effort immobilized me.

"Mrs. Raymond," my uncle said with a smile. "How are we this morning?"

"Not so bad, not so bad. It's been a quiet night," she said. "But I am famished."

"Of course, you are, and I have brought some breakfast for you and the other matrons."

She accepted the basket from my uncle and stepped backward toward the door. "I'll just take this down to our station to share with the others. I'll be back in a shake."

"If you don't mind, we'll just visit until you return."

Once alone, the two moved quickly to the table farthest from both entries, and I followed, placing the valise on its top. Unburdened, I now turned to my mother, and she quickly enfolded me. After a moment, she placed a hand under my chin and studied my face. "My dear Sherlock," she said with a sigh. "I do believe you've grown at least an inch since we left you at school."

Her lips turned up in a smile, but the skin about her eyes continued to droop as they had when she'd entered the room. I also noted a greyness I hadn't seen before. But perhaps her wan color also related to her wearing no powder or rouge. Her hair was pulled back into a severe bun. Other than these changes, I caught no difference. She was still the tall, elegant woman I had always known. While

Mycroft resembled my father, I resembled my mother in height and leanness, not to mention the pronounced sharp nose of our French ancestors.

"We only have a little time before the matron returns," Ernest said. "Let's get to it."

When I turned back around, the table had been set for breakfast, including a cloth to cover the table.

"How kind of Mrs. Simpson to think of this touch," Mother said, fingering the linen. "Please thank her for me."

Before sitting, she cleaned her hands on a wet cloth set on the chair next to her place. "One must continue to practice good hygiene, regardless of the situation," she said with another of those forced smiles.

"That reminds me," Ernest said and dug about in his coat pocket. He held out his hand, palm down and dropped something into hers, which she quickly slipped into a skirt pocket. "I hope that keeps you for a while."

She turned to me and finally gave me a genuine smile in response to my obviously quizzical study. "Soap. More important than gold here. I've had mine stolen twice already."

I watched as she cut the ham and chewed it slowly. Despite what I was sure was a ravenous appetite, she had not lost her sense of decorum.

"Uncle Ernest told me you wanted to see me. Why?"

"Because, my dear Sherry, I need you to get me out."

I stared at her. Had I heard her correctly? Surely she

was speaking to her brother, but she returned my gaze over her cup as she sipped her tea.

"Unfortunately, my arrest and detention has appeased Mr. Brown for the moment. The constable sees no reason to seek Emma's true assailant. You are my best hope."

My mouth dropped open. "But-but Mycroft—"

"Don't underestimate yourself. Mycroft has a brilliant mind but would not be willing to go about to collect information. You have both the logical skills and the ability to gather new information as needed without raising suspicions."

I tilted my head to the side, considering her observations. Mycroft had made it clear he was not interested in visiting the garden with me. For the first time I realized I *did* offer a unique skill in this situation.

She took a piece of paper from her pocket and held it out to me. "I have written down everything I can remember about the morning when I found the body. I'm afraid I'm having some trouble concentrating here. Use your own skills to see what I haven't been able to. I *know* you can do it."

I fingered a corner, ready to open it, but she shook her head. "Not here. Keep it safe."

"I'll study it later," I said and slipped it into my pocket.

"Violette, dear." Ernest cleared his throat. "We must discuss the inquest."

"Another time, please, Ernest. The matron will be back shortly, and I don't want to think—"

As if on cue, the door slammed against the stone wall

with a *boom* and the matron stood in the doorway. "The superintendent will be coming in soon. You have to leave."

"Right away, madam. Right away," my uncle said.

He stood and gathered up the remains of the breakfast, motioning me to help, as the matron tapped her foot.

As soon as all was put away, Mother shook Ernest's hand and patted me on the head. "I'll see you both soon."

I forced a smile as she had done earlier. My palms moistened when I contemplated again the responsibility she had just placed on me.

She stepped to the doorway and faced us. Her eyes glistened, but her voice remained strong. "Thank you for coming." With that, she followed the matron into the hallway.

Once the door shut soundly, Ernest jerked on his waistcoat. "We must be going as well."

When we exited the room through the other door, the formerly empty hallway now buzzed with activity. Two rows of women marched past in opposite directions. Ernest and I pressed ourselves against the inner wall to let one group pass us. All were dressed in a similar style of rough-woven blue dresses and with a grey apron over them.

"Convicted prisoners," Ernest whispered to me. "Heading to breakfast I would guess."

They appeared to be assembled according to age, the oldest at the front of the line. As the last of the column passed us, I noted the last one—a young girl of about my age or a little older—glance in our direction.

A moment later, she stumbled and fell to her knees. I rushed to her side.

"Oh, thank you, sir," she said in that rough accent associated with the lower classes.

As I supported her elbow, she rose and studied me and my uncle. "You're not criminals, are you?"

I chuckled. "No. We're here to see my m—my uncle's client."

"He's a solicitor, then?" A glance at her shoes, and I could see then why she stumbled. They appeared several sizes too big—as if she were wearing boxes. "I wish I had a solicitor. I might not be in this place if I had."

"What were you accused of? Perhaps my uncle might help?"

"Liftin' a pocket watch off an old man." Her emerald gaze searched my face and filled with tears. "But I didn't. Honest I didn't. He'd given it to me just to let me have a look, but I think he was a little forgetful and didn't remember. That's why I had it."

My mouth dropped open. Never had I heard such a travesty of justice. How could anyone think such a young, innocent girl could commit such a crime? I sought my uncle's gaze to see if he was as indignant as I. His head gave the barest of shakes. Whether it meant he couldn't help or that it was too late, I was unable to decipher.

"I'll see what I can do."

"Oh, thank you, sir. You're a regular right gent, you

are." Her arms wrapped around me before I could even protest.

"I—"

"Constance," the matron at the front of the breakfast procession shouted down the hallway to us. "No fraternizin' with visitors. Get back in line."

"Yes, ma'am. Right away, ma'am."

She shambled back to her place in the column, and the group shuffled away. We followed them for a moment before turning right to the antechamber where we'd entered about an hour earlier.

Once in the carriage, my stomach rumbled. Having seen my mother was relatively safe, and even given some ideas on what to consider in her defense, my appetite had reappeared. The cinnamon bun I'd eaten in the kitchen was long ago digested. Recalling the bread Cook had provided me, I reached into my pocket and found it…empty.

Ernest caught my movement and shook his head. "I should have warned you, I suppose. Recall where your mother is. These are not members of the genteel class with whom you're accustomed to socializing. They are deceivers. Criminals. Not to be trusted."

"So, Constance—"

"Is a pickpocket, and truly did steal that man's watch. Be glad you didn't have anything more than a slice of bread in your coat pocket. She's young and her mother died recently. Your father put her in there as a lesson. She'll be out soon."

"You know her?"

"Seen her in a previous visit. I inquired and got the details from your father."

We bounced along the road back to our estate, and I considered what I had learned that morning. How had that girl been able to take the slice without my knowing it? It seemed to be a skill that could prove useful in certain situations.

With no other sustenance available, I returned to the more pressing issue of my mother's innocence. I removed her notes from my pocket and studied them. Halfway through, I stopped to re-read her account of finding the body of Mrs. Brown. I glanced at my uncle. Still sleeping.

He roused himself when I called to him. "What? Back at Underbyrne already?"

"No. I have a question. My mother's clothes. The ones she was wearing when she found Mrs. Brown. Do you know where they are?"

"I would suppose Mrs. Simpson arranged to have them laundered."

"We need to examine them when we get back."

"Of course, dear boy, of course," he said with a yawn.

I turned to ask my uncle about the magnifying glasses, but found he'd fallen back to sleep.

No matter, I already knew my next step.

CHAPTER THREE

B y the time we arrived back home, the sun was already warming the day. I helped carry the basket and valise into the kitchen. Ernest headed on to the breakfast room, but I paused to speak to Cook.

"How was your mother?" she asked without glancing up from the dough she was kneading.

"All right, I guess." I traced my finger through the flour on the table. "She said to thank you for the food."

With a click of her tongue, she said, "It's the least I can do. Poor woman."

I watched her continue punching the dough for a moment more before broaching my next subject.

"What do you remember of that morning?"

She stopped, her hands deep in the white dough. Her gaze shifted to the door leading to the garden. "Dawn was just breaking. You know your mother's an early riser. Said she wanted to get some things from the garden before it got too hot. No sooner had she gone out than she came back in, callin' for your father."

"Was she—" I stopped, unsure how to ask the question. "Did you see a lot of blood?"

Her brows formed a line. "Now what kind of a question is that for a young boy to ask? Don't you be thinkin' on such gruesome ideas."

She went back to pounding the dough, and I knew she wouldn't answer any more questions along this line. I decided on another topic. "What was she wearing that day?"

A shrug followed her burying her fist into the bread. "One of her house dresses."

"Has it been washed?"

"Has it—?" The violence with which she now worked the bread caused small clouds of flour to rise about the edges. "How should I know? I'm the cook, not the laundress. Ask Mrs. Simpson."

With a sigh, I dropped my gaze to the floor. I had hoped—

My body tightened when I focused on my shoes. With a jerk, I raised my head. "What about her boots? Was she wearing her gardening boots?"

"Her boots?" She blinked at me. "I don't recall, but she must have been."

Without waiting for more information, I rushed through

the door to the rest of house and down the hallway leading to the conservatory.

Just inside the entrance, however, I pulled to a stop. The scents of damp earth and of green, growing things enveloped me and carried with them memories of my times helping my mother. I could clearly see the sunlight dance on her face as we traversed the various aisles and she quizzed me on the names of the plants she cultivated. In later years, I came to understand how different her collection was than most. Hers was an assortment of very specific species of medicinal plants selected for their treatment of different illnesses. Even the usual trees found in greenhouses—such as lemon and orange—were there because of their healing properties.

Following a deep breath, I passed between the rows of the pots in search of my mother's gardening boots. This required me to push aside the leaves to check underneath them as well.

My heart pounded against my ribs. What would I do once I found them? And what would they show? To calm myself, at each pot, I recited the Latin and common name for each as well as what my mother had taught me about their different properties.

Mentha × *piperita*, or peppermint, good for nausea. I picked a leaf and chewed it, further calming myself.

Rosmarinus officinalis. Rosemary. Good for memory. Mother always complained about Cook stealing stalks for her kitchen. Still, she never confronted the woman about it, and I knew she truly didn't mind it.

Eucalyptus oblique. Eucalyptus. Good for skin eruptions.

I continued down the aisle in this manner. Nothing. At the end was a small stand, similar to a clerk's table, holding her books, a series of journals inventorying the plants and their growth. She'd been experimenting with different soil enhancements. One lay open on the stand, waiting for her next entry. I picked it up to study her notes, and a pocket-sized volume fell to the floor.

As I stooped down to pick up the smaller book, my gaze fell upon a set of dried, muddy footprints on the floor. They had to be my mother's.

I slipped the volume into my pocket and followed the prints up the next aisle. Halfway down the passage, I found her boots, lying on their side, as if kicked off in haste. I picked one up and studied the bottom. Mud, dried to a tan color, caked it and the sides. Along the top, more mud splatter.

Getting on my hands and knees, I examined the prints still on the wood planks of the greenhouse. Luckily, Mother didn't allow servants into the conservatory, or else the tracks, the same color as that on the boots, would have been cleaned away.

But where was the blood?

If Mother had stabbed the woman with a pitchfork, wouldn't there have been blood on her? Or her boots?

Certainly I would find it in the garden?

After a moment's hesitation, I grabbed the boots and slid them under the table holding the pots. Once safely concealed, I dashed from the greenhouse and up the servant's staircase to descend again down the front stairs to the breakfast room. Both my father and brother still sat at the breakfast table, each perusing part of a newspaper.

My father observed me over the top of his paper. "*Bonjour.*"

"*Bonjour,*" I said in response.

I'd almost forgotten my parents' practice of speaking different languages at the table. As a result, we were all conversant in French, German, and Spanish.

"Dressed already?" my father asked in the language of the day.

"I'm going to the garden. I want to check the vegetables. For Mother."

He scrutinized me for a moment before picking up the paper and hiding himself from my view. After losing the bread to the pickpocket at the gaol, I found myself quite hungry. I filled my plate with the crisp bacon, toast, and eggs from platters on the sideboard and, as fast as decorum allowed, polished off my breakfast.

"Not missing Eton's porridge now, *n'est ce pas?*" Mycroft said with a smirk.

Ignoring the remark, I asked Father, "May I be excused?"

The top of his head moved behind the paper. I noticed he held it open to the same page as when I sat down. I took his gesture for agreement, and I left for my uncle's workshop to pick up the magnifying glasses.

On the way there, I glanced to the bushes from which Mrs. Winston had appeared. I froze as I recalled our conversation. I had entirely forgotten to ask my mother about the seeds she'd requested.

How could I explain this to the maid when she returned?

My head dropped forward. I promised her and had failed to keep it. My only hope would be to ask Mother on the next visit, which I hoped was soon. I'd planned to ask my uncle that very question as soon as I got to his workshop, but as I approached the building, I could hear his snoring through the door.

I felt it safe to enter without waking him, despite my surprise greeting the night before, and let myself in. True to his word, Ernest had located his magnifying glasses, and he *did* have a number of different ones—all displayed on a small work table to the left. The collection included several of the normal ones—round lenses with a metal handle—in various sizes. A few others were probably his own design. I picked up what appeared to be a pair of spectacles with a series of lenses attached to it. These could be rotated down over the spectacles' lenses to create a form of binocular.

I put them on and flipped different lenses into place, studying their various magnifications of the table's wood surface. I found it impossible to focus well using both sides at once, but if I used it as Mother had taught me to use a microscope—with only the lenses for the right eye—the magnified image appeared in a much crisper focus and my brain concentrated on it. In the end, I selected one of the hand-held glasses as well as the spectacles and went to the garden.

With no idea what I would find, I was surprised at how easily I could identify the area where the body had lain. Being autumn, most of the garden now lay fallow, with withering stalks poking up through the raised rows. The remaining vegetables, onions, potatoes, and other root vari-eties as well as the fall squashes, occupied the back portion of the garden, nearest to a stone fence separating the plot from a pasture beyond.

Just inside the wall, vegetables had been smashed into the earth and the ground about it churned up and flattened by many footsteps. As I had seen hunting dogs trained to search for foxes, I paced the perimeter of the flattened area first, studying for anything out of place in the area not disturbed by the constable or others.

Nothing.

I then continued my survey making smaller and smaller concentric circles around the area. Mostly I found only more footprints in the rows until I came upon a flattened, dying onion stalk about two feet from the center. On the leaf was a brown stain.

Blood?

I knew it could turn brown after time. If only I had a way to know for sure.

I first tried the spectacles, and then the regular hand glass to examine the mark. Despite making the stain larger, neither provided more insight.

A few more stains appeared when I reached the center, but never in great quantity. Even when I studied the area with a magnifying glass.

I sat back on my heels and glanced about me. My interest fell upon the stone wall at the end of the garden.

The stone structure came up to my waist, and I leaned over it, hoping to find virgin territory for my investigation. Instead, I found the same trampling as on the other side, but with more footprints and less churning.

I clambered over the wall at one edge of the churning and conducted the same type of review of the grounds, starting with the perimeter and moving inward. Even less to be found on this side because I found no brown stains as I had on the other. Upon reaching the wall, I slid down the stones to sit in the earth, not caring that I might be staining my pants' seat or that Mrs. Simpson would probably scold me for it later.

Melancholy slipped over me. I so wanted to have discovered something the others had missed, but had come up with nothing. I pounded the back of my head against the wall. Pain shot through me, and I cursed myself for being so ridiculous as to give into my emotions. Mother had always taught me a detached mind produced better results. Dipping my chin, I rubbed the back of my neck. In that position, a fluttering between the stone wall and the grass caught my attention.

Flipping onto my hands and knees, I focused on the object. A piece of coarse material was snagged on the jagged edge of a rock. With my thumb and forefinger, I removed the small square—no bigger than an inch—from the wall and studied it. The material was too rough to be from a person's clothing, but from what other object, I wasn't certain. With one of Ernest's magnifying glasses, I took an even more detailed examination. The fibers along the edges were frayed, but their color wasn't faded. Whatever it had come from, it hadn't been there long.

I wrapped the piece in my handkerchief and stuffed it in my coat pocket. There, my hand hit the book I'd found earlier in the conservatory. I removed the slim volume and examined it. It appeared to be some sort of ledger with columns lining each page. While I recognized my mother's script, I couldn't make heads or tails of the entries. The writing appeared to be in some sort of cipher.

What was the purpose of the record, and why would she feel the need to use a code?

Perhaps my uncle would have an idea?

I scrambled back over the wall and returned to the workshop. The snoring had been replaced with a loud banging similar to the one I'd heard last night. I reached for the latch, but stayed my hand halfway to the door. I had no interest in a repeat of last night's near miss. I pounded on the door until Ernest opened it.

"Sherlock," he said, "why didn't you just come in?"

"Could you remove the *hira shuriken* from the bow?"

"Good idea. I'll move it to another bench as well," he said, stepping back into the workshop and toward the workbench with the crossbow.

I followed him into the workshop. "I'm returning your magnifying glasses."

"Already been out there? Did they prove useful?"

His rounded gaze told me how much he wanted to hear the affirmative.

"Very," I said and waited until after he removed the stars from the crossbow to approach him. "I did find something odd."

"And what was that?" he asked, turning to me.

"This was caught on a rock in the wall at the back of the garden." I opened the handkerchief and passed it to him, the piece of cloth resting in the center of the white linen.

He peered at it, then moved to the door to examine it in the sunlight. "It's too fine for burlap. Too coarse for linen. Perhaps I'll show it to Violette."

"Will you be seeing her again soon?"

"I'll probably take her breakfast again. Good time to have a private conversation, you know."

"May I come too?"

He paused. "She only gave me instructions to bring you this morning. We took an awfully big risk, deceiving your father like that. I don't like lying. I'll pass on your request to her, though."

My shoulders dropped. I had so many things I wanted to ask her, but for the moment I would have to depend on Ernest.

"I do have another observation about the garden. I found no blood."

"It must be there. I saw some on the pitchfork tines myself."

"But none on Mother's boots, or on the plants." My words picked up speed as I could see Ernest's gaze drifting from me. "Last year when Mother hired that medical student to tutor me in biology, he had me dissect a frog. When I opened it, blood sprayed out all over my hands and the dissecting tray. He said it wasn't dead and I'd hit a vein. Because the heart was still pumping, the blood spurted out. When they dissected the cadavers in medical school, very little blood leaked out because it wasn't flowing. The person was *dead*."

My uncle frowned, as if he were weighing the information I'd just shared. "Why would someone put a pitchfork into a dead woman?"

"I don't know. But you see, if the constable claims Mother killed Mrs. Brown by stabbing her—"

"She's innocent of the crime." Ernest's mouth widened into a broad grin, and he slapped me on the back. "Good show, my boy. Good show. I must share this with your mother directly."

"Shouldn't you tell Father?"

He paused to stare at the wooden beams crisscrossing

under the building's roof. After a moment, he refocused on me. "I think it's best for us to keep your father out of it at the moment. After all, as a local justice of the peace, he might be denounced for favoritism or some other bias given that the accused is his wife."

With a sigh, he glanced about the workshop. "I have so much to do, but Violette must come first. I don't think I'll wait until tomorrow. I should go now."

Having made the decision, he scurried about the workshop, preparing to return to town and the prison. In a matter of minutes, he was back in his suit, valise in hand. "Come and see me when I return, and I'll share your mother's thoughts."

When he waved me toward the door, I passed the workbench and spied my handkerchief still lying on it. "What about that bit of cloth?"

"Cloth? Yes. Quite right." Pausing at the bench, he carefully folded the handkerchief and dropped it into the bench's top drawer.

On the way back to the house, I put my hand in my pocket and remembered the ledger I found in the greenhouse. I needed to decipher the entries noted inside.

Mycroft.

My brother had the ability to sort out things just by studying them for a moment. The skill had served him well in chess. After only two or three moves, he would tell the other player what their moves would be and the inevitable outcome of them being checkmated. Most people refused to play with him after a single game.

I found him in the library, gazing out the window on the far wall, tea cup and saucer in hand.

From the doorway, I asked, "May I come in?"

With a slow turn, he faced me. "What do you want?"

"I...I need your help."

He drew back his chin. "Go on."

"I...I found this—" I pulled out the ledger. "I don't understand it. I thought you might—"

He held out his hand and drew me forward with his fingers. "Let's see it."

I placed the leather-bound book in his hand and watched him study the pages. A frown wrinkled his brow, and I shifted my weight from one foot to the other. After a moment, he handed it back to me.

"Where did you get this?"

"From the greenhouse. You know that little stand Mother has by the back door?" When he didn't respond, I asked, "Can you read it?"

"It's a simple code." Following a moment when he stared at me as if seeing through me, he strode to the book-shelves, pulled out one volume, and passed it open to me. "They describe it in here."

Sure enough, markings similar to the one in the ledger were described there. "Why would she need to write in code?"

"Because she's prescribing medicinal herbs."

"Is it"—I glanced behind me before asking in a low voice—"legal?"

"It all depends, I guess, what they are given for."

After considering that bit of information, I asked, "Do you find Mrs. Winston listed there?"

After a quick check of the code description, he took back Mother's ledger and ran his finger down one column of the last page of entries and stopped about two-thirds down. "Here's a Rachel Winston. Isn't she one of the Devony's maids? Says here, 'Queen Anne seeds. One ounce, crushed.'"

"Queen Anne seeds," I said, letting the name roll around on my tongue. In my mind, I could see the plant growing in various pots along one bench in the conservatory. Mother would harvest the seeds from the tiny white flowers.

"What is the plant for?"

"*Daucus carota*," I said, reciting my mother's instructions, "Also called the wild carrot because the root is edible and similar to the carrot. It can be used for digestive problems and to stimulate urine."

"That's it?" he asked, raising an eyebrow.

"And caution must be taken not to confuse it with hemlock."

"Does any of that make sense for Mrs. Winston?"

I thought for a moment. "She needed the seeds. Crushed. And said something about babies.... They somehow inhibit having babies. But why would—?"

"Because children can be a burden, you fool. Think about the Stratons, for pity's sake."

The Stratons were tenants on the estate next to ours. Everyone could recite the woes of the recently widowed John Straton. His wife had died after the birth of her fifth child, and the village congregation had taken up a collection for the family to cover her burial.

As I contemplated this bit of information, Mycroft's frown deepened, and he put his hands on his hips. "Do you know where children come from?"

We had farm animals, so I'd heard Father and others discussing— "You mean mating? Like animals?"

"We *are* animals, you know. Some a lot closer to them than others, I suppose." He turned to the bookshelves again and removed another book. "Here, study this and leave me alone."

Without examining the book, I gathered it, the one on codes, and the ledger and carried them to my room. The bed had already been straightened, but I clambered upon the covers and propped myself against the pillows after kicking off my shoes to avoid Mrs. Simpson's scolding about mussing the coverlet.

The tome Mycroft had given me was a sort of medical text written in French. I flipped through the pages and immediately recognized my mother's notes in the margins of some of the pages. Notes covering different ailments and treatments—all in some way related to the plants growing in the conservatory.

When I turned to the section entitled *Anatomie*, I slowed my study. While I had seen drawings of the various organs in my previous biology studies, I had not seen these types of graphics before. Here were detailed illustrations of both the male and *female* bodies. I ran my finger over the page-sized reproduction of a mature woman's breast, stomach, and the dark triangle where her legs met. A strange warming raced through me and settled in my groin.

I turned the page to a detailed drawing of a penis, standing stiff away from the body. Various arrows indicated the technical terms for the parts. On the adjoining page was that dark triangle exposed. Just a few quick strokes indicated the thighs, but what lay between them appeared in great detail with the names of all the parts duly noted. I touched the oval in the middle marked *le vagin*, and another rush pulsed through me, setting my groin throbbing.

My entire body grew hot.

A moment later, I snapped the book shut, unable to continue. My heart drummed against my chest, and I checked the door, certain someone was going to enter and see me with this book. I must have broken some moral code or rule of etiquette by even viewing these pages, despite the scientific nature of the book.

After several deep breaths, my heart rate slowed and my agitation lessened. Then, the hall clock chimed one, and my throat tightened. I had only a few minutes before I would be called for dinner. I leapt off my bed, and quickly searched the room for a place to hide the book. I had just slipped it and the other volumes between my old lesson books when Mrs. Simpson rapped on the door.

"Dinner is ready," she said through the wood.

"Be right there."

After splashing some water on my face, I rushed downstairs to the dining room.

When I entered, Mycroft lifted one side of his mouth and asked in French, "What took you so long?"

Once again, heat flooded my face. He *knew* what I would find in the book, and my reaction. What's more, I was certain that it'd been his intention all along. Now, he was taking a great deal of amusement out of the whole act.

"I was checking that book of codes," I said, hoping to divert the subject. "Most interesting."

"I'm sure," he said and chuckled at his plate while he cut his meat.

My knuckles whitened as I gripped my own knife and fork. I felt as if the whole world could sense my secret.

How would I ever face my mother?

Ducking my head, I poked at my food, too afraid to meet my brother's or father's gaze.

I'd only managed to choke down a few bites of meat when the thumping of heavy boots announced Uncle Ernest's arrival. Anticipation of my mother's reaction to my discovery regarding the blood pushed out all other thoughts.

"What's for dinner?" he asked, rubbing his hands together.

Father raised his gaze from his plate and studied him. "Where have you been?"

"Out."

Ernest leaned back in his chair slightly to allow Mrs. Simpson to place his meal in front of him.

My gaze jumped to his, but he gave a hint of a shake with his head. Whatever had passed between my mother and uncle was not to be shared at the dining table—or not with my father.

"But you went into town," Mycroft said. "I heard the carriage leave this morning."

"Yes. I have to prepare for the inquest. We have discovered—"

My father held up his hand. "Please, Ernest, not at the table. As a justice of the peace, I should not be discussing such things outside the court."

"Of course. Of course," Ernest said and turned his attention to his plate. A moment later, he asked him, "Do you plan to butcher a pig this week?"

"A pig?" His forehead creased. "I would have to check with the foreman. If you are in need of additional bacon—"

"No. No. It's not about bacon. I have need of a butchered pig." He chewed a potato slowly and after swallowing, said, "I guess I will have to discuss it with Mr. Simpson after dinner."

"Do you need it to test another weapon?" Mycroft asked.

"In a manner of speaking," Ernest said. "I'm not

allowed to discuss the matter here, but it's of vital importance for the hearing."

My father scrubbed his mouth with his napkin and threw it on top of his plate. "Fine. I'll ask Mr. Simpson to ask the tenants who has a pig they are planning to take to market."

"Thank you."

Father pushed his chair back from the table with great force and strode into the library.

Once we were alone, Mycroft asked, "Do you have a defense planned?"

"Thanks to Sherlock and Violette, I do," he said, a smile broadening on his face.

My brother pulled back his chin. "How?"

"You'll see. You'll see," Ernest said with a chuckle.

I stared down at my plate, unable to share in my uncle's enthusiasm. A sense of dread overwhelmed me. What if I was wrong, and my observation failed to free my mother?

Even if she were freed, until the true killer was identified, the scandal wouldn't completely die. I knew I couldn't rest until the Holmes name was fully cleared.

CHAPTER FOUR

After dinner, I returned to my room. My gaze immediately went to the case with my old text-books and, hidden among them, the anatomy book Mycroft had given me earlier. The slow burn I'd experienced at dinner rekindled itself, and I cursed him for his now obvious maneuvering. It was like playing chess with him, only on a more personal scale.

No longer able to even bear knowing the book was in my room, I picked up the volume to return it to the library.

This time, however, the door was closed. I paused before knocking to check for voices. My father and brother's loud conversation passed through without distortion.

"It's your duty to the family, son," Father said, a sharp edge in his tone.

"The world's changing. You may not be able to see the

trends, but I do. Clearly. The village may have been the center of your world, but mine is much grander. I have absolutely no interest in—"

"Interest? Interest? I don't give a bloody damn about your interests. As the first born—"

"Don't lay your concept of responsibility on me. I see a much larger one for me. If you can't accept it, disown me and pass this 'duty' on to Sherlock. See if I care."

"You'd care well enough if I let your *grander* duty support your lifestyle. All your fancy foods, that group of yours—"

"The Diogenes Society is in its infancy. Once established, it will be self-sustaining."

"The only sustaining at the moment appears to be on the backs of my tenants."

One of them approached the library door, and my hand tightened its grip on the book. I took a step backwards, ready to turn and run before I was caught eavesdropping. Just before reaching the door, the steps stopped and retreated. Given the strides' quickness and light tread, I decided they were those of a young man. Mycroft had to be pacing, but it must have calmed him because when he finally spoke, his voice was low and sedate.

"I need to get back to university. My responsibilities lie there. My studies, the contacts I've been making, I've even been working on a treatise that will lay out some of my current observations and conclusions regarding the changes I see on the horizon. Take the war that just concluded in

America. The resulting defeat of the seceding states will reshape that country."

"I don't see why you wouldn't be able to make your observations here at Underbyrne in the meantime. As long as this scandal hangs over our family—"

"I need more immediate access to information." He sighed. "It arrives too late by post. And I need—no I *require* —intellectual stimulation to form my conclusions. The sedate life of a country squire may be all right for you, but not for me."

"Why are you putting this on me now?" My father's voice was worn, troubled. "With your mother in gaol?"

"Because I feel the clock ticking. Every day I'm away from Oxford and my studies delays my whole future and the contributions I can bring."

"What about your mother? Aren't you concerned about her at all?"

"Once she's free, my presence won't be necessary."

"What makes you sure she'll be freed?"

"Because—"

I ruined my chances to hear Mycroft's analysis with a sneeze. Not a polite exhalation of air through the nose, but an explosive snort worthy of Uncle Ernest. I spun about, prepared to step around a corner to avoid being caught. Before I could take two steps, a hand clamped down on my shoulder and turned me back around.

"How long have you been listening, you little sneak?" Mycroft asked.

"I-I-I just got here," I said and held up the book. "I was going to return this."

He snatched it from me. "I'll take care of it. Go. Find some other door to listen at."

I glanced behind him toward my father. His mouth was a hard line, but I couldn't tell if he was angry at me or the conversation he'd been having with Mycroft—or both. In any case, I knew not to argue with either.

With a quick bob of my head, I returned to my room but found I was unable to sit, as thoughts swirled in my brain. That Mycroft had no interest in returning to Underbyrne after his studies made no sense to me. How could one not want to stay here? Of course, Mycroft had always been much more cerebral than I. He was not one for hunting with Father. And what about his remarks about the future and how things were changing? Did he truly believe that Underbyrne would not remain as it was? More existed to the argument between the two than I'd heard, but Mycroft's predictions were enough to make me pace the floor.

After several circuits between the window and door of my room, I noticed my violin case on the desk. I recalled my promise to my mother and crossed the room to open it. After running my fingers across the instrument's neck, I fitted it under my chin and tuned it. Tentatively at first, but with growing confidence, I worked on the piece I had practiced with my mother. For some reason, I found myself able to pour my emotions into the music, providing it with a depth I had never experienced before. When I hit a sour note, I didn't rebuke myself, I simply continued until I finished the entire score.

Having completed it once, I repeated the entire composition again—this time with fewer mistakes. I found myself relaxing as my thoughts quieted in the process. By the end of the second repetition, I came to the conclusion that whatever plan my uncle and mother had developed would succeed.

Halfway through one execution, someone knocked on my door. I had been so engrossed in the music and my thoughts, I hadn't heard anyone approach.

When I opened the door, Mrs. Simpson said, "Your father sent me to fetch you for supper, Master Sherlock. He and your brother are waiting."

Supper? How long had I been practicing?

But I had a more pressing question.

"Will my uncle be joining us?"

"He asked that I bring his to the workshop. Do you want me to hold it for you to take to him later?" I nodded. "Get a move on, then. You don't want the meat to get cold."

She turned to leave but turned back to face me. "That was lovely playing, Master Sherlock. Your mother will be proud of your progress when she returns."

"Thank you, Mrs. Simpson."

A quick smile at me, and she headed back to the stairs.

The two men sat at the table, drumming their fingers on the linen covering.

"Another minute and we would have started without you," my father said in Spanish.

"Sorry, sir," I said, shifting to that language. "I was practicing and lost track of time."

My father studied me for a moment. "I heard some of it. You are improving."

"But you are having a problem with the C-sharp on the arpeggio," Mycroft said.

Before I could respond about the difficult fingering for that section, Father glared at him, and he dropped his gaze. We all three fell silent, the only sound the scrape of our forks and knives on the china.

After finishing, I hustled to the kitchen to pick up my uncle's supper. As I stepped outside, I remembered Mrs. Winston, but no one stopped me as I crossed the yard. Had she solved her problem on her own?

The clanging from within the workshop differed from the preceding evening—tinnier and not as loud. He actually heard my knock and opened the door to me.

His appearance almost made me drop the basket. Blood splattered an overcoat he wore over his clothes—not to mention more of it coating his face and hands.

"Sherlock, you came at quite a fortuitous time. I could use an extra hand. Come in."

If my uncle's condition hadn't been enough to disturb me, the stench greeting me when I entered certainly completed the task. A pig's carcass lay on its side on an oilskin cloth in the middle of the room. A number of puncture holes covered the exposed side. The iron scent of blood permeated the building, and I truly regretted having eaten my meal before visiting Ernest.

My uncle followed my gaze to the dead, pierced pig and cleared his throat. "I'll explain that in a moment. Come here and help me."

He strode to his workbench where a pitchfork lay. One of the tines was bent, and Ernest pointed to the fork's handle. "Put down the basket and hold this steady for me while I straighten out this one point."

Striking the tine with a hammer, he spoke between beats. "The fork...must have hit...a rib or...something.... Didn't go in...like it should.... I'll need...to make sure...my aim's true."

With the tine straightened, he picked up the pitchfork and balanced it in his hand as if estimating its center of gravity. Without any warning, he gave a loud roar, ran to the pig's carcass, and jammed the fork into its side almost to the handle. I stared at him, my whole body quivering uncontrollably.

With the fork now imbedded deep in the animal's body, my uncle turned to me. His wide smile faded when he focused on me. "Boy, you're absolutely pale. Are you all right?"

I swallowed to keep my supper from rising higher in my stomach. "Are *you* all right?"

"Never better," he said, his grin returning. "Downright

ecstatic, actually. Your mother and I have worked out a plan, thanks to you. She should be home by Friday night."

Had I heard him correctly?

"Friday? But—"

"The coroner has set the inquest for Friday morning. After we present this evidence, the man will have to release her immediately."

I stuffed my fists into my pockets to keep them from shaking. This whole ordeal would be over in just a few days? Was this what Mycroft referred to during his argument with Father? I studied the scene, seeking to piece together what my uncle and mother's plan could be.

"The pig is the evidence," I said. "You're going to show how a dead pig doesn't bleed when stabbed with a fork, but a live one does. That's why you have blood on your clothes."

He glanced down at the blood-covered smock. "I truly didn't expect such a burst from the live one. I'm glad I had on the smock. Not quite sure why I didn't anticipate it. After all, in Afghanistan…"

His voice faded off, as did the light in his eyes as he stared at a point somewhere above my head.

"Uncle Ernest," I said after a moment. He shook his head and refocused on me. "Are you going to bring pigs into the inquest?"

"I don't see any other way, my boy, to prove my point. That should put on a good show, don't you think? Might be a bit messy, though," he said, glancing at his smock. "Perhaps the street…"

"Will it be that one?" I asked, jutting my chin in the direction of the now-impaled swine.

"No, Simpson is coming to pick up this one to smoke it tonight. I've already asked for some of the bacon from it, and the live one I stabbed earlier. Maybe some of the sausage from the one we use on Friday as well. Seems fitting, doesn't it? To devour some of the animals serving to set your mother free? Like the African warriors eating the heart of their kill." He placed a finger to his lips. "Not a word of this to anyone. Especially your father. Your mother's orders, again."

THE REST of the days between my uncle's pig practice and the inquest were unbearably long and fretful. My father paced about the house, Mycroft kept to the library, and I worked at finding tasks to do and keep my mind occupied. I moved my violin practice to the schoolroom on the top floor to avoid further critiques from my brother. Given the number of hours I was able to devote to my music, I progressed rapidly and anticipated showing my mother the perfected result.

When not practicing, I spent time in Mother's greenhouse. Her plants required daily attention. The first afternoon when I tended her plants, as I went down the rows watering each pot, I noticed several in need of pruning. After retrieving some small shears from her workbench and donning a pair of work gloves, I removed dead or dying leaves as I worked through the aisle. About halfway down the second row, I came across a pot containing tall, thin stems topped with white flowers. I picked a leaf and crushed it between my gloved fingers, expecting the pleasant scent of mint from a pennyroyal plant.

Only a sharp odor similar to urine filled my nostrils instead. I studied the plant more closely, and my mouth dropped open.

Hemlock.

With a rush of urgency, I pulled off the gloves to confirm the sap had not penetrated the heavy fabric and then ran to the water barrel by the back door to scrub my fingers. The juice I'd extracted by crushing the leaves could be absorbed directly through the skin. Thank goodness I'd put on the gloves as Mother had always insisted when working in the greenhouse. I knew from helping my mother that hemlock and pennyroyal were very similar, but the subtle differences, such as the scent given off, could mean the difference between life and death.

Once I felt I had removed any traces of the plant, I pulled on another pair of gloves, placing the contaminated ones in a special basket Mother kept for such accidents. Poisonous plants were kept on a separate table to prevent the type of error I'd almost committed. This plant had obviously been misplaced. I returned it to its proper table where a space marked its absence. As I positioned it on the table, I also noticed a smudge of dirt just below the rim and turned the pot so it wouldn't show.

Who could have been in here and moved the plant?

Just as no one disturbed my father's insect collection, the whole household knew not to enter the greenhouse or move any of the plants. After checking about the area, I found no indication of any other plants having been moved and returned to my former duties of watering and pruning. In the back of my mind, however, I hoped my actions for keeping things up for her return weren't in vain.

THE DAY of the inquest into Mrs. Brown's death dawned appropriately dreary. A fine rain pelted my bedroom window, and judging by the clouds, wouldn't be ending any time soon. I'd spent a restless night. Of greatest concern was my uncle's demonstration. Only knowing how much my mother trusted him kept me from despairing completely.

As a result of my inability to go or remain asleep, I was already washed and dressed in my best black suit when Mrs. Simpson knocked on my door to call me to breakfast.

Judging from the lined faces and dark circles under the eyes of both my brother and father, I wasn't the only one who had passed an uneasy night. Everyone's brooding silenced our morning meal even more than usual. Unlike most mornings, neither of the older men hid behind their newspapers. Instead, they stared down at their plates, keeping any thoughts to themselves.

Mrs. Simpson passed through with a pot of hot tea and offered to freshen our cups. I took the opportunity to enquire about my uncle.

She shook her head and clucked her tongue. "The poor man came home after midnight. I know because he woke me to ask about his suit for today. I told him it was already laid out on his bed in his workshop. He thanked me and said he'd be leaving for town early to make arrangements for the pigs—whatever that means."

"He plans a demonstration with them," I said. The other two at the table turned to me, and I shifted in my seat. If my uncle's appearance and performance the other night in the workshop were any indication of what he planned for the courtroom, I decided it would be best for Mycroft and my father to see it firsthand and at the proper time. "But I'm not sure exactly what."

My father's eyebrows drew together. "I do hope Ernest won't make a scene. I have my reputation as a magistrate to uphold."

I poked at my eggs, unable to think of actually chewing and swallowing. I did, however, manage a bit of toast and the tea. The day promised to be a long one, and I knew I needed enough sustenance to endure the hours. A glance at the others' plates suggested their appetites were similar to mine. Even Mycroft finished only about half of what was on his plate.

My father wiped his mouth with his napkin and said, "Let's get on into town. I can't abide this waiting."

Mrs. Simpson followed us out to the carriage and reached in and grabbed my hand when I took my seat. "Give your mother my love. Let her know I've been praying for her."

I nodded, and she shut the door.

Like my uncle during our visit to the gaol, Mycroft immediately rested his head against the seat's back, shut his eyes, and within a few minutes commenced snoring. My father, on the other hand, kept up a steady rhythm with his foot on the carriage floor. Every few minutes, he would interrupt the tapping to lean forward and glance out the window. At one point, he studied the sky before settling back into his seat.

"The weather's just bad enough to perhaps deter some of the crowds." He scrubbed his face with his hand and said, "She's such a private person. All this attention. She'll... she'll just have to soldier on."

Following that remark, silence pressed down upon us again.

After what appeared just short of an eternity, the carriage pulled to a stop in front of the tavern where the inquest would occur. A huge crowd—those unlucky enough not to catch a space inside—had already gathered around the steps leading up to it. So much for the weather deterring attendance. The constable's men kept an eye on the assembled, ensuring none blocked the street. The spectators parted when we stepped forward. As we pushed through, the stares from those assembled created a physical sensation against my skin. I could *feel* their scrutiny—a heaviness on my arms, back, and shoulders. I dropped my gaze to avoid meeting their gawking ones.

As part of my duties as a squire's son I'd also attended the preliminaries for the assizes when a circulating judge arrived with great ceremony to oversee hearings in the shire hall. And given my father's position as justice of the peace, I knew about court hearings, quarterly assizes, and coroner's inquests from my father's discussions of various cases. But never had I actually attended one. I still found it odd these were held in the village's largest public house, but knew it was the traditional venue.

I paused after stepping inside to take in the transforma-tion of the large, open room. A sort of courtroom had been created, complete with twelve chairs for the jury lined in two rows on the right side of the room. A platform bearing a tall desk and chair was situated against the back wall, and a witness box stood just to the judge's left. Chairs and tables for spectators had been placed in rows to form an *L* to the left and in front of the court-like area. These were already occupied, and all heads turned in our direction at our entrance. Along the left wall stood the bar, already conducting a brisk business for those waiting for the spec-tacle to begin.

Had my mother's freedom—and possibly her life—not

been in jeopardy, I might have been caught up in the crowd's festive mood, some of which resulted from heavy imbibing of the tavern's wares. Among those at the bar, I recognized the recently widowed Mr. Straton supporting himself by his forearms at the end farthest from me. An empty glass stood nearby. A young girl approached him and pulled on his arm. He jerked from her grasp and raised a hand as if to hit her. She ducked her head into her shawl and stepped away from him, moving to the edge of the throng. Now facing me, I recognized her as Constance, the bread-thief from the gaol and, given her coloring, one of Straton's offspring.

Having moved away from her father, she now paused next to an older gentleman and let those gathered about push her against him. At this distance and through the assembled, I wasn't able to observe her as I wished, but I was certain she was helping herself to something in his pockets as she'd done to me. Between two breaths, she retreated back into the crowd and toward her father where she slipped something to him.

I knew I'd witnessed a crime and had a duty to call her out for it. At the same time, however, I found myself admiring her stealth and audacity.

Mycroft resolved my dilemma when he glanced in the direction of the bar and snorted. "Vultures."

My back straightened as I agreed with his assessment of the others in attendance. They *were* vultures, here to gawk at my mother and her predicament. I owed them no sympathy or assistance should some misfortune befall them in the process.

Father glanced over his shoulder at us. The slight gathering of his eyebrows warned us of the need to maintain the Holmes dignity and position. Mycroft transformed his sneer into an impassive expression similar to Father's, and I followed suit, but with the satisfaction of knowing at least one had received some retribution.

Unlike outside, we had to push our way through the throng to the first row of seats in front of the witness box. Uncle Ernest guarded three empty seats. He rose when we stepped to him. "Glad you got here. I've had to fight off quite a number to keep them for you."

"Thank you," Father said. "Have you seen Mrs. Holmes today? How—" He coughed. "How is she doing?"

"A trooper. Stiff back, upper lip. All that." He glanced about. "I've got a bit to confirm before the inquest begins. I'll be back."

He gave me a quick wink and pushed himself through the crowd toward the tavern's entrance.

Not long after we'd taken our seats, a murmur passed through the crowd, followed by cheers from those at the bar. Twelve men moved to the jury box and jostled about a bit until they all had found a seat. They remained standing, and a tall man in a wig and black robe stepped into the cleared area in front of the jury. I recognized Mr. Thompson, the village coroner from his visits to our home. Until that moment, I'd never questioned his position or ability. The man was a solicitor and had no medical background that I knew of. What made him capable of determining my mother's—or for that matter any other person's—fate with respect to a charge of murder?

The others in the room rose to their feet, mimicking the jury. I wasn't sure if they stood out of respect for the coroner or if they wanted to get a good view of him. Either way, no one sat until he instructed them to do so.

"We are here today to consider the circumstance surrounding the death of one Emma Brown..." Mr. Thompson said.

The next part of what he said I couldn't make out despite our proximity to the platform because of the two women sitting behind us.

"I still can't believe dear Emma is gone. She brought both my babies into this world," one said.

"She was the only one I trusted. How can you expect a *man* to know what a woman goes through?" the other said.

The two continued, commenting on the reputations of Dr. Farnsworth, Mr. Harvingsham, and the late midwife. Both agreed Mrs. Brown was, by far, the one most knowledgeable of women and their needs. And that her husband, God bless him, was putting up a good front and continued to deliver the honey he harvested from his bees despite his deep mourning. They also discussed the coroner's appearance and current marital status (still single, but a good catch), the rowdiness of those by the bar, the presence of acquaintances also in the tavern and those who failed to make it in.

Both my father and brother, regardless of social conventions requiring decorum at all times, shifted in their seats. Father leaned forward in an apparent attempt to catch more of the coroner's opening remarks. Mycroft's foot tapped a tattoo that failed to drown out the ladies but did a rather exceptional job at making Mr. Thompson's opening remarks unintelligible. He stopped only when Father's glare froze him in mid-tap.

The next words I caught from the coroner were, "You may begin, Mr. Brown."

The command elicited a series of *tsk, tsk* from the commentators behind us, and I was grateful when one of the women reprimanded the other when she remarked on the widower's appearance. "Quiet now, I want to hear."

The assembled turned their heads in the direction of movement near the jury area, and Mr. Brown stepped forward. While the whole town knew he was in mourning, it would've been difficult to tell simply from his dress. The man made a habit of wearing black throughout the year. His ensemble resembled a vicar's—with a high, white collar and black coat and trousers.

As he stepped toward the platform, several low murmurs and additional *tsk, tsk*'s indicated he had the sympathy of all present. Except for the three of us. Mycroft stiffened in his chair, and Father straightened his spine. We all knew our mother's current situation came from this man's efforts, and he found no quarter among us.

The man glanced about him, shuffled his feet, and coughed. "My lord—" A slight squeak in his voice forced him to cough again. "I will prove that Violette Holmes of this parish did willfully end the life of my wife, Emma Brown. The circumstances being that Mrs. Holmes stabbed her to death on her property following an argument in the village square where, in a voice loud enough for others to hear, said that she would ensure Emma stopped her practice."

"Do you have any witnesses?"

"Yes, I would like to have Constable Gibbons answer questions first."

Heat rushed from my chest throughout my body. I'd had little contact with the man other than when he visited my father as part of each other's duties. From the moment he appeared in my line of sight, only the public setting and my father's presence kept me in my seat and not with my hands about his neck. My father and brother must have had similar thoughts because I could feel them stiffen as well.

Gibbons moved into the witness box and took an oath to tell the truth. Mr. Brown asked him to tell about being called to our house. The constable described Mr. Simpson delivering the message, going to the garden, finding Mrs. Brown, and examining the pitchfork.

"Thank you, Constable Gibbons," he said at the conclusion.

A man called out from behind us. "My lord, may I ask a few questions?"

I pressed my lips tight to bottle the laugh that bubbled up my throat when Uncle Ernest spoke up. Was this the big display he'd planned?

I dared a glance at my father and brother. While the older man's face remained impassive, Mycroft worked his jaw as if he were fighting to keep some exclamation from leaping out of his mouth. I followed their examples and composed myself, but within, my stomach and heart raced each other toward my throat.

In contrast to our silence, the rest of the spectators voiced shock and surprise. The ones at the bar were especially vocal with shouts such as "Where does this toff get off?" "Sit down, you old fool." "He's a few tiles short of a roof, that one."

Uncle Ernest ignored their derisions and strode to the platform for affirmation of Mr. Thompson's consent.

The man pounded on his desk and spoke to the crowd. "Silence. Interested parties have the right to question the witnesses. And he does have an interest, having been part of the original group finding the...er...Mrs. Brown."

"But he's a Holmes," Mr. Brown said. "He's a witness himself."

"I am *not* a Holmes. The name's Parker. And I'm quite proud of it," Ernest said. He turned to Father. "Sorry, Siger."

Father raised his hand to show he took no insult from my uncle's correction.

Mr. Brown's face turned a deep vermillion, and the room echoed his sentiments with angry mutterings and shouts.

Mr. Thompson rose to his feet, two patches resembling Mr. Brown's color forming on his cheeks. "I run this inquest, and as coroner, I will allow Mr. Parker to interrogate the witness. Any man who has questions should see me after these proceedings."

The widower studied Thompson, now standing and pulled to his full height, rightful indignation in his stare. Anger drained from Mr. Brown's face, and he stared down at the floor.

"You may proceed, Mr. Parker," the coroner said.

"Thank you, sir," he said and stepped to the witness box.

"Constable Gibbons, when you arrived at the home, where was the pitchfork?"

"Mrs. Holmes handed it to me."

"It wasn't in the body?"

"If it had been, Mrs. Holmes would have had to be a lot stronger to lift both."

The courtroom chuckled along with the witness. My disgust for the man grew. Not only had he arrested my mother, now he made light of the fact he was trying to have her condemned to death.

After the other's mirth subsided, my uncle continued. "How much had the body bled?"

"Excuse me?"

"How much blood was on the body?"

Crimson crept up the man's neck and colored his face. "There were spots. Where the pitchfork had been."

"What about the ground beneath her? Any blood there?"

"Again, some spots."

"And just to be clear, you believe that Mrs. Brown died after being stabbed by a pitchfork?"

"She was skewered through and through. There were holes in front—by her bosom too."

"And it is your contention that Mrs. Holmes killed her with the pitchfork?"

"Exactly."

"Which is why you arrested the woman?"

The man sat up straight and met my uncle's gaze, stare for stare. "Yes. I determined her to be the murderess of Emma Brown."

My uncle turned to Mr. Thompson. "My lord, I ask that you find Mrs. Holmes not involved in the death of Emma Brown, charge the jury to find the cause of death unknown pending further investigation, and order the constable to release Mrs. Violette Holmes forthwith."

That statement caused the whole room to gasp and then buzz to the point that any remarks from the platform were impossible to comprehend. The chatterboxes behind us reminded me of two squawking magpies as they expressed their shock.

Constable Gibbons pulled himself taller and pointed at my uncle. "Now wait just a God-damn minute—"

Another pounding by the coroner cut off the man's curse and the droning in the courtroom. "Why should I do what you suggest?"

"Because, my lord, she could not have possibly done what the constable accuses her of. It's a fact of science. Mrs. Brown was not killed by a pitchfork."

"Are you disputing the fact that she was stabbed by a pitchfork?"

"No, your lordship, only that Mrs. Brown was already dead when she was gored by it."

I wiggled in my seat, barely able to contain myself, knowing I had initiated this conclusion.

"Well played," Mycroft whispered, more to himself than to those about him. And a smile crept over his face.

At that point, I allowed myself to also let a small, satisfied smile emerge.

"Constable Gibbons contends that Mrs. Holmes stabbed Emma Brown with a pitchfork, killing her," my uncle continued. "I can prove the evidence does not support this assertion—if this inquest will indulge us."

Mr. Thompson's mouth turned down and studied Uncle Ernest for a moment. He then considered the constable whose face still flamed scarlet, and Mr. Brown, who stood stiff, fists at his side. The crowd stilled, waiting for the man's decision. After another brief interval while he contemplated the scene, he leaned back in his chair and said, "Very well. Provide your evidence."

"Thank you, my lord," my uncle said, and gestured to the tavern door. "If you will follow me outside."

The rush to the street proved to be a chaotic jostling as those at the back of the room tried to make it through the doors first. I held my father and brother back, letting the others push around us.

"I want to see——" Mycroft's cheeks puffed out with the words.

"You don't want to be in front," I said, cutting him off. "We'll be able to see everything from the steps. And we should be safe from the blood."

Both turned to me, but after a glance at the quickly emptying courtroom, they followed me as the last of the crowd exited the building.

Outside, I stepped to one side of the small porch at the tavern's front. Over the heads of those around and beyond us, I could see a small pen set up in the street directly in front of the tavern. The crowd had gathered on all four sides, blocking the few carriages and carts passing each way. Those in the vehicles, however, appeared more curious than annoyed, with some standing up to get a better view of the event.

Inside the pen, a mature hog squealed and grunted at all the attention focused on him. The constable's men fought a losing battle to keep everyone back but were able to make room for the coroner and the jury near the enclosure.

When my uncle raised his arms, the assembled quieted, with only the hog's continued grunts punctuating my uncle's speech.

"My lord, as I noted inside, the evidence indicates Emma Brown did *not* die from stab wounds despite Constable Gibbons' assertions. I will now conclusively demonstrate this fact."

Mr. Simpson stepped to the pen and handed Ernest an oilcloth coat, which he donned over his suit. He then accepted a pitchfork from our steward, and before the coroner could open his mouth to question this preparation, my uncle gave the same terrifying yell I'd heard in the workshop and reached over the barricade to jam the instrument into the animal just below its shoulders. Simultaneous with the pig's loudest scream yet, blood spewed from the wounds covering the front of my uncle's overcoat and several of the bystanders who'd decided to get the best view they could. The animal's wails weakened along with the liquid spurting about the fork still in its back.

It also evacuated its intestines, releasing a stench that caused many of the onlookers to cover their noses and mouths.

"That's why he asked about..." my father muttered under his breath.

I pressed my lips together to hold back the laughter desiring to manifest itself. Ernest's demonstration had gone off without a hitch, and I had been the impetus for the proof that my mother hadn't stabbed the midwife.

Ernest turned to the coroner and the jury, his features grim. Even from my distance, however, I could catch the gleam in his eyes revealing his satisfaction with the display.

"As you can see, stabbing a living animal—be it pig or human—would result in a large quantity of blood. It would cover the aggressor as well as the surrounding area. None of which Constable Gibbons reported observing on Mrs. Holmes or the garden."

Mr. Thompson turned to Gibbons, and his question traveled over the heads of those between them. "Did you find any evidence of such blood about the place where Mrs. Brown was found?"

The constable's color had paled some, but his nostrils flared wide—despite the reeking brew of pig waste and blood. "No, sir."

"Did Mrs. Holmes have any blood on her?"

"No, my lord, but she could have—"

"What about the pitchfork? Was its handle covered in blood?"

"No, my lord."

The coroner turned to the jury men and said, "Given this demonstration, I now charge you to meet in private to deliberate the cause of the death of one Emma Brown."

"No. Wait." The honey man shouted at the coroner and held up his hand to stop the jury. "My wife was murdered. I know she was. How can you say—?"

"She may have been murdered," the coroner said, placing a hand on the man's shoulder, "but not by a pitchfork wielded by Mrs. Holmes or anyone else. Her death needs additional investigation."

At that moment, my attitude toward the widower shifted. While I had considered him vindictive, holding some sort of grudge against my mother, watching the man's back round into a slump, I realized he'd endured a great loss. The cause of his suffering still remained unsolved, and his pain all the greater for it.

Mr. Brown dropped his hand and let the jury push past him. My uncle, who now had passed the overcoat to Mr. Simpson, followed them to the front of the tavern and joined us there.

Before any of us could congratulate Ernest or even share our relief, the coroner spoke to the constable again. "I would suggest you release Mrs. Holmes immediately before you're made an even bigger fool with the jury's decision." He then waved his hand at the scene on the street. "And clean up this mess."

I turned to my father, elated at this announcement, but his grim features squelched the rush of joy that a moment ago had surged through me. Mycroft had a similar stony posture.

A smile, however, creased my uncle's face. "A bloody good show, what?"

"Yes. Although it might have been done with a little less spectacle." My uncle's smile wavered, then disappeared. Father took a step toward the street and spoke over his shoulder. "Come along. We'd best go and collect your mother."

"I'll stay here," Ernest said. "I want to observe the final decision."

My feet fairly floated me to our carriage, and even the glare the constable gave us as we passed didn't diminish my giddy mood.

My mother was in my father's arms the moment she stepped through the door. She fell into his embrace in the same antechamber I had entered when I accompanied my uncle to visit her. Such different circumstances. Such different emotions. Trepidation and anxiety had been replaced with a renewed sense of order and peace. As much as I wanted to place my arms about her as well, Mycroft's hand on my shoulder reminded me this moment was for them.

After the first public display of affection I'd ever seen between my parents, my father went further by taking a step back and holding her face in his hands. I thought he would kiss her, but instead he only studied her countenance. She responded with an examination of her own. Her eyes glistened above a wide smile that parted her lips.

"I take it Ernest's demonstration was successful," she said.

"Violette, my dear, don't tease at a time like this," he said, his usually steady voice shaking. "I was so afraid I was going to lose you."

"Never, Mr. Holmes. Never."

He pulled her to him again. Over his shoulder, her gaze

fell first to Mycroft and then to me. She pushed back against my father and said, "Come, boys, give us a hug as well."

I was in both my parents' arms in the next moment and enveloped in the familiar scent of my father's cigars and the heavy gaol odors.

Behind my back, I heard the door to the street open and close, and my mother stiffened at my side. When I turned to see what had caused the change, I found the constable, still fuming, standing, a step behind my father. A hot flame coursed through me. I checked the others in my family, and they all had the same hard squint as I.

"What a touching scene," he said. "Your whole blasted family has made a fool of me."

"It wouldn't have happened, if you had listened to me," Mother said, raising her chin.

The constable took a step forward. "Now see here, no *woman*—"

My father blocked the man's way.

"How dare you speak to my wife in such a manner," he said.

His voice held an almost animal-like growl. Never had I seen him in such a state. His eyes had cleared and were as hard as his tone. Crimson colored his cheeks, and I actually feared for the constable's safety.

Gibbons must have had similar concerns because he took *two* steps back.

"You leave my family alone," Father continued. "I stayed out of your investigation and the coroner's because I didn't want to be accused of favoritism or meddling with justice. As a result, I still hold a respected place in this community. You, however, are simply a town servant. I can arrange your replacement, should I have a mind to do so."

The constable's glare darted from my father to Mycroft and me (still in our mother's arms), and finally rested on her.

"This isn't over. You may not have stabbed Emma Brown, but you're mixed up in this in some way. I'll not rest until I find out how and bring you to justice."

My father took a step forward, but Mother placed a hand on his arm. "Let's not make a scene, my dear. The man is beneath you. I want to go home. I have need of a bath."

After a moment, he turned his back to the constable and spoke to us in a clipped voice.

"Simpson is waiting."

He turned, took a step toward Constable Gibbons and met the man eye-to-eye. After a moment where I feared one might actually take a swing at the other, Gibbons stepped to the side and let us pass to the street.

Perhaps we shouldn't have left our carriage in front of the gaol, because outside we discovered our presence had been noticed by many in the village. The crowd, while not anywhere near the size of that at the inquest only an hour ago, surged forward as we exited the gaol. Father and Mycroft quickly flanked my mother, and I was left to take up the rear.

Given the constable's response to the inquest's findings

and the threat he'd just delivered, I had assumed a similar reception by those outside. To my surprise, the assembled, mostly women, cheered at the sight of my mother, and many reached out to her as we passed to the carriage.

"I prayed for you, my dear."

"I knew you couldn't do what they said."

"So glad to see you free."

"I'll be by later. For…you know."

My brother and father pushed at those bearing down on us, but their numbers were too great. My mother must have sensed their frustration because she raised her hand and the throng stilled.

"I appreciate your good wishes." She sought out the village women as she spoke. "I am a simple woman who desires nothing more than to return to her home and family. I feel deeply for Mrs. Brown's family and hope the true murderer will be apprehended. Now please let us pass so that we can return to our lives."

The group responded to her request and opened a path for us. Mr. Simpson jumped down from the driver's seat to open the carriage door.

At that point, I noticed several men with paper and pencils scribbling furiously, some shouting questions over the heads of others.

"Were you aware of the stunt with the pigs?"

"Why do you suppose the body was left on your property?"

One particularly aggressive reporter stepped in front of the carriage, blocking our progress.

"Can you tell us what you fought about with Mrs. Brown?"

My mother paused, but before she could respond, Mycroft bolted forward, pushed the man to the ground, and grabbed the paper and writing instrument from his hands.

"Leave my mother alone," he said, ripping the paper into shreds. "You...you... scavenger."

The man scrambled to his feet and dropped back into the crowd. Mycroft's display had sobered the others, and everyone took a few more steps back. I held my breath as if somehow it would make me smaller and allow me to slip unseen into the vehicle after the rest of my family.

Only after taking a seat did I exhale.

As the carriage lurched forward, Mycroft, still flushed and panting from his exertion, reached about and pulled down all the shades to block out the view of the crowd. When he settled back onto the bench, I glanced at him with a new sense of admiration. I'd never seen him display quite as much strength or emotion as he had in that one event. For the first time I saw his sense of superiority and contempt for others—usually directed at me—had served a useful purpose.

Following a huff, he said, "Damned press."

"Was that display necessary?" my father asked.

"Yes."

My father opened his mouth, but Mother restrained him

with a shake of her head. "No arguments. Not now. Thank you, son, for your efforts to protect my privacy."

The two men settled back in their seats, and we rode in silence, each in his own thoughts. A moment later, however, a chuckle bubbled from Father's lips. It grew into a full laugh which lasted long enough I feared he'd lost his senses. When it subsided, he took Mother's hand and managed to say through hiccups, "You should have seen it, Mrs. Holmes. I thought the coroner and the jury were all going to have seizures right there in the street when Ernest stabbed that pig."

"I'm surprised more of them didn't get blasted when the blood spurted out," Mycroft said.

"Please share the particulars."

"Don't you want Ernest to tell you, my dear?" asked Father.

"I'll get his review later. I'd like to hear your impressions as well."

"I do have to say it was a most effective way of showing the poor woman hadn't been stabbed to death," Father said and proceeded to describe Ernest's questioning of Constable Gibbons and the spectacle in the street. By the end, he was laughing again with the rest of us joining in. The tension that had gripped us for the past week dissolved into the tears we swiped from our cheeks as we recalled the observers' shocked countenances.

When our mirth had died, Father shifted in his seat to face her and lifted her hand to his lips. "I'm so glad you are free. Underbyrne hasn't been the same without you. I realized how much your presence completes the home."

Mother blinked, glanced at the shuttered window, and pulled the shade open before turning back to him. "It is I who am the fortunate one."

Mycroft coughed and the two of them flinched and turned to face us. Their fingers, however, remained entwined.

"With this inquest now behind us," Mycroft said, "I assume we'll be returning to our duties?"

I gulped. All the joy I'd experienced with my mother's release evaporated at the thought of entering Eton again. Despite the heavy atmosphere at home with my mother's imprisonment, I'd had the freedom to roam about and a sense of importance in the work I was doing. Returning to school for me was the equivalent to Mother's time in gaol.

"Why don't we discuss that later?" Mother said. "I want to revel in this moment. With no thought of the future." She took a deep breath. "I never knew freedom had a scent until now."

Without any thought, I took a deep breath as well, drawing in the tang of the carriage's leather, the dust of the road, and the green fields beyond. As with her, I now knew the aroma of freedom—its source lay in Underbyrne. At that moment, the two were the same.

She rested her head on my father's shoulder. The two continued their grip on each other's hands. That small gesture and the tenderness with which he now stroked her thumb with his own gave me a new view of my parents' bond with each other. I had always considered their relationship as something akin to a business arrangement—with my father providing the income and my mother maintaining home and family. For the first time, I understood marriage might also involve an emotional connection.

The carriage turned onto Underbyrne's private drive, and we passed over a rut. The carriage swayed, and Mother cracked open her eyes. She straightened herself in the seat and drew in her breath. "Oh my. What day is tomorrow?"

"Saturday, dear," Father said, opening his eyes as well. "I suppose it's difficult to keep track of time while in—"

"It's not that. My ladies' luncheon is tomorrow."

"Surely, Mrs. Holmes, you don't mean—"

"Mr. Holmes," she said with a tone that, while soft, carried a hidden warning within it that she would not be swayed. "If we are to return to normalcy in our home and our place in the community, we must maintain our social obligations. That includes my monthly ladies' luncheon. I'll make certain that Mrs. Simpson has the staff prepare as I planned prior to my...to my absence. And you, Sherry dear..." She shifted her gaze to me. "I think it's time for us to consider that duet we selected before you left for Eton."

I nodded, elated I had practiced the piece while she'd been incarcerated. My heart swelled with pride, knowing she'd be pleased with my progress.

The next moment, however, my mouth fell open when

Mycroft glanced out the window and asked, "What the devil is that man doing here?"

"Truly, Mycroft," Mother said with a sigh, "is cursing necessary? I have told you, one doesn't need foul language to express—*Bloody hell*, how dare that man show his face at our home."

CHAPTER FIVE

Mrs. Simpson must have heard the carriage pull into the yard, because she rushed out of the house and down the steps. When she turned her head to her right at the bottom, she halted, frozen on the driveway, yards from the carriage. From the window, I saw her pull herself to full height and march in the direction of a man and horse waiting beyond our coach. Mr. Brown stood by his steed, a package in hand. My surprise at his presence shifted to the same indignation Mother expressed when she saw him.

The carriage swayed as all the occupants descended, one after another. The honey man took several steps back when Father, Mycroft, and the Simpsons approached him like the Roman army advancing on the Huns. Only the horse prevented the man's further retreat.

Mother and I caught up with the others in time to hear Mrs. Simpson say, "God's teeth, you have some nerve to show yourself at this home."

The five grown-ups formed a semi-circle around Mother's accuser. I hung back, knowing my father wouldn't have approved of my presence in a matter involving adults.

The beekeeper must have forgotten about his horse because he tried to step back again. He was trapped, only able to stare wide-eyed at the five fuming before him. Finally, he dipped his head and shoved the package toward them, almost as if making an offering to some heathen deity.

"I brought honey for Mrs. Holmes' luncheon tomorrow. Same as always."

I stood still, expecting one of them to slap the bundle from his hands before sending him off draped over his horse's back. At least, that was my own inclination in response to his appearance at our home. I could only stare as my mother stepped forward. When she reached out, his flinch was visible even from my vantage point.

"How kind of you to remember my upcoming event," she said. "It wouldn't be the same without your contribution. How much do I owe you?"

After glancing at her outstretched hand, he placed the parcel in it. "I-I can't accept anything from you. Not after what I put you through."

Had I heard her correctly? She was accepting his apology? I checked the others' backs to see if I was mistaken. All four still stood rigid as if prepared for battle. One, however, didn't remain immobile.

"*Put her through.*" My father stormed forward and grabbed the man's shirt and vest in his hand. Father's color passed red and bordered on purple. "You had her *arrested*. Put in *gaol*. Ready to be *hanged*. Without one lick of evidence."

The man sputtered, and his face darkened, progressing beyond my father's color. "I-I didn't... P-please... S-sorry."

"Mr. Holmes," Mother said, tugging lightly on his outstretched arm. "Mr. Holmes, let him go. *You* don't want to be accused of murder as well."

"It'd be justifiable homicide. No jury would convict me," he said, fairly lifting the man off his feet.

The honey man gave a strangled gasp.

"Regardless, your reputation would be tainted. You don't want to hand that on to your sons."

Father glanced at his wife, then at the man, and dropped him to the ground. Mr. Brown fell onto all fours and took several deep breaths between coughs. Mother knelt next to him to observe him while his color faded to something more normal. When his breathing slowed, she gestured to my father to help him up.

Once he was on his feet again, Mother pointed toward the house. "Why don't we all go inside? A cup of tea might help restore you."

"Mrs. Holmes, really—" Father said, unable to even complete the sentence.

Mother raised her hand and gestured to all assembled toward the house. "Mrs. Simpson, will you lead the way?"

The men fell in line behind the two women, Mr. Brown holding back a moment to give some distance between him and the others. I followed even later. While we entered the house, Mr. Simpson tied the beekeeper's horse to the carriage and took both toward the stables. I overheard him talking to the two animals as he did so.

"Finest example of Christian charity I've ever seen. The man accused her of killing his wife and now she's having him to tea. Not an angry or bitter word toward him. Aye, true Christian charity."

My lips turned up at the edges. I was quite certain he'd have a different opinion of my mother if he'd heard her oath earlier in the carriage. I had no doubt her resentment and anger ran quite a bit deeper and stronger than what my father had displayed. Something else had motivated her to invite the man inside.

That realization spurred me to hasten inside just in time to find my family and Mr. Brown already seated in the parlor. I slipped into the room and took my usual place toward the back, following my father's admonition that boys my age in the presence of company should be "seen and not heard—and in most cases, not even the first."

I observed Mr. Brown had taken off his gloves, which now rested on his knee. Even from my vantage point, the sticky sheen of honey on the fingertips was visible. Surely one of the hazards of his trade—beyond the obvious bee stings—would be the impossibility of ever being fully free of their product.

Mrs. Simpson apparently took it upon herself to bring out the tea and a substantial arrangement of food. She must have brought out some of the food already prepared for celebrating my mother's return. As Mother accepted a plate from our housekeeper, she turned to the beekeeper. "Surely, Mr. Brown, you didn't come here to risk the Holmes' anger simply to deliver some honey—although I do appreciate your wares. What is it that you truly want?"

Mrs. Simpson served our guest and stepped back to the tea tray to make another plate. I leaned forward to catch the man's explanation.

He shifted on his chair, making the teacup rattle in its saucer. As he did so, he grimaced and glanced in my father's direction. He took a sip of tea, glanced at the plate and set it on a small table next to him.

"I-I came to apologize. I should have"—he pulled at his collar—"uh...known you weren't capable of such a crime. It's just that...poor Emma, she deserves her peace."

My father coughed, but I knew it was to mask a sound of contempt that bubbled up unbidden.

"I was just so certain—although quite mistaken, mind you—my Emma had been stabbed to death. With the display your brother so graphically completed today, it's quite obvious her death occurred by other means. Mr. Parker did such a fine piece of investigation and demonstration, I was hoping he'd consider continuing to search for her true killer and bring the person to justice."

I entwined my fingers, the knuckles turning white, as my uncle was given credit for my discovery.

"I'm afraid my brother isn't here at the moment," she said. "He stayed in town to observe the rest of the inquest. But I will pass on your request to him. I think he'll be glad to help you identify the perpetrator. I would suggest you share your request with Constable Gibbons as well. He might have his own notions of who might be suspect."

"Oh, no. He was quite grateful for the information I gave him concerning your argument with Emma." He stopped and crimson crept up his neck and into his face. "I mean...er...he reported to me having no evidence beyond finding...her in the garden."

At this point, his voice cracked, and he swallowed hard.

Despite my earlier resentment and anger at the man, I found myself sympathizing with the widower. Perhaps he grasped at the first straw that seemed to explain what happened?

My father and brother must have had a reaction similar to mine because they both cleared their throats and shifted in their chairs. Mother, however, reached out and touched the man's hand.

"I'm sure I can convince my brother to help you determine who did this to your wife." Mrs. Simpson huffed from the far corner of the room. Her employer turned to her and said, "That will be all, Mrs. Simpson. I'll ring if we desire anything else."

The woman shuffled off, but her muttering commenced as soon as she stepped into the hallway. Her retreat sparked something in Mr. Brown as well. He searched about for a moment, then set his cup and plate on a small table next to his seat. Relieved of his burden, he stood and faced my mother.

"I want to thank you for your kind forgiveness and hospitality. I recognize this has been a trying time for you. And for me. I should let you enjoy reuniting with your family."

We all escorted the man to the door, and he took his leave, heading to the stable to pick up his horse.

As soon as the front door closed, Father spun about and said with a voice that failed to exhibit the reserve he always lectured us to maintain, "Has your time in gaol addled your brain, Mrs. Holmes? I find it incredulous that Ernest would consider helping him find the true culprit when the man was willing to have you hanged."

His shallow, rapid breathing suggested he might pass out from his efforts to control his emotions. My mother must have feared the same because she stepped to him and ran a light caress up his arm. When he turned to her, she met his gaze with the same calm I had seen her show one of our injured animals as she placed a poultice on its wound.

"I recognize it appears to go against reason. But when he came here today and put in his request, several things became clear to me. Our family's reputation is far from redeemed—despite the inquest today. A shadow still hangs over our name, and Constable Gibbons is going to exploit that unless we are able to show beyond all doubt we were not involved in poor Emma Brown's death. The most efficient way to do so is to find the true culprit. While Mr. Brown says he's convinced we were not involved, I am not certain he truly believes it. Let us not forget the teaching of Sun-Tzu, '*Keep your friends close and your enemies closer.*' I can't abide any cloud darkening your standing in our community."

Father's breathing had slowed as she spoke, and he now studied her in deep contemplation. After a moment, he glanced at Mycroft and then me. "You mother is right. I'm afraid it also means you boys can't return to your studies until we resolve this matter. The scandal would haunt you there as well."

Both Mycroft and I sighed at this pronouncement, although I was certain for different reasons—Mycroft out of frustration and me, relief. He opened his mouth to speak, but Father spoke first.

"This is not open for argument. As long as I'm paying for your studies, I will decide when, and if, you return."

"I think, Mycroft," Mother added, "you might find this an appropriate incentive to put your intellectual skills to the task confronting us." She smiled, letting her gaze rest for a moment on each of us. "Now if you'll excuse me, I am overdue for a bath."

Mrs. Simpson stepped from the shadows, and I realized she had an ability for stealth I hadn't observed previously. "I already had the chambermaid prepare one for you. The water, however, might not be warm enough. I'll have her bring some more."

"Thank you. Will you also send a plate up? I'm afraid I wasn't able to partake of much during Mr. Brown's visit. Perhaps two," she said after taking a few steps toward the stairs and turning back to us. "That is, Mr. Holmes, if you care to join me?"

A kind of secret communication passed between them, and the corners of his mouth lifted slightly. He stepped to the stairs, took her hand and raised it to his lips.

"It sounds…delicious."

Mrs. Simpson's cheeks reddened. "I'll have the girl bring up a tray to your sitting room." "Thank you, Mrs. Simpson," my mother said.

Her hand still in my father's, the two headed to the second floor. Mrs. Simpson, my brother, and I watched them ascend. While I had no desire to remain downstairs, I felt following them to go to my room almost bordered on an intrusion of their privacy.

When they had passed out of earshot, Mrs. Simpson sighed. "Now the home is complete again. I thought your father would die when they took her away. Come along, boys, I'm sure whatever you had in the parlor wasn't sufficient. There's more in the dining room."

"Breakfast was rather light," Mycroft said.

We followed her to the dining room, and as I took my seat, I glanced at the two empty places set for my parents. I had to agree with Mrs. Simpson. Even though they were not at the table, I found myself at peace—as if a missing puzzle piece had found its proper place and the image completed. Simply *knowing* they were in the house was enough to create a familiar contentment.

With a plate of food in front of me, I attacked all I had been served with great relish. I glanced across the table at Mycroft and found him slumped over his plate. While he consumed his repast, he didn't do so with the same enthusiasm he normally showed. But for me, even the impending monthly invasion of mother's luncheon invitees tomorrow couldn't dampen my spirits for the moment.

PLANNING AND EXECUTING one of my mother's luncheons took as much coordination as the campaigns in Afghanistan my uncle had described to me. First were the preparations of the dining room and parlor, for not only did the invited village women eat, mother also provided them with entertainment and a lecture. The women assembled in the parlor for the entertainment (such as the duet my mother and I had practiced), moved to the dining room where they were treated to tea, finger sandwiches, cold meats, and an assortment of desserts, and then returned to the parlor for a health-related lecture.

This required the servants to arrange the parlor furniture into rows and the dining room for twenty-five or so guests. All the servants were enlisted in one way or another to clean, move furniture, or assist Cook in food preparation. Given my mother's absence and the uncertainty of her fate until the day before, some of the anticipated work had not occurred and now arrangements were being hurried along. My father and brother had disappeared shortly after breakfast, and had I not been slated for the duet, I would have followed their example.

When the hour for the guests' arrivals chimed, I descended the stairs, dressed in the same suit I had worn the day before to the inquest. Mother had donned one of the ensembles she usually reserved for church services, and her activity during the preparations had brought a flush to her cheeks, enhancing her appearance.

With none of the guests yet received, Mother suggested we practice our piece until they came. The pianoforte had been pulled out of the corner to a more central spot in front of the audience. We went through the duet twice before the first carriage wheels crunched up the drive to the front of our home.

Mother fairly jumped from her seat at the sound, a hand to her chest. A nervous gesture I had never seen her express previously.

"I was so afraid the women might stay away," she said more to herself than to me and pulled the red ledger I had found in the greenhouse from her pocket and placed it on the far corner of the pianoforte.

I heard Mrs. Simpson greet the guest, and their footsteps clicked on the floor as they entered the parlor. A woman I didn't recognize extended her hand and smiled. "Mrs. Holmes, I hope you will excuse me for not accepting your previous invitations to your luncheons. Unfortunately, other duties had always called me away." Her expression faltered a bit when my mother released her hand, but she continued. "All the same, I'm here now."

"I'm so glad you could join us today, Mrs. Gibbons. I'm sure you'll find the afternoon a most pleasant diversion."

Gibbons?

The name fairly pierced my brain. The constable's wife had chosen to visit our home only one day after my mother was released from gaol—where her husband had put her?

"Would you care for a cup of tea while we wait for the others to arrive?" Mother asked with a smile. And not an *I-plan-to-gossip-and-insult-you-behind-your-back* smirk, but a genuine beam as if they were long-time friends.

After our first guest had been served, the ensuing silence allowed us to hear clearly the grandfather clock ticking in the hallway and the faint clink of Mrs. Gibbons' cup on her saucer as she sipped her tea. Sighs escaped both Mother and Mrs. Gibbons when another set of carriage wheels rolled up the drive.

Several carriages arrived in quick succession after that, and although their number reached the usual proportion, the group seemed much more subdued. Father always referred to them as "clucking hens," but today they chirped more than clucked. In addition to most of Mother's usual guests, Mrs. Adams, the vicar's wife, also made her first appearance. She and Mrs. Gibbons drifted to the edge of the crowd as the others served themselves tea or lemonade. Once the assembled settled into seats, Mother and I presented the day's entertainment.

The duet went off flawlessly, if I do say so myself, and after the appropriate applause, Mother invited all to the dining room for the light meal. Because I'd been part of the group, she suggested I also stay in case some wished to comment on my performance. I took a chair at the far end of the table near Mmes. Gibbons and Adams. Neither seemed completely at ease among the spouses of the community's prominent landowners. They kept glancing about and only nibbled at the food on their plates.

As I had previously observed, the adults talked over my head as if I were invisible. This attitude suited me fine. I found the effort to maintain the sort of social chitchat required for such functions both tedious and unproductive. Until they touched on the subject of the Straton family. Having recently made the acquaintance of the oldest daughter, I listened more intently to this topic.

I pretended to concentrate on the tomato aspic on my plate while I listened to their discussion.

"Yes, I agree, the situation with the children must be

addressed," Mrs. Adams was saying to the constable's wife. "We should take up a collection."

Mrs. Gibbons pulled back her chin. "The only collection they need is one where they are all gathered up and sent off to a workhouse. My poor husband just despairs about the havoc they having been causing the whole village. Not to mention the fights he's had to break up with the father at the center. While their mother was alive, she kept them in check, but with their father now turned to drink, they've gone completely wild."

"Caught the oldest, that redheaded devil, with two tins of milk in her pocket," said Mrs. Gillis, the wife of the village's general shop, joining in on the conversation. "How she got behind the counter, I have no idea. I should've called your husband, but when she began to cry and promised not to do it again, I let her go."

"You're too soft-hearted, my dear. Mr. Gibbons always says the best way to avoid additional criminal behavior is to put them in a place where they have time to contemplate their transgressions."

"But don't you see?" Mrs. Adams said. "That's exactly why we must take up a collection. Think about it. She didn't steal candy or a toy. She tried to get milk. Probably for the new baby. My husband and I have discussed this at great length, given we plan to start our family now. Children are a blessing and must be cared for by all of us. He's to make an announcement from the pulpit on Sunday. He's also planned a series of homilies related to the love and care of our neighbors."

Before either woman could respond, my mother rose and announced dessert and additional tea would be served in the parlor during her lecture. The women all returned to the other room, and I joined them long enough to snatch one of the desserts (a compote of some of our own preserved fruits in a tall glass) and accept a few more compliments on my musical skills before taking my leave.

As the parlor door closed, I heard my mother raise her voice from her position in front of the pianoforte. "My dear ladies, as you know, I have focused my talks of late on hygiene and its importance to overall prevention of disease. Today, however, I would like to deviate slightly and to share my opinion on the corset and its effects on women's bodies..."

A murmur passed through the audience, and I shut the door with a firm hand. I knew one did not discuss undergarments—whether for men or women—in mixed company, and my presence would certainly be considered an intrusion. The topic, however, did give me pause as I considered what exactly these items looked like and their purpose. These thoughts then gave rise to what lay below all the clothing and to the images I'd seen in the medical text. A slow heat crawled up my neck and into my face.

A sound at the end of the hallway—probably one of the servants clearing away the luncheon items—brought me out of my reverie. Fearing I might be caught red-faced outside of the parlor, I strode toward the back of the house. With no determined aim in mind other than getting away from the parlor, I found myself headed outside and in the direction of my uncle's workshop.

I could hear the banging from halfway across the yard and waited until it stopped to knock on the door. After he opened the door, he turned and rushed back to his work-bench, throwing a "hello" over his shoulder. Only when I reached the other side of the table, did I see the high crimson color in his face and the beads of sweat trickling down each cheek. He had certainly worked himself into a lather working on....

I checked out the item before him. A misshapen *hira shuriken* lay on the table. He raised a mallet and smacked the star-shaped metal with it. Between each strike, he explained what he was doing. "I determined..." *Smack!* "That the pieces..." *Whack!* "Were too heavy..." *Thump.* "Which is why..." *Clang!* "The trigger became ..." *Clunk.* "So sensitive."

He paused to peer at the piece before him. While defi-nitely flatter, all the blades were squashed into odd shapes, their points now rounded. He lifted it by one blade, raising it to his eye-level.

"I guess I have some filing to do." As if he had only just seen me, he pulled his chin back. "Sherlock, my boy, I'm very busy today. Do you need me for something?"

"Not really," I said and sighed. "I just wanted to get out

of the house. Mother's luncheon, you know. I was hoping you wanted to go hiking."

"Can't today, boy. I want to see if I can solve the trigger problem. Violette said she wanted to speak with me later. Something about the Brown issue. I want to get this done before she's free."

I considered asking if he needed help, but he was already pulling out a foot-operated grindstone—truly a one-man activity. I excused myself and left him to his business.

I knew my father and brother were probably both in the library and contemplated joining them—even possibly suggesting a game of chess with Father. Mycroft deemed only Mother a worthy opponent for him in chess, explaining she was unpredictable.

If Father had already found another pursuit, however, I would still have to seek out some other diversion. My gaze landed on the door to the greenhouse, and I chose to devote some attention to Mother's plants.

I'd made it about halfway down the second aisle of plants when I heard the sounds of horses and carriages. The chiming of the clock in the hallway followed. Were the ladies already leaving? With a shrug, I returned to my efforts and snipped off a dried leaf from a basil plant. The item fell from my grasp, and I bent down to pick it up.

That was when I heard two voices approaching. I recognized my mother's and, then, that of Mrs. Gibbons coming toward the greenhouse. When they entered, I was still on my hands and knees, hidden from view. At first, I'd planned to stand and greet them, but when I realized their conversation was rather heated, I hesitated. Would they consider my behavior as eavesdropping—even though it had been unintentional? In the end, I decided to remain concealed, and I hoped, undetected.

"Won't you change your mind, Violette?" the other woman asked as they traversed the next aisle.

I held my breath but was certain they could hear my heart drumming in my chest. They passed me without even pausing.

"I'm sorry, but this really is a matter for Mr. Harvingsham."

"But I've heard from a very reliable source that you do supply some with pennyroyal. And with Mrs. Brown—"

I could almost hear my mother straighten her spine. "Mrs. Brown was a quite capable midwife, but she had a limited knowledge of botanicals. And you are mistaken. While I have the plant in my collection, I do not dispense it because of its toxicity. Even a non-fatal dose can seriously damage the liver."

"So what is it that you do dispense?"

"The usual. Rosemary. Eucalyptus. Mint."

"But you said you do have pennyroyal. Can't you give me just a small bit? That's all I ask. You know..." Mrs. Gibbons dropped her voice almost to a whisper. "For ladies' problems."

A pause followed. Finally, my mother said, "I think it

best for you to see Mr. Harvingsham about the subject. I'm sure he will be able to advise you better than I."

"Then you won't—"

"No. I'm sorry. It's too risky."

"Then what about—"

"Again, I suggest you consult Mr. Harvingsham."

"Yes. Well. Thank you. I can see myself out."

"I believe you'll find Mrs. Simpson farther down the hallway to lead you out."

A swish of skirts signaled Mrs. Gibbons' departure. After the door closed, Mother said, "You can come out now, Sherry."

I swallowed hard, hesitating for a moment before rising and asking, "How did you know I was here?"

"Your footprints on the floor. How many times have I asked you to clean your boots before entering the house?"

She headed down a row, the ledger in her hand, toward her work desk. Her mouth turned down, and I feared she was angry with me.

With some trepidation, I followed and asked, "Is everything all right?"

"We had a spy in our midst today."

"I'm sorry. I should have said something when you came in."

"Not you, my dear. Although it wasn't proper etiquette to listen in to someone else's conversation. I was referring to Mrs. Gibbons. She came here to spy for her husband." The creases in her forehead deepened. "I believe you're aware of what I do for the women of our village. Mrs. Winston came early this morning to see me to let me know how glad she was I was let out of gaol. She mentioned how she asked about the Queen Anne's Lace seeds the other day."

"I meant to ask you about it when I visited you in gaol. I just…forgot, and she never returned."

"Don't worry. She told me she'd taken care of it another way and didn't need any more seeds at the moment." She placed a hand on my head. "You have to understand, son, I do what I do for the health of the women. Having so many children—"

"Makes them die young. Like Mrs. Straton. Mycroft told me."

"Exactly. Unfortunately, not everyone believes in preventing so many births. Queen Anne's Lace seeds do exactly that. When crushed and taken properly, women will avoid pregnancy."

"Then why did Mrs. Gibbons ask about pennyroyal?"

"Because it causes a woman's monthly bleeding to occur. I believe Constable Gibbons sent his wife here for precisely that reason. To determine if I share such plants with women."

She studied me for a moment and must have seen something in my face because she noted, "I think we should discuss the topic of what occurs between men and women more, but at a later moment."

The images from the medical text flashed across my consciousness, and my face warmed as I remembered the reaction they sparked. More scrutiny from my mother. I dropped my gaze and mumbled to my shoes. "Mycroft shared something with me...a book."

"I think I know which one. Mycroft found it quite... educational when he was about your age." A cool hand on my cheek turned my face upward. A small smile flitted across her mouth, but her tone was serious. "There's nothing to be ashamed of. It's a natural part of being human."

While I appreciated Mother's forthrightness on the subject, I found such a discussion with her quite uncomfortable and made a concerted effort to change the subject. "Does Mr. Harvingsham provide women with pennyroyal like Mrs. Brown did?"

"Not that I know of. I only want Mrs. Gibbons to report back to her husband that I wouldn't give her anything and sent her to consult with the surgeon and perhaps divert his attention away from me."

"Do you think you succeeded?"

Mother glanced at the door separating the greenhouse to the main house. "I hope so. Only time will tell." She sighed and said in a lighter tone, "I need to speak to Ernest about Mr. Brown's request. He's in his workshop?"

I nodded. "He said he's waiting for you."

"I need to prepare him for tomorrow. Mr. Brown is sure to want an answer then."

CHAPTER SIX

The next day, Sunday, began sunny and breezy. Out the window, the light reflected off the crimson and gold leaves twisting in the wind. I could almost feel the crunch of the freshly fallen ones under my feet, the crisp tang of the autumn air in my lungs, and drew on all my willpower not to pull on my boots and jacket to wander among the woods. For on Sunday, as one of the county's leading families, the Holmeses went to church.

As with the rest of my education, Mother took a special hand in assuring I had proper instruction in the basics of theology. I had several tutors who provided me with an in-depth understanding of world religions, the history of the church (both Catholic and Protestant), and catechism lessons. Not to mention the Latin and Greek a superior education required.

Despite all this preparation, what truly compelled me to attend services—beyond my father's expectation his family would fulfill their duties to the community—were the rituals and the assurances behind them. The predictability in the prayers and litanies, the following of the same calendar each year, even the benches' unyielding pressure on my thighs as the vicar drew a deep breath, signaling he was but halfway through his homily produced a sense of order and inner strength that comforted me.

True to his wife's words, Reverend Adams did include an announcement about the Straton family and the plan to take up a collection. He asked for anyone wishing to contribute to see his wife following the service.

By the time church ended, the sun had risen high in the sky and sweat beaded on my forehead and upper lip almost as soon as we'd stepped outside and headed to the carriage.

About halfway to our carriage, someone called from behind us.

"Mrs. Holmes." Mr. Brown waved at us from the top step, his black cloak flapping with the movement. He tripped quickly down the stairs and ran to meet with us. "Please excuse the intrusion, but I wanted to ask if you spoke with your brother, as we discussed yesterday?"

"You can ask him yourself. Ernest, I believe you were going to speak to Mr. Brown about accepting his request to investigate his wife's murder?" she said, turning to my uncle.

"Yes, of course," he said, settling his shoulders and clearing his throat. "With all humility, Mr. Brown, I will continue the investigation I had already begun on behalf of my sister. Thank you for your confidence in my abilities."

Mr. Brown took my uncle's arm and dropped his voice. "I wanted to make you aware of certain events that point to the perpetrator, if I may be so bold. Might we discuss this in privacy?"

"My dear sir," Ernest said, straightening his back, "anything you have to share with me, you can have the utmost confidence will be kept within our family."

The man's eyes darted back and forth in their sockets as he studied each of us. After shifting on his feet and dropping his gaze, he raised his head to speak to my uncle. "I think you need to look carefully at Straton. The man has an evil temper. And blamed my Emma for his wife's death. In public. At the Pig and Spider."

"You frequented a pub?" Mother asked. When the two men faced her, the color rose in her cheeks, but her voice remained steady. "Excuse me for interrupting, but I was under the impression you were a teetotaler, Mr. Brown."

He raised his head and glared at my mother. "I don't believe in strong drink, that's true, but I do have a business to run, and they have as much need of honey as any other establishment." He turned his back to my mother and continued speaking with my uncle. "Although my wife was innocent of what he claims, I am certain his temperament is such that he could be capable of murder if properly provoked. Ask any at the pub. You'll hear all of them testify to his threats against my wife."

"Interesting insights, sir. I'll take that under considera-tion. Now, if you'll excuse us, we were about to return home for Sunday dinner."

"Yes. Of course." The man fairly scraped the ground with his bow. "You will follow up, won't you? You'll see. Straton is your man. I'm sure of it."

We took our leave of the honey man and boarded our carriage. Once moving, the carriage's methodical rocking put all of us into a dreamy stupor until Mother spoke up to no one in particular.

"An interesting discussion on the part of Mr. Brown, don't you think?"

"Straton certainly has a temper," Father said. "He's been in my court more than once on charges. But murder? I guess if carried too far…"

"Pity we can't simply visit the Pig and Spider to deter-mine if others actually did hear him threaten the woman," Mother said.

"Mrs. Holmes, I refuse to allow anyone in this family to lower themselves to fraternize with those who frequent the front room of such an establishment."

"The word is *proletariat*. At least that's what the Germans, Marx and Engels, call them in their treatise." Mycroft's voice was clear without any hint of drowsiness. He'd been resting his head against the carriage's panel but hadn't been asleep despite appearances. "These men have described a rather bleak situation for them and predict a violent revolt should conditions not change."

"Marx and Engels?" Mother asked. "Do you have a copy of this treatise? I would like to read it."

"Revolutionary poppycock," my father said, almost spitting the words. "I've heard they call for the confiscation of all lands. Everything to be owned by all. They call it *communism*."

His mouth turned down, and he squished his face as if he'd tasted something bitter.

Mycroft leaned forward, his words almost tumbling out of his mouth with an enthusiasm he rarely displayed. "Whether you support their cause or not, this is one of the shifts I've noted in my studies. History has shown that when the masses are discontented, change will occur. Look at the colonies, and their revolt against the crown. The same passed in France. Calling it poppycock doesn't mean it can't occur. That's why I need to return to Ox—"

"And you shall," Mother said. "But I don't care to discuss it at the moment." Mycroft pressed his lips together, thwarted in his effort to bring up the topic of his return to his studies. He leaned back against the cushion and scowled at us the rest of the way home. For my parents and myself, we slipped back into silence.

Driving up to the house, however, the sight of the gamekeeper waiting in the yard caused us all to sit up and shake off our pensive attitudes.

"What's the matter, Benson?" Father asked, alighting from the carriage as soon as it pulled to a stop.

The man frowned. "I've found another one, sir." He spat onto the ground. "Ripped a lamb up good this time."

"After dinner, we'll go out after it." Father turned to Mycroft and me. "Care to help us hunt a wild pig?"

My brother immediately shook his head, but the desire to spend the day outside I'd experienced in the morning returned and compelled me to respond. "I will."

"Sherlock and I will see you then in an hour or so, Benson."

The anticipation of spending some time with my father led me to rush through dinner. Once upstairs, I changed into my hunting clothes, including the deerstalker cap I received last Christmas. Once again, I found them a little tight, but could do nothing about that at the moment. I raced down the stairs and found my father already putting on his boots by the back door. I tried to do the same with my own but couldn't seem to get the first one past my ankle.

"Good heavens, son," my father said as he helped me extract my foot. "We're going to have to order you some new hunting gear. I guess you'll just have to wear your regular boots today."

He handed me a rifle, and we headed off through a field to the woods surrounding our grounds. I'd been hunting and shooting guns for a number of years now and knew how to carry the rifle for proper safety.

Once outside, we headed to the left, passing the stables and moving through the field beyond, fenced to hold a small flock of grazing sheep. Benson waved at us from the far side, just inside the fence. Behind the fence, the woods began. When we approached him, I could see a circle of blood from the slaughtered lamb. Also visible were two broken rails where the pig had broken through. The grass and ground about the bloodied area and on the other side of the fence were churned and trampled with hoof marks.

"He went back into the woods the same way as he came," Benson said, pointing to the pig's trail. "It's too old for tracking, but at least we know where to begin."

Father pointed to the right. "Benson, you head in that direction. Sherlock and I will take the other. I suppose we'll know if you find anything. We'll hear it."

"Yes, sir," the gamekeeper said with a nod.

Once we split, Father and I loaded our weapons before tramping toward the first trees. The going was too narrow for us to go side-by-side, and I let him lead the way. He spoke over his shoulder. "Stay near. I don't think the animal would attack a human, but if it gets cornered, it might."

I shuddered. More than one governess had put me to bed with tales of the evil befalling children who disobeyed their parents—most of which involved an event in the woods. Even armed with a weapon, I wasn't all that confident. Not that I hadn't been in the woods or gone hunting before. But stalking and shooting a deer wasn't the same thing as tracking a wild pig.

We took a path running parallel to the woods' edge. Father checked broken branches in the underbrush or other signs the animal had passed. At one point, we found more stirred-up earth and a tuft of hair caught on tree bark.

"Not wool," Father said, holding the strands in his palm. "Too straight. Probably from that beast."

He dropped the hair to the ground, and we continued trudging through the area, seeing nothing more ferocious than a rabbit when it crashed through the underbrush and appeared almost directly in front of us. Father and I both started, then chuckled at our unfounded fright.

No sooner had we exchanged our silent joke than a high-pitched wail echoed from deeper in the woods, directly ahead. My father put a finger to his lips and pointed in the direction of the noise. He motioned me to step behind him, and we marched single file through the brush. I gripped my rifle tighter, my palms now damp and slippery on the wooden stock. Another wail, now on our left, followed by a rustling in the brush, made us both freeze. We shifted our direction, moving with even greater caution and now almost side-by-side.

Tiny rivulets of sweat ran down the rifle's barrel, and my tongue traced my lips. I barely dared to breathe. We crept forward, placing one foot as silently as possible in front of the other. Father pushed back a limb and exposed a huge black and white pig, shrieking at something in a tree. Huge teeth rose like yellowed claws from its pink, foamy mouth. My heart pounding, I watched the animal lower its head and ram its brow against the tree's trunk. The wail that had originally alerted us to the pig's presence emanated from the trees' branches. A blue-clad figure—about my size—showed through the crimson and mustard-colored leaves. The person must have seen us because a girl's voice called out.

"Shoot it. The branch is breaking. If I fall, he'll rip my throat out."

As if on cue, the lower branches shuddered, sending a shower of dead and dying leaves upon the pig, which, in turn, crashed into the trunk again to add to the deluge of foliage.

Father motioned me to follow him into the clearing, and I mimicked his stance—rifle raised, finger near the trigger, ready to fire—as I drew abreast of him. Once I was beside him, he shouted at the pig. The sound caused the animal to turn and lunge toward us. We fired almost simultaneously, the cracks of our weapons echoing off the trees and sending all the fowl in the area into the air. The weapon's stock recoiled into my shoulder, and my nose filled with the acrid stench of gunpowder.

Over the ringing in my ears, the pig's screech sent a jolt down my spine, freezing me in place. Unable to move, I saw the animal slide to a halt a few feet in front of us, its breath puffing out of its mouth. Its rear muscles twitched, and I braced myself for it to continue its charge straight at us. Instead, it gave a second squeal—only slightly less intense than the first—and spun about to race off into the underbrush.

"Come on, Sherlock," Father said, cocking his gun and

reloading. "We have to find it and kill it. It's even more dangerous now it's wounded."

"What about the girl? Up in the tree?"

He squinted at the figure hidden among the branches. "Constance? Is that you up there?"

"Yes, sir."

"You come on down, and don't you run off. I don't want to have to go looking for you too. If Benson comes along, you send him after us."

"Yes, sir."

A rustle in the branches suggested she would soon be on the ground, but Father was already on his way to the area where the pig had pushed through the underbrush. I followed, my rifle reloaded and ready.

The blood trail allowed for easy tracking, but still Father paused every so often to listen before proceeding. I understood why a few minutes later when he again stopped and turned his body slightly, his jaw tense. Heavy, slow snorting blew dead leaves and other debris from underneath a growth of saplings. He motioned me to keep in step with him.

The pig lay on its side, its labored exhalations indicating both pain and anger. When we were almost upon the animal, Father stepped on a branch. The pig jerked its head up at the crack and pulled itself to its feet, facing him.

The beast tightened its haunches, prepared to charge. Without hesitating, or even thinking, I raised my weapon and fired at its side. Already having lost blood, the shot was enough to down him. He collapsed at my father's feet.

In the shot's aftermath, my body responded by rebelling against every part's natural state. My earlier, heavy Sunday dinner formed a weight in my stomach and threatened to return. The bones in my legs lost all rigidity and were poised to melt onto the leaves and twigs under my boots. With great effort, I raised my gaze to my father. He, too, appeared quite affected by our ordeal. His eyes rounded, he shifted his focus between the pig, its snuffling becoming a death rattle, and me.

My hands grasped the still-raised rifle even tighter until a broad grin split his face. "Well done, son. Good show."

My grip relaxed, and the gun sank to my side.

Pounding footfalls and a general breaking through the brush caused us both to spin toward the noise. Benson appeared, his rifle at the ready. When he stepped up to us, he lowered his weapon. A girl, clad in blue, peeked at us from behind the gamekeeper.

"You killed 'im, then?" she asked.

"Sherlock did it," my father said, his voice now strong. "I couldn't get a good shot with it charging right at me."

Benson stepped up to the pig, his rifle again at the ready. He gave the beast a kick in the side. "A good, clean kill. Well done."

My shoulders dropped, and my chest rose at the second "well done." Rarely had I had the opportunity for someone outside my family to recognize an accomplishment.

"Take care of it, will you, Benson?" my father asked. "I think we should all enjoy some sausages and bacon from the beast." He glanced at the girl still standing at the spot where she and the gamekeeper had first stopped. "You want to tell me why you were in my woods, Constance?"

"I weren't doing no harm," the pickpocket from the gaol said, raising her chin. "Just pickin' some wild berries here's abouts."

As if to prove her point, she put her hand into a dress pocket and pulled out a handful of bilberries. Their juice had stained her palm and tongue.

"She *has* been eating them, Father."

His mouth pulled down. "These are private lands. Another owner might have you arrested for poaching."

"For taking a few wild berries? For my brothers and sisters?" The girl had more cheek than I'd ever witnessed. Even Mycroft wouldn't have confronted my father as directly. "Besides, I wasn't *looking* I just *saw* and thoughts to myself, 'such berries would make a tastier treat for the young ones than they would for the birds.' So I took a few."

My father's mouth twitched, and at first I feared he planned to actually have her put in gaol. Instead, the corners went up, and he chuckled. "I suppose you have as much right to them as the birds."

"Thank you, sir."

"That still doesn't explain why you were in the woods in the first place."

"The path, sir. Everyone knows abouts it. Leads straight

through the woods to the village. We all use it. I'm always meetin' people on the way to town or to Hanover Manor."

Father glanced at Benson, who nodded. Even the game-keeper seemed to know about the apparent shortcut. My father shifted on his feet and gazed about him. He was planning to dismiss the girl and leave the pig to Benson's attention. Perhaps inspired in part by Constance's boldness, I spoke, expressing a thought without weighing its full consequences.

"She's obviously hungry, Father. I know the church is taking up a collection, but perhaps we can send something back with her until the other is ready?" Before he could answer, I turned to her. "Come back to the house with us. We'll get you something to eat and a basket to take back to your family."

"Truly? You would do that for me?" I nodded, and then she paused before asking, "What do you want in return?"

"Nothing. Consider it…Christian charity," I said, recalling the conversation at the luncheon the day before.

Father cleared his throat, and I faced him, fearing he had decided to countermand my offer. Perhaps he had, but when he glanced first at me and then Constance, who blinked her eyes, making a face as heartfelt as a dog begging scraps at the table. He shifted on his feet and cleared his throat once again. "Christian charity. Of course. Come back to the house with us."

The return trip to the house seemed much longer than when we went into the woods. We finally emerged near the field where the sheep grazed. While I'd been prepared to offer Constance assistance in passing over the rails, I never had the chance. Without hesitating, she hopped nimbly over the barricade. As she did so, I noticed her shoes for the first time. The toes had been cut out of them as if to make room for her growing feet.

Once we were all on the same side, I asked her. "Aren't your feet cold?"

"I'm used to it," she said, studying her shoes. "I usually wrap the ends in rags, but they fell off when the pig chased me."

"Father," I asked, turning to him. "May she have my old boots? They don't fit me and she needs them."

"She was the one who found the pig, in a way." He rubbed his chin. "At least she alerted us to its whereabouts. I suppose she saved the life of more than one lamb. You can share them, if you wish."

When we reached the barn, both Mr. Simpson and my uncle stepped out, deep in conversation. Father hailed them both, and we stopped not far from the kitchen door. Constance's stomach rumbled, and I knew she was anticipating our "charity."

"The pig won't be bothering us anymore." He slapped me on the back, and a warmth spread through me from that spot. "Sherlock here got him when it charged me."

My uncle placed a hand on the other shoulder. "Good show, boy."

"He's a right good shot," Constance said and sent a smile in my direction.

My uncle stared at her and frowned. "Who are you? No, wait. I've seen you before…"

"She's one of the Straton children. Constance. The pig had her treed."

"What's she doin' here?" asked Mr. Simpson.

"Sherlock invited her," Father said. He faced me. "Go on and take her to the house."

With a nod, I passed my rifle to him and motioned the girl toward the house. With each step, her shoes slapped up and down between her feet and the ground.

Mother must have been in the greenhouse and seen us approaching from its windows. She arrived in the kitchen the same time as we did. She still wore the apron she would put over her dress when working there. She smiled at us when we entered.

"Constance, how good to see you again," she gave her a smile. "Did the men find you in the woods?"

The glow I'd experienced when my father had reported on my shot of the pig re-ignited with my mother's inclusion of me among the "men." If she realized the effect of her remark, she appeared not to notice and focused on the girl.

The girl nodded. "I was picking berries. For my family."

"I told her we'd fix a basket for them," I said.

"And give me somethin' to eat now."

"Of course," Mother said with a smile. "Let me prepare a plate for you. I'm afraid Cook has the afternoon off, so it will have to be cold, but there's bread. And milk. Of course, you need to wash up before you eat. Let me show you to the facilities."

When they returned, the girl's transformation caused my breath to catch. Her face, now scrubbed clean, displayed a pale complexion with just a sprinkling of freckles across her nose and cheeks. From my mother's own efforts to avoid direct sunlight and the resulting darkening or freckling of the skin, I knew it was not fashionable, but in Constance's case, I found them quite becoming. Mother had also managed to tame Constance's hair, brushing it smooth and tying it with a ribbon in the back. She also provided her with a white servant's apron to cover her dress.

"You look…" I stopped when I saw scarlet creep into her cheeks. I fumbled for a moment for the proper words, and finally said, "Like you're ready to eat."

She stared at the plate set on the table before her. "That's all for me?"

"Yes, dear," Mother said and motioned to me. "Sherlock, please pull out the chair for Miss Constance."

I rushed over and drew it out, pushing it back in once she was seated.

"Lords, I feels like a lady," she said, glancing back at me.

Mother moved to the other side of the table and said to me, "Let's join her, shall we? Sherlock, would you mind bringing us two cups of tea?"

While I prepared the teapot using the water always kept hot in the kettle over the kitchen fire, Constance attacked her food. She grasped the fork in her fist and shoveled the cold meats and vegetables into her mouth as if someone might pull the plate away at any minute. By the time I returned to the table, she'd consumed three-quarters of the meal. Mother and I sipped our tea while she finished off her plate, pausing only to take a bite of bread or drink some milk to help swallow what she had in her mouth.

After she scraped the plate clean with her fork and used the bread to pick up any stray pieces, she leaned back and belched.

"Lords, that was tasty. That meat, it was roast beef, wasn't it? I don't think I've ever had such tender meat. Of course, when my mother was alive, we'd eat good—like this."

"Your mother was a good cook?" Mother asked, leaning forward. "What dishes did she prepare?"

"Chicken, for one," she said, glancing away and adjusting herself on the seat.

"You must miss her very much."

"I do." Her eyes glistened. "She went to bed one night and never woke up again. I was the one who found her."

"How horrible for you."

Her head jerked up and down in quick succession, then she lowered her voice. "It was a shock, findin' her de—that way. All cold and stiff."

She shuddered, and my mother placed a hand over hers. "I didn't mean to bring up painful memories. Let's speak of other things."

The girl gave a nod but lowered her head to stare at her hands. I imagined how I would feel if I lost my mother. She had been my teacher in so many things, and the hole she would leave in my life wouldn't be filled. To assist the women and myself, I changed the topic.

"Mother, Constance's boots are all broken, and I have a pair I've outgrown. I told her she could have them."

"An excellent idea," Mother said. "Why don't you bring them here?"

With great enthusiasm, I pushed back my chair and rushed to the garden door to retrieve the boots I had left earlier. I presented them to her with a flourish.

"Try them on."

She kicked off her foot coverings with the missing toes, and I gasped before I could stop myself. Mother squinted at me, her mouth a hard line, before addressing Constance.

"Those cuts must hurt."

"I'm used to it, ma'am," she said, studying the various abrasions across her toes. Had they not been covered with dirt and crusted with some dried blood, I was certain they would appear even worse. "It's the blisters that can make it hard to walk."

When she pointed to the tops of her feet, I recognized the raw places where the shoes had cut her skin.

"I have some ointment that might help with all those," Mother said. "But we need to clean them up first. How about we wash your feet, and I'll bandage them so that the new boots won't irritate them? You can take some ointment home to put on them until they heal."

The girl tilted her head to the left and studied first my mother and then her feet as if pondering the offer. After a moment, she asked, "Is it going to hurt?"

"It might sting some, but I promise it will help in the end."

Another moment, then she nodded. "All right."

Mother turned to me. "Sherlock, why don't you get a pair of your socks? That will help hold the bandages in place after I'm through with Miss Constance."

By the time I had raced upstairs, located a pair of socks, and returned, they had moved to the greenhouse where Mother kept her ointments. Both of Constance's feet soaked in a bowl of water, and her injuries appeared more pronounced once they had been removed of dirt. Never had I seen the effects of no resources and poor hygiene as up close as I did at that instance. While my pity for her grew, her stoicism as my mother bandaged the tender skin impressed me even more.

"Now," Mother said, rising to her feet. "See how it feels to walk."

Constance slid off the stool and took a few tentative steps. "I can walk all right."

We helped her put on my old boots, which were slightly large for her. Once we stuffed the toes with some clean rags, however, she managed quite well in them.

We returned to the kitchen to fill a basket.

"Sherlock," Mother asked when we had completed the task, "will you escort Miss Constance home, please? And carry the basket for her?"

Her back straightened. "I can take it myself."

"Nonsense. That basket is far too heavy for you."

My cheeks burned, but at the same time, my heart quickened at the thought of spending time with the girl. She intrigued me. I had never known a thief, and her ability to take the bread from my pocket without my knowledge was something I'd never encountered before. In addition, my mother trusted me with a task she might have passed to Mr. Simpson or another adult.

For the second time that day, my maturity was recognized.

I ran my arm through the basket's handle and followed Constance to the door. Mother held it open for us, and I turned toward the road, planning to follow it in the direction of the village. When I realized Constance wasn't following me, I turned to see her still by the kitchen door.

"The other way is shorter," she said, pointing in the direction we'd come with Father.

I glanced toward the road and then to the fields beyond the wall. I'd eliminated the pig problem and could think of no reason not to learn about the path she'd referred to earlier. I certainly couldn't appear less inclined than a girl. With a shrug, I said, "Lead the way."

After crossing the walls and the fields, we arrived at the woods. She walked along the edge for a while and then turned in when we came to an opening between two bushes. A short time later, we were walking in the cool shadows under the trees. As she promised, a clear path ran perpendicular to the trail we'd used to enter the woods and parallel to the woods' edge. She pointed to the left.

"That way leads to the Browns' house and the village, and this way," she said, pointing in the other direction, "is Hanover Manor. You know you're gettin' close when you find the stream that runs onto their land."

I glanced in both directions. The path was clearly well traveled with packed dirt visible under the current dried leaves. "I can see it's much quicker than the road."

"If you have to walk."

I shifted the basket in my hands. "To the left, then?"

We continued side by side for a while in silence. With the pig menace now removed, I found myself open to other sights and sounds in the woods. The call of various birds, the rustle of leaves as different creatures hid from us, the rasping of the wind among the tree branches. I shifted the basket in my hands and checked the sky. The sun was dropping to the western side of the forest.

"It's getting late. Is your father going to be cross with you for being out?" I asked.

She trudged on a few moments before answering. "He's probably still working. He comes home very late, and sometimes not at all. We watch each other, mostly. I'm the oldest, but with my mum sick for a long time before she… before she passed, we'd been taking care of each other for a while. Mrs. Brown told her she'd had too many babies too close."

"I've heard that," I said. When she turned to stare at me, I quickly explained my remark. "I've heard, in general, too many babies can weaken a woman."

She didn't reply, but simply continued putting one foot in front of the other. A tear slipped down her cheek. She didn't try to wipe it away, but let it slide down her chin and drop onto her chest, making a tiny dark spot there.

I wanted to say something to her, but had no idea what would be an appropriate sympathetic remark and so remained silent. Although Mother's incarceration had been rather short, the specter of her permanent absence lurked in the back of my mind. The very thought of her never returning caused a melancholy to descend upon me. If only the *possibility* of such a loss created that sensation in me, what would the *reality* produce? I shuddered at the very prospect and forced my mind to shift to another subject and decided to do the same for Constance.

"I saw you at the inquest on Friday."

"It was quite a show," she said, her face breaking into a smile. "I'd've paid to see your uncle stab a pig like that."

I nodded, a smile also crossing my lips as I remembered the scene on the street. "He did put on an impressive performance."

"Better than the circus."

I opened my mouth and snapped it shut, not sure if I should broach the question that popped into my mind.

"What is it?" she asked and poked my arm. "You were going to say something."

"I was going to ask something, actually."

But still I hesitated. While never addressed specifically by my father's etiquette admonishments, I doubted it was appropriate to ask about certain behaviors from someone who was almost a stranger.

She turned to me and jammed her hands to her hips, a stance that reminded me of one of the lead soldiers I'd used as a commander in all my make-believe battles. "Spit it out."

"I saw you…. There was an elderly gentleman near the bar…and the bread at the gaol…."

Her eyes rounded, and I feared she was angry with me. Instead, when she opened her mouth, she laughed, and continued on the trail. "That was you? It was the most delicious thing I'd eaten. Ever."

"Would you…? Could you…?" I cleared my throat and dropped my voice even though we were alone in the darkening woods. "Teach me how you did it?"

She stopped and tilted her head to study me. "What for? You don't need to."

"Maybe not, but it seems a skill worth developing," I said, jamming the toe of my boot into the ground.

Another momentary pause while she scrutinized me.

"You goin' to tell your father on me?"

"Never. He'd not approve. I'm sure."

"I can't do it in a day. It takes time. You gots to practice."

"I'm willing."

"Let me think on it." She picked up her speed and mumbled to herself. "A judge's son wantin' to learn dippin'. What's the world's comin' to?"

I did my best to keep up with her in spite of the increasingly heavy basket. Despite the ill-fitting boots and the wounds on her feet, she had quickened her pace. Shortly after this exchange, she turned onto the faintest of trails, pushed through some brush, then stopped, apparently waiting for me. When I reached her, she pointed to a cottage about twenty yards ahead.

"That's my home," she said.

My first impulse was to disagree with her. A person could not possibly live there, let alone a family as large as hers. The cottage couldn't have been more than one room. The thatched roof showed thin spots, which probably leaked when it rained. The area around the house was packed earth.

She took a few steps and called to those in the cottage. When the door opened, three children of various ages ran out to meet her. The oldest among them carried a bundle in his arms, and I realized it had to be the youngest baby. They stopped, however, when I stepped beside her. They squinted at me, and a boy who walked on unsteady legs hid behind the skirt of a girl I guessed to be five or six. A boy of about ten glared at me.

"This is Sherlock," she said, heading toward her brothers and sister. "He's Squire Holmes' son. He's brought us something to eat."

At the mention of food, the children's mouths spread into smiles, and the girl ran her tongue over her lips. Somehow, I didn't think the berries Constance had found earlier would have been sufficient for her siblings. The vicar had better hurry in collecting for the family.

When we reached the others, the girl made a grab for the basket. "What's in there?"

Constance slapped her hand.

"Mildred, where's your manners? You, Victor, and Harold go to the pump and clean your hands. Mrs. Holmes, she told me we could get sick if we didn't clean up. I'll take Daniel inside."

They all stood for a moment, and Mildred stared at her before asking, "Is that why your face is all white? 'Cause you washed it?"

"And she brushed my hair," Constance said, running her hand down her back. She turned so that Mildred could touch it. "Feel it. It's all silky."

"Ooo," the younger girl said. "Can you do mine? After we eat?"

She nodded, and the others ran to the side of the house. Now burdened with the baby, she stepped to the house and motioned me to follow her inside. The moment I entered, I was assaulted by an odor not unlike that of a barn. The interior was dark, with only a light in the fireplace at the wall opposite the door providing any illumination. A kettle hung over the fire, but no other scents of cooking could be detected. Three platforms covered by some old blankets appeared to serve as beds. Constance stepped to a box on the floor and placed the baby in it. It made some very weak mewing sounds, and I thought I would suggest to Mother the child might need additional attention.

She took the basket from me and said, "Thank you, Master Sherlock. I'll feed the others. You best be getting back before dark."

I checked over my shoulder at the sun, sitting just above the treetops. With a nod, I turned and had taken two steps outside when the three younger children ran past me, their hands and faces still wet, but definitely cleaner than when I'd arrived.

Despite the encroaching twilight, I was able to find and follow the trail back to Underbyrne with little difficulty. Without the burden of the basket, the trip was also quicker.

Once home, I sought out my mother to inform her I had completed my task. She was in her sitting room next to the bedroom she shared with Father. Only after visiting other homes when I was older did I learn how Mother's sitting room was not typical. Other ladies of her time might embroider, paint, read, or observe other "feminine" pursuits. Mother did read in the room, primarily scientific treatises, but she also had a microscope.

When I arrived, I found her deep in thought, a volume open on her lap. She lifted her gaze. "Back so soon?" She pointed to the book. "Just reading the book Mycroft loaned me. Quite interesting view of economics, particularly the role of women and the family."

Which seemed an appropriate way to transition to the Straton family. I made my report of the cottage and the baby, and she promised to see about arranging for appropriate milk for the infant.

"May I ask you something?" I asked at the end of that discussion and continued with her assent. "It's Mr. Straton. Or rather, Constance's description of him. I didn't see him at the house, and it appears the children care for themselves. But she talked as if he provided and cared for them."

"I've seen this before," she said, shaking her head. "With her mother. Like her, Constance wants to believe what she says about him. She needs to."

"Why would she do that?"

"Love. Or what she takes for love. I've seen women deny when men hit them because they believe their husbands love them."

After I recovered from the idea that a man would hit a woman (something my father had taught was never done), I considered her observation about such relationships in light of my own parents. I could never imagine her accepting violence from my father, but would she vouch for or repeat my father's lies? Certainly my father had defended his wife when accused of murder, but it had been obvious she was innocent. What if she had been guilty? What would he have done then? And what if it had been the other way around? Would my mother have lied for him?

Was loyalty to the point of blindness a part of love? I had a hard time imagining my having such love for any person beyond, perhaps, my parents. And maybe Mycroft.

Before I could ask her more, a rapid footfall on the stairs caused us both to turn toward the door of the sitting room. One of the parlor maids stood in the open doorway, panting to regain her breath.

"Madam…the door…constable."

"Constable Gibbons?" Mother asked, and the maid nodded in response. "Please inform Mr. Holmes. I'm sure it involves some infraction—"

The maid shook her head violently. "No. He says he's got a warrant to search the house."

CHAPTER SEVEN

By the time Mother and I made it down the stairs, Father, Uncle Ernest, and Mycroft were already in the front hallway, blocking Constable Gibbons from passing any farther into the house. Behind the constable stood three deputies, all as sour-faced and grim as their superior. Several veins bulged on Father's crimson neck and face, and he was shouting at the officer.

"This is an outrage. The inquest put to rest any question of my wife's involvement in the death of Emma Brown. What makes you think you can come in here, and—"

"This warrant," Gibbons said, holding up a folded sheaf of paper. "Signed by Judge Montgomery."

"Let me see that."

Father fairly snatched the paper from the man's hand and perused the document. "It says here you have the right to search the greenhouse. That can be reached from the *outside*. Go around the house to the back, and we will let you in there."

Behind me, my mother drew in her breath. Because everyone's attention focused on the exchange between the two men, no one else seemed to have heard her. She had to be recalling Mrs. Gibbons' sudden interest in my mother's luncheons and the contents of her greenhouse.

Did the constable have a similar interest?

She didn't make any verbal protest, which I was certain reflected an effort to keep from drawing more attention to her activities.

In addition, Father's acquiescence to the search suggested he was not completely aware of Mother's plants or their purposes. He might not be concerned, thinking nothing would be found to connect her to Emma Brown's murder, but would he be so detached if he knew about the information the little red volume held? I recalled how it lay in plain sight on the pianoforte. Mrs. Gibbons was bound to have seen it. Observed any notations Mother made. And its return to the greenhouse after the luncheon.

Cold sweat beaded on my upper lip. I saw no way of avoiding its discovery if that was what he truly sought.

The four officers of the law spun on their heels and marched back through the front door. As soon as the door shut behind them, the five of us rushed through the halls to the conservatory and waited for the men to reappear.

After gazing about the room and the plants for a

moment, Gibbons said, "We will now execute the warrant. You will not pass the threshold during the search."

On his superior's orders, one of the officers accompanied us to the interior entrance to the greenhouse and remained there to prevent our entry.

The remaining three poked about the various pots and studied the recesses under the tables.

"What exactly are you searching for?" Father called to them.

"Pennyroyal," Gibbons said.

Mycroft said, "A common enough plant."

Gibbons straightened up and faced us. "Perhaps. But there are rumors going about that Mrs. Straton was poisoned by pennyroyal. And it came from this greenhouse."

The process was exceedingly slow. The pulse in my neck thrummed as they moved toward the pennyroyal plants. Mother, however, remained straight-backed and still. When they reached the pots with the aforementioned plants, they passed them by, giving them no more attention than they had with any of the other plants.

My pulse quickened as my worst fears seemed realized. The pennyroyal was merely an excuse for the search. I checked my mother and saw the color rise in her cheeks as the constable stepped back again toward the outer door, focusing on the books and papers scattered about the top of her workbench.

I held my breath as Constable Gibbons flipped through

the pages on one and then another of the notebooks on the table. I reminded myself to remain impassive as he opened the coded notebook, frowned, and tucked it under his arm. I allowed myself a glance at Mycroft. Had he recognized the ledger as the one I'd shown him? He wore the same bored, inscrutable expression he showed when playing chess.

The constable completed his inspection of all the items on the table, spun around, and strode up the room's central aisle to where we stood. He held out the ledger and displayed it to all there.

"Would you care to tell me what this is?" he asked.

"It's a diary," my mother said. Her chin was high, her gaze steady.

"Of what?"

My uncle cleared his throat. "Violette, dear, as your solicitor, I would suggest—"

She held up her hand to silence him. "I appreciate your concern, Ernest, but I can answer that question." She faced the constable. "Of my activities."

His brows drew together, but he said nothing. He thumbed through the pages again and placed it in his pocket. His gaze traveled about the room and my family gathered in front of him. "I guess we're through here."

With that pronouncement, he marched back to the outside door, his men following behind. None of us moved from the area until the greenhouse's back door closed soundly. Our simultaneous exhale resembled a chorus of bellows.

Mycroft was the first to speak.""You must get that diary back, Father."

"I don't see the importance of—"

"It represents years of scientific research. I can't lose all my notes," Mother said.

"I understand, Mrs. Holmes, but he had a warrant and as a magistrate, I must respect the law. Once he determines they are research notes, he'll return it."

She opened her mouth, shut it, glanced at the door Constable Gibbons had exited, and then at us. After a moment, she straightened her back, as if she had decided something, and said, "Let's retire to the schoolroom."

"But that's on the third floor. Whatever do you want up there?" Father said.

"The blackboard."

She spun on her heel and headed to the stairs. The four of us glanced at each other and then at my mother's retreating back. After a moment, Father shrugged and followed my mother.

"Since supper won't be served until Mother and Father request it," Mycroft said, his mouth turning downward, "I suppose we might as well appease them."

"Sort of singing for our supper, wouldn't you say?" Ernest said. "Shall we, boys?"

The three of us trooped up the stairs behind my parents. Ducklings heading to the pond. Only the pond was a miniature classroom complete with a large slate attached to the left wall. Generations of Holmeses had studied here, and the odor of chalk dust and old books permeated the walls and floor. The ceiling sloped down to a set of windows on the right. Because I had been using the room to practice for our duet, a music stand occupied a space at the center window to catch the light. My violin case rested on a chair next to the stand.

Two long tables and six chairs faced the slate, their backs to the windows. A desk and chair—used by the tutors— occupied the back wall to the left of the slate. Mother positioned herself at the blackboard, a piece of chalk in her hand. The rest of us seated ourselves in the chairs. Because Mycroft and I had used the room for our early studies, the desks and chairs were smaller than such regular furniture. After taking my chair, I glanced about and couldn't help but smile at how the adult men had to accommodate their longer legs to the furnishings. To a man, they all pushed back their chairs and stretched out their legs to fit under the desks.

"All right, Mrs. Holmes," Father said, his voice still tinged with the same exasperation he'd expressed to the constable. "We're here. What's this all about?"

"*This* is about Mrs. Brown's murder." She sighed. "The invasion we just suffered exemplifies how much under a cloud we remain. The constable would have never been so bold as to take my personal property *before* my incarceration. I had Ernest agree to help Mr. Brown primarily to keep the man at bay. Now I see the decline in the Holmes' reputation is more pervasive than I had thought. We must restore it."

Father stilled as he considered her words, then said, "I've always upheld the law to the best of my ability. While I've never been this personally involved in investigating a crime, I can see how we might need to be in this case. The cheek of that man."

Like Father, I could see the logic in her argument. If we identified the true murderer, the constable would have no choice but to return the ledger.

Father straightened in his chair. "Where should we begin?"

She paused, staring first at the blank slate and then at us. Tapping her finger against her lip, she faced us and said, "With a review, I suppose. What do we know at this point?"

The four of us exchanged glances, but it was Father who spoke first. "The victim."

"That seems an appropriate place to start," Mother said.

She wrote *Mrs. Emma Brown* on the board. Underneath, she wrote *Midwife*.

"We also know she wasn't stabbed," Ernest said, raising his chin. "I proved that."

Under Mrs. Brown's name, she wrote, *Cause of death: Unknown.*

"But was she murdered?" Mother asked.

Father sat upright in his chair, "Are you suggesting—?"

"I'm not suggesting anything. I'm stating that without knowing the cause of death, making a judgment as to whether it was an accident, murder, or an illness is based only on speculation. We must determine *how* she died."

"Pity no autopsy was done," Ernest said, his mouth turning down. "Constable Gibbons was so convinced—thanks in part to Mr. Brown—that Violette had stabbed her, he didn't call Mr. Harvingsham in."

Mycroft shifted in his seat and coughed. "For the sake of argument, shall we assume Mrs. Brown was murdered? If so, it leads to the question 'by whom?'"

"Mr. Brown says it was Mr. Straton," I said.

"Very good, Sherry dear. Because that leads to a possible second murder. Mrs. Straton."

Again, she wrote the name on the board.

The letters, white on black, stared back at me. My palms grew damp as I realized the impact my pronouncement would have on Constance and her brothers and sister. If Constance's father was arrested, the children would be sent not to the workhouse Mrs. Gibbons had mentioned, but to an orphanage.

"Other than her husband's accusation at the pub, do we know how she died?" Mycroft asked, breaking into my thoughts.

"Another time Harvingsham wasn't called in. Everyone knew she'd been in ill health since the boy was born. Gibbons told me the surgeon signed the death certificate without even examining her," Father said.

"But she'd seen Mrs. Brown, and I'm almost certain the midwife gave her pennyroyal." She stared at the slate but seemed not to be seeing it. She continued, more to herself than to us. "But something happened. She needed more."

"Mrs. Holmes, what makes you think she was given pennyroyal and needed more?"

Mother shivered as if awakening and turned to face us. I noticed the same color in her cheeks as when the constable had taken her ledger.

She hadn't told him.

Father had no idea about the seeds she was giving to the women. She'd lied to him—if nothing else, by omission. What if Father discovered her sin? I had no desire to see any rift between them. Without any more thought, I spoke up.

"Constance."

The others all turned to me. Warmth spread up my neck to my face, but I said in a calmer voice, "Constance Straton. She told us about her mother seeing Mrs. Brown and then finding her mother dead. Remember, Mother?"

"Yes," she said, the color fading in her cheeks. "I had a long talk with the girl while she ate. She shared that her mother had consulted Mrs. Brown before she died."

Father tilted his head and stared first at Mother and then at me. I mimicked Mycroft's passive expression during the search of the greenhouse. After another moment of silence, he spoke slowly, as if choosing his words, "It appears we need to know more about what happened to Mrs. Straton. Perhaps another talk with Constance may be in order."

Father's stomach rumbled, and he stood. "For now, however, I suggest we have our supper. This day has been most upsetting, and I could use some nourishment."

"An excellent suggestion," Mycroft said, also rising.

As the others filed out of the room and headed down the stairs, Mother touched my arm and whispered, "Wait a minute."

The footfalls of the three men faded as they descended the stairs, and she faced me to still speak in a low voice. "Sherlock, you need to speak to Rachel Winston."

The idea of having a discussion with an adult woman seemed beyond my comprehension. I was used to speaking to servants, but only to make requests. I couldn't fathom interrogating her. The very idea made my palms sweat.

"Wouldn't she be more comfortable with you?"

"Perhaps, but I would be recognized at Hanover Manor."

"Hanov—? You want me to go there? But I'd be recognized too."

"Not if you were disguised as a tinker's apprentice."

My jaw fell as my mother's request became more and more bizarre. "You wish me to disguise myself as a tinker's apprentice and ask for Mrs. Winston? Won't they suspect me if I ask for the woman by name?"

"Not if you ask about any tin ware needing repair. Rachel is in charge of the kitchen utensils. She'll be called to talk to the tinker's man. As for the disguise, you recall we have quite a number of used clothes for when we have played *tableaux vivant* with your father's family."

I nodded. My father's sisters came to visit at different times, and while Mother found them rather tedious, they did fill the house with more noise and activity than usual.

Among their interests was dressing up and depicting various famous events or paintings. Their greatest joy was to demand Mycroft dress as a woman. I might have considered it more amusing if they hadn't also dressed me as a young girl.

"It's very important for you to speak with her. We need more information about what Mrs. Straton got from Mrs. Brown. Perhaps Mr. Straton is right. Mrs. Brown may have poisoned the woman."

I nodded as the gravity of my mission became clear.

When I turned to leave, Mother spoke one more time. "Thank you, Sherlock, for deflecting your father's question today. I truly appreciate it." She draped an arm over my shoulder. "Let's not keep the others waiting. Supper should be ready."

As we descended, I allowed myself a smile. A special mission, her gratitude, and the full use of my name. Then I sobered. I had to do well at Hanover Manor. Anything less than gathering the information she desired could destroy the trust she now placed in me.

AFTER ALL THAT happened that day, I was glad to return to my room after supper. But after what seemed like only a minute after I closed my eyes, someone roughly shook me awake. Through cracked eyelids, I made out Mycroft holding a candle. He was still dressed as he had been for supper.

"Get dressed and meet me at Ernest's workshop."

I sat up and rubbed my eyes. "What for?"

"We have to get Mother's ledger back."

When I arrived at Ernest's workshop, I found my brother and uncle in the workshop's sitting area. As with my brother, Ernest remained in the same clothes he had worn all day. I'd glanced at the grandfather clock in the downstairs hallway. One o'clock in the morning. Was I the only one needing sleep?

As soon as I sat down, Mycroft turned to our uncle. "We must retrieve Mother's diary before the constable has an opportunity to translate the cipher."

"How could botanical experiments be—?" He paused and squinted at him. "Violette lied to the constable?"

Mycroft paused as if recalling the exchange between our mother and the constable. "I suppose, technically, she didn't. She said it was a record of her activities. She never specified what sort. It's in code, but the risk is that the constable will find someone who can decipher it."

"You did straight away," I said. "Without the book you loaned me."

Mycroft pulled on his waistcoat. "Of course, I did. An average person like the constable won't be able to do it on his own, but someone familiar with ciphers would recognize it and be able to determine its true meaning. It contains names of Mother's clients."

"I conclusively showed she did not stab Emma Brown, so I don't understand the concern over the names of a few village women."

"Some of those names are of local prominent women."

He drew back his chin. "Prominent? Really? I've never seen them skulking about our back door."

"Do you truly believe Mother *enjoys* all those visiting days? Listening to all their gossip and prattle?"

I considered Mycroft's observation. The women arriving in their carriages, drinking tea in the parlor, taking a tour of the...*greenhouse*. I saw these seemingly mindless female pursuits in a whole new light. But another question surfaced and flew out my mouth before I could stop it.

"How long have you known this?" I asked my brother.

"I'd always considered some hidden agenda for their calls, given their almost precise frequencies and patterns. But it wasn't until you showed me the ledger that the final piece fell into place." He turned to Ernest. "Gibbons is now bent on seeking a way to smear our mother. That stunt with the pigs—while brilliant—discredited him. He wants revenge. Do you see how important it is to recover the book? We need to find a way of doing so. Are there any legal arguments that could be used to regain its possession?"

"He had a warrant. I'm not sure..."

"I'm never going to get back to Oxford at this rate," Mycroft sighed. "We must find a way—legal or not—to rescue that notebook."

A thought occurred to me, and I drew in my breath.

"What if we don't try to retrieve the book? What if we were to *replace* it instead? We could create another ledger in code that *did* have data from botanical experiments in it."

"We can't very well just walk into the constable's office and say 'Sorry, old chap, you picked up the wrong book. Here's the right one,'" my uncle said and chuckled at his own joke.

Mycroft tipped his head upward and stared at the beams crossing the workshop's ceiling as if considering my suggestion and spoke more to himself than to the two of us. "It would have to be done clandestinely."

"You're assuming he has it in his office. He could keep it at his home," I said.

"Office. Home. It doesn't matter," Ernest said, straightening his spine. "You're talking about breaking the law. As an officer of the court, I can't be involved in this."

I leaned forward in my seat to meet Ernest's gaze. "Uncle, we're not doing this for us," I shot a glance to Mycroft to ensure he wouldn't contradict me. "But for Mother. As Mycroft said, Constable Gibbons seems to be seeking some way to arrest her again. You weren't with us at the gaol when she was released. He said then he was going to see her returned to prison. You know her. She has only good intentions in helping the women here. We can't let the constable end that."

My uncle blinked several times. "How, then, would you propose we break into the constable's office and replace the ledger?"

"I don't think we are the best people for this type of work," Mycroft said. "We lack the skills to successfully carry out a robbery. It takes training to be able to break in. Someone who has the knowledge…and the tools—"

As he shared this thought, one popped into my mind as well. Before I even realized it, I said it out loud. "I know such a person."

When the other two turned in my direction, I added, "Or at least I think I do."

Mycroft and I each left with a task. My brother was to create another ledger. His eidetic memory (more highly developed than mine) would ensure an almost identical replica of the ciphered contents. I would speak to Constance about assisting us with replacing it.

But before seeking her help, I had to complete the errand to Hanover Manor.

MOTHER ASSISTED me with the disguise after breakfast. She found a pair of canvas trousers that, once the legs were rolled up, fit me well enough. With a shirt, jacket, and cloth cap pulled low over my eyes, I almost didn't recognize myself in the mirror in Uncle Ernest's workshop.

"The clothes appear to be fine, but there's something missing," she said, tapping her finger against her lips. A moment later, she smiled. "You're too clean. That's the problem."

She rushed outside and returned with a handful of soft dirt which she rubbed on my face and hands.

She accompanied me to the workshop door. "Remember, have Mrs. Winston explain why Mrs. Straton needed more pennyroyal. It may be she exceeded the dosage, but we need to determine if that's what she took."

I nodded and headed toward the woods.

"Where are you going?" she asked. "The road is in the other direction."

"Constance showed me a way that leads to Hanover Manor more directly. I'll save time. Besides, that's what a tradesman would use. She says they all do, including Mr. Brown."

She studied the tree line where I was pointing. "Really? You'll have to show me. I had no idea."

"I didn't either until I took the basket to the Straton cottage yesterday. The opening's in there between two bushes. You can see how it's thinner there."

Despite my father's position in the village, I had only seen Hanover Manor from the outside, but even from that perspective, it was obvious Underbyrne would fit neatly into one wing of Lord and Lady Devony's home. The grey stone walls rose high above the verdant lawns surrounding it, and the roof held a cupola at its center with a rooftop walk surrounding it.

The trail ended at the back of the structure, perfect for tradesmen seeking the servants' entrance. Had I arrived at the front of the mansion, I might have had some warning about what happened next. I did note the absence of any activity in the barns or stables to my right, but I had assumed the staff were on a different schedule than at Underbyrne. When I reached the servants' entrance, I knocked and waited for someone to answer.

When no one opened the door in what I considered a reasonable time, I rapped again. Louder.

This time, the door swung open, and a woman in an apron filled the opening. Several strands of her hair hung out from under her white cap as if she'd stuffed it on in a hurry. Most impressive, however, were her red-rimmed and puffy eyes.

"What is it you want?" she asked.

Her words were clipped and tinged with more than just a bit of annoyance. The sight of the woman in obvious distress took me by surprise, and I was forced to gather my thoughts.

"I was wondering, miss. If you…might you not have…?"

"What it is, boy?"

"Tin ware. Do you have the need for any repairs?" I forced out in one breath.

She pulled back her chin as if I'd struck her. "Tin ware? You want to know if we have any tin ware at a time like this. Get on with you, boy. I haven't any time to collect any tin ware for you."

My heart skipped a beat. I was failing in my mission. When she moved to close the door, I shoved against it.

"Please, miss. Can you check with Mrs. Winston? Maybe she'll know of some items to be repaired."

At that remark, the woman pulled her apron to her mouth and fresh tears ran down her cheeks. "You silly sod. Leave us to our mourning. Rachel Winston's dead."

CHAPTER EIGHT

I ran back along the trail as if someone were pursuing me after I'd run to the corner of the manor and peeked around to the front and saw the surgeon's carriage. While I knew it seemed illogical, I was overwhelmed by a desperate desire to get as far away from the manor house as quickly as possible.

When I arrived back at Underbyrne, I made straight for Ernest's workshop to change into my clothes before reporting to my mother.

To my surprise, Mother was visiting my uncle in the sitting room at the back. A tea tray sat on the table between them. He must have shown her the crossbow because she had the leather sleeve she used for archery on her arm.

They both turned toward me as I approached them,

taking in gulps of air while I massaged a stitch in my side from the run.

"Sherry, darling, whatever happened? Are you all right?"

I nodded, but still found no breath to answer.

"You ran all the way from Hanover Manor?" Uncle Ernest asked.

Again, I nodded but found my breathing had slowed enough that I could gasp out a few words. "Mrs. Winston. Dead."

The announcement pulled both of them to their feet. Mother raised her hand to her mouth.

"Dead?" she asked. "How? When?" She pointed to an empty seat. "Sit. Catch your breath. Have some tea."

While she poured a cup, I forced out an answer to her questions. "Don't. Know. But. Surgeon. There."

Her eyebrows pulled together, and she handed me the cup. "Mr. Harvingsham was called in? How do you know?"

"I saw his carriage," I said, managing a full sentence after several sips of tea.

"A third woman," Ernest said, shaking his head and making little *tsk*-ing noises. His gaze landed on my mother. "You know, Violette, there's a connection between you and all these women. I hope no suspicion will fall—"

"Don't be ridiculous, Ernest. We have shown conclusively I had not stabbed Emma Brown, and I haven't been near Rachel Winston since the constable arrested me." Her eyes glistened, and her tone dropped. "Poor Rachel. She was such a young and beautiful creature. And so much in love."

I held my peace and finished my tea, even though I could now speak in full sentences. My stomach knotted at the reasoning behind my uncle's statement. Mother *did* have a connection to all three women, and given Constable Gibbons' determination to find her guilty of some criminal activity, he might weave enough ideas together to do just that.

"Quite right," Ernest said with a sigh. "All the more likely she did not die of natural causes. I hate to say this, but you may have another murder to solve."

"Let's not jump to conclusions, Ernest. The poor Winston woman might have fallen down the stairs or had a bad heart. Did they say anything about murder to you, Sherry?"

"They didn't say much of anything." I summarized in just a few seconds the extent of my conversation with the servant at the back door.

Mother tapped her finger on her lips. "Not much to go on there. If Mr. Harvingsham's been called in, it's possible something suspicious *did* happen to her. Mr. Holmes, as magistrate, might be involved. Still, if the death appeared accidental, we may never know. A professional call on the good surgeon, however, might supply some answers."

I stared at her. Mother didn't trust the man to treat us for most illnesses. "You want to visit him for a medical consultation?"

"Unfortunately, it appears to be the most direct approach." She gave me a studied gaze. "You definitely appear a little peaked to me, Sherry, dear. A severe case of dyspepsia, I believe."

I was being tasked to assist her again?

"Why me?"

"Because that will give me an opportunity to speak with *Mrs.* Harvingsham. There are two things I know about that woman. She has intimate knowledge of all his cases, and she is a severe gossip. I will have no trouble learning from her whatever occurred to poor Mrs. Winston." She consulted a watch she wore pinned to her dress. "We have to give her time to collect the information. I suggest we go first thing in the morning. I'm afraid, dear, that means no supper or breakfast for you."

"Don't be cruel, Violette," Uncle Ernest said, coming to my defense. "He may need to appear to be in digestive distress, but you don't have to starve the poor boy."

"All right. Some broth tonight, but no breakfast. The surgeon must hear something to suggest a reason for the visit. An empty stomach certainly creates gastric issues."

While I considered adding a protest to that of my uncle's, I recalled Rachel Winston the night of my return home. Mother's description of the woman as pretty was accurate. For her, I could endure a brief starvation.

"Don't worry, Sherry," she said, rising from her seat, "I won't allow him to give you anything. Whatever he suggests as a treatment, I will insist on administering myself. Will you accompany me back to the house?"

I shook my head. I still needed to talk to Constance. "I think I'll stay and help Uncle Ernest."

"Please enjoy the rest of the sandwiches with your tea. I'll see you then at supper." She smiled and covered her mouth with her hand. "Excuse me. Supper for us. Broth for you."

The edges of her eyes crinkled, but I failed to find the same amusement in her statement. I was also distracted as I considered how to approach Constance for the tremendous favor I had promised Mycroft and Ernest I would ask of her.

Once she left, Ernest turned to me. "You going to see the Straton girl?" When I nodded, he studied me for a moment and said, "I wouldn't change if I were you. Raise less suspicion for another of her station to visit their cottage than a squire's son."

I'd forgotten about my disguise for visiting Hanover Manor. "I believe you're right. Care to go with me?"

"I need to work here. I think I've made something of a breakthrough with the crossbow," he said. "Care to see? Only a moment to set up the target."

Before I could answer, he stepped to the work area and pulled out a bale of hay. He'd painted a set of concentric circles to form a target on its side.

"The secret was the coil. I tried a heavier one and found that while it made the trigger harder to draw, it did keep it from being too sensitive. The lighter projectiles compensated for the stiffer pull."

My uncle stepped to my side and handed me the loaded weapon. I took aim and found the trigger more resistant than that of my rifle, but with extra effort, the pointed star flew from the box and embedded itself into the hay bale. A second star slid into place ready for the bow to be drawn and fired again.

He squinted at the bale and said, "It appears it may still pull to the right. What about the trigger?"

"Definitely harder to pull, but not too difficult."

I placed the crossbow back on the worktable, making sure to point the still-loaded device toward the back of the workshop.

"My whole purpose was to be able to shoot a number of these stars in quick succession. I think I told you that the *hira shuriken* were designed to disable, not kill, an enemy. A number of them shot one after the other, however, might prove more deadly—or at least capable of disabling a group."

"I think the project is progressing."

He scrubbed the side of his face with his hand and studied the crossbow. His eyes carried a far-off glaze to them, and I knew he was about to shift all his concentration onto the weapon. With his attention now elsewhere, I determined it was an appropriate time to take my leave.

For the second time that day, I found myself on the path through the woods Constance had shown me.

When I found no one in the Straton yard, I knocked on the door. Constance answered. She placed a finger to her lips before I could speak. After a moment's study, her mouth dropped open, and she pushed me back into the yard, closing the door behind her.

"Lords, Master Sherlock," she said in a harsh whisper. "I didn't recognize you at first. Whatever are you doing dressed like a 'prentice?"

"I...uh..." I felt exposed in the yard, as if the clandestine act I planned to ask her to accomplish should be shared privately. "Might we speak inside?"

She shook her head.

"Papa's sleeping. Best not disturb him. When he's got one of his headaches, it's best to keep quiet."

Somehow I suspected there was more to the story than just a headache, but I couldn't pursue it at that moment.

"You didn't bring more vittles, did you?" she asked, glancing at my empty hands. "The vicar's wife came by and left a basket. We won't need some for a while."

"No. I came to ask a favor." I checked the dust on the tops of my boots. "Have you... Did you ever..."

How did one ask someone about their criminal activity? My concern for my mother spurred me to continue with my proposal as I searched for the words.

"Well, what do you want? Don't go hemming and hawing. I need to get back inside and keep the others quiet so's Papa can sleep."

"The constable. He took something. Something that

belongs to Mother."

When I paused, unable to think how to continue, she squinted at me, not waiting for me to proceed as much as weighing what I had already said.

"You wants it back. What the constable took."

Not a question. A statement. I nodded.

"What was it?"

Her forthrightness spurred my own. "A book. If he determines what's in it, it would ruin my mother. My whole family."

Another studied squint. "You want to steal it back?"

"Yes…no…. Replace it actually. With another."

"All right." My heart thrummed at the thought of her acceptance, but she dampened my enthusiasm in the next minute. "But you have to come with me."

"But I—"

"You said you wanted me to learn you to be a dipper. It ain't dipping, but we have to start somewheres. And the constable's house is as good as any." She checked over her shoulder toward the cottage. "I can't do it now, though. Come back later. After dinner tomorrow. He should be up and out by then."

I nodded and turned to leave. I'd only taken a few steps when she spoke once again.

"We gots enough food at the moment, but if you've got some of the bread you brought to the gaol, you can bring that along tomorrow."

Although the very thought of Cook's bread reminded

me of my restricted diet until after the visit to the surgeon tomorrow, I responded over my shoulder, "I'll see what I can do."

Upon my arrival at Underbyrne, I stopped again at my uncle's workshop to change into my proper clothes and to report to my uncle that I had been able to successfully recruit Constance into service for retrieving Mother's ledger.

With no sounds emanating from the structure, I concluded he had already gone to the main house for supper but knocked anyway. Uncle Ernest opened the door as soon as I rapped once.

"Come in, boy," he said.

He searched around the yard before stepping aside to let me in.

"Are you looking for someone?" I asked as he closed the door behind me.

"That honey man. He came by for a moment. Asked about progress. If I had any new information to share with the constable."

"Did he speak to Mother too?"

"No. Just me. But then he thinks I'm the one doing the investigating." He shook his head. "Poor Violette. She's always been so much more clever than I."

His gaze dropped, and I could see the slump in his shoulders. I understood his feelings of inferiority. Mycroft's ability to foresee people's actions and future events made it difficult to consider any intellectual achievements of my own. On impulse, I noted to him, "But you're clever in your own way. You came up with that crossbow idea. By the way, have you worked out the problem of the pull to the right?"

He shook his head.

"No time with Brown visiting. Told him about the Winston woman's death. He seemed quite upset about it and asked what we knew. I said not much until we had a chance to talk to Mr. Harvingsham."

Given his earlier ethical concerns about replacing the book, I decided it best not to mention Constance's condition that I accompany her on her mission. Instead, I asked, "Would you be able to arrange a horse for tomorrow afternoon? If I asked for it, Mother or Father might question why I need one. And Mycroft rarely goes riding. I need it... to help Mother."

"A horse?" He paused as if again considering whether he was aiding and abetting a crime, but in the end, he nodded. "As far as I know, you simply don't want your parents to know that you are visiting the Straton cottage again. Very well."

I changed into my clothes, leaving the others for my visit tomorrow, and returned to the house for my supper of broth.

THE SUN WAS FULLY up and flooding into my bedroom when Mother came in the next morning. I rubbed my eyes and sat up in bed. "Why didn't anyone wake me?"

"With your having to miss breakfast, I thought it best to let you sleep a little longer," she said, and kissed me on the forehead. Her mouth turned down. "Quite a normal temperature. How unfortunate we have no way to make you appear feverish. We can however, have you wear yesterday's clothing. At least then you'll appear disheveled. Remember, you have a bad case of dyspepsia."

I slid from my bed, and as if on cue, my stomach rumbled the moment my feet touched the floor.

"Very good," she said with a smile. "I heard that one myself." She placed an arm about my shoulders. "I truly do appreciate your willingness to participate in our little charade."

"I don't mind it so much," I said. "I do want to catch whoever killed poor Mrs. Brown."

She pulled me closer. "You're growing up so quickly. I almost have to reach up to touch your shoulder. In a little bit, you'll be taller than I. You get your height from the Parker side." Facing me, she studied me more intently and touched my nose. "Also the nose. A fine aristocratic example, if ever there was one."

Another squeeze on my shoulders, and she left me to dress.

When I met her downstairs in the kitchen for Mr. Simpson to drive us to the Harvingshams', the scent of baking bread greeted me as well. My stomach gave another protest.

"Excellent. Perhaps we should have a loaf with us? You can sniff it just before the surgeon examines you."

I opened my mouth to protest then remembered my promise to Constance to bring some and nodded my assent.

"I'll meet you at the carriage."

Mr. Harvingsham's house was on the edge of town. I supposed he chose the spot to be near both those living in the village as well as in the countryside. His surgery had its own entrance as a separate wing on his first floor. I followed my mother into a small waiting room. A man sat in one of the chairs lining the room's walls, his hand wrapped in what appeared to be a rag. Mother and I took two chairs more or less across from him. Groans emanated from a closed door at the far end of the room.

"That's my mate in there," the man said, nodding to the door. "We were shoein' a horse when the beast bit me, then kicked poor Joshua in the chest. I think he broke all my fingers, but I'm more afeared for Joshua."

Another groan from the other room made the waiting man wince, and I involuntarily copied him. Mother's hands gripped her reticule until her knuckles grew white.

"I suppose we could've gone to the cottage hospital, but since the surgeon had already visited there for the day, we came here."

"I'm sorry, Sherry. I hadn't considered him having patients with such urgent needs. Perhaps—"

Before she could complete the thought—which I hoped involved returning home and dinner—Mrs. Harvingsham stepped into the room through a side door. "Violette," she said. "I thought I recognized your trap outside. Whatever brings you here?"

"It's Sherlock, Elizabeth. I'm afraid he's suffering an extreme bout of dyspepsia."

I forced an expression between woe and pain. In an effort to emphasize the malady, I imagined some of Mrs. Simpson's boiled beef, and my stomach accommodated my wishes with a loud rumble.

"Oh dear," Mrs. Harvingsham said after my sound had dissipated, "I'm afraid you're right. But why didn't you have Mr. Harvingsham come to your house?"

"I thought perhaps the fresh air might help him, but I'm afraid the ride didn't have the effect I'd hoped."

Mrs. Harvingsham's gaze shifted from me to the man with the bandaged hand. "Why don't we wait in the parlor? I'll let his nurse know he should attend you there."

The woman stepped to the far door and rapped on it. When the door opened a slit, Mrs. Harvingsham spoke in low tones to whoever answered. As the door closed, another moan escaped—only this time it was weaker and lower than the others.

His shoulders dropping lower, the man with the broken fingers clucked his tongue. I gathered he held little hope for his friend.

Following the surgeon's wife to the parlor, we maneuvered around a number of small tables displaying various *objets d'art* to arrive at the sitting area on the far side of the room. I marveled at both women's ability to avoid knocking any of the tables despite the width of their skirts.

Taking a seat, she said, "I spoke to his nurse. My husband still needs to attend the two men before he can see your son. Would you care for some tea in the meantime?"

"So kind of you," my mother said. "Of course, I believe it best for Sherlock to abstain until after your husband's examination."

She rang a silver bell on the table next to her. "It shouldn't be much longer. Mr. Harvingsham is quite efficient at setting bones. I've seen him do so in less than two minutes, including the binding."

"But there is the matter of the other patient. I believe he was kicked by a horse."

The other woman glanced away before responding in a low voice. "I was told there was nothing to be done for him. Internal injuries. He was administering morphine to him when I knocked—for the pain."

My mother paled, and my stomach gave a bit of a lurch. The woman's nonchalance at a man's apparent impending death took me aback. But perhaps being a surgeon's wife simply hardened her to the thought?

A maid opened the parlor door, and Mrs. Harvingsham's voice had a lilt I found disconcerting given the slow death occurring in the next room. "Betsy, please bring in some tea. Only two cups."

The maid curtsied and returned shortly with the requested pot as well as some finger sandwiches and a sliced fruit. My stomach recommenced its concert—a little more *fortissimo* this time.

"My goodness," Mrs. Harvingsham said. "Perhaps I should suggest my husband consider prescribing some laudanum for him. You must be in a great deal of pain."

I placed my arms over my stomach and inclined over them slightly as if in pain. "I don't think that's necessary."

"But my dear—"

"Why don't we wait and hear what Mr. Harvingsham suggests?" my mother said.

"I suppose...." the woman said, eyeing me over her teacup.

I forced a wan smile, hoping to appear to be suffering bravely, and gratefully relaxed when Mother called our hostess's attention toward her.

"I say, Elizabeth. This is most excellent tea. Wherever did you get it?"

"It was a gift. From Lady Devony. Mr. Harvingsham had been treating one of the servants there. A very grave case. I'm afraid she passed despite his efforts to bleed out the illness."

"Rachel Winston, wasn't it? One of Cook's friends mentioned it to her this morning. She didn't say what happened. Some sort of illness then?"

"A very severe case of—" She glanced in my direction and lowered her voice. I still made out the next word despite her attempts to keep it from me. "Dyspepsia."

"Truly?" my mother asked and was answered with a nod from our hostess.

"As I said, a very severe case." She turned to me. "I'm certain you have no reason to worry, dear boy. Hers was accompanied by a great deal of—" She stopped herself again before whispering, "She was quite sick for several days."

Mother's eyebrows came together. Perhaps it was the years she'd spent in France, but while Father had impressed upon us the need to refer to certain delicate conditions with less specific terms—such as "sick" for "vomiting"—Mother had always preferred the more precise and medical terms. Out of deference to her husband, however, she often would revert to French in such cases.

"Did he ever determine any cause?"

The woman shook her head. "He determined it was something she must have eaten, given the symptoms and the lack of fever. That's why the Devonys had called him in. To ensure that she was not contagious. When none of the other servants became...*sick*, he did what he could to treat her, but as I noted, she succumbed all the same."

Mother took another sip of tea and glanced at the clock on the wall. Her ability to collect this information on poor Mrs. Winston's death without the woman even knowing she was sharing information was not lost on me. Such a skill could prove useful in a variety of settings, and I promised myself to consider just how she did it.

Before she could ask for any additional information, a

set of rapid footsteps cut off the conversation.

A woman wearing a nurse's cap and apron opened the parlor door with such force all the items on display in the room rattled and threatened to topple off their tables.

"Come quick, something's happened to Mr. Harvingsham," was all she said before spinning on her heel and rushing away.

Mother and Mrs. Harvingsham glanced at each other for a moment, both with mouths opened as if seeking an explanation from the other. While they froze in this position for a moment, I leapt from my seat and headed out the door. From behind, I could hear the swish of fabric and knew they were now making their way through the maze of tables. With my head start on the women, I reached the surgery first. Finding the waiting room vacant, I rushed through the open door into the examination room beyond.

The man with the broken fingers and the nurse knelt on the floor next to the writhing surgeon. His nurse held down his shoulders, and the man from the waiting room lay across his feet, holding his injured hand aloft as if to keep from re-injuring it as Mr. Harvingsham thrashed about the floor.

Behind them on a table lay a covered figure, which I assumed was the man's now deceased friend. Two cabinets, one with glass doors and another with small drawers covered the wall at the dead man's feet, and across the back wall, a tall workbench holding a number of instruments the surgeon used in his practice.

Mrs. Harvingsham reached the examination room door

before my mother, and stopped at the threshold, her hand to her mouth. I could hear my mother's voice from behind the woman blocking the doorway.

"What is it?" she asked. "What's going on?"

"He's having a fit," the man with the broken fingers said over his shoulder. "I heard a crash and come in to find him floppin' about like a fish out of water."

"Let me through, Elizabeth," my mother said. "I need to see what's going on."

Mrs. Harvingsham remained where she was.

I stared at the poor surgeon. He continued to convulse. Now, however, a bit of spittle formed at the sides of his mouth.

"Sherry, are you in there?"

"Yes," I said, unable to take my gaze off the man on the floor.

"I need your help, dear." Mother's voice, while low and without emotion still carried a hint of urgency. "I need you to get Mrs. Harvingsham out of the way. I must get into that room."

With great effort to pull my attention from the scene in front of me, I forced myself to turn my head in the direction of the blocked door and step to Mrs. Harvingsham. Her chest moved rapidly up and down, and the air whistled between the fingers over her mouth. She definitely wasn't breathing correctly. I pulled her hand from her mouth, and she dropped her gaze to me—although I could tell she didn't recognize me.

"Mrs. Harvingsham, you're turning white. Why don't you sit down in the waiting room? Let me help you to a chair."

She remained still a moment longer, as if her brain was trying to make sense of what I was saying, but finally she nodded and allowed me to lead her from the room and onto a chair. Once she was seated, I turned back to the examination room.

As soon as the entrance had opened, my mother had dashed through. She now knelt at the man's side, her fingers on the inside of his wrist. After that, she placed a hand on the man's forehead.

Without glancing at me, she said, "Sherry, I want you to check the surgeon's medicines. See if you can find a box of asthma cigarettes and matches."

Swallowing hard, I pushed myself to rush around the dead man on the table, avoiding a direct study of the form, to search the various boxes and bottles in the cabinet for the cigarettes.

"What do you think you're doing?" the nurse asked in an octave higher than when she'd come to the parlor. "The man can't smoke now."

"I don't expect him too," Mother said, her voice strained. "He's having an allergic reaction. The cigarettes—"

A thump made me check on the scene behind me. The man was arching upward as Mother was untying his tie and opening his collar.

"The cigarettes contain belladonna. Sherry, we'll need a funnel, too, to send the smoke into his lungs. We need to open his airways or he'll choke to death."

A wail came from the adjoining room. "Good lord."

"Mrs. Harvingsham, are you aware of any allergies for your husband?"

"I-I-I—" His wife's response ended in a sob.

"Bees," the nurse said.

"That explains the welts on his hand," Mother said. "I saw them when I checked his pulse."

Mother must have pointed out the injury because the nurse now barked at me as she struggled with her employer. "The cigarettes are on the top shelf. The matches...by the lamp. The funnel...in the drawer...on the same table."

"Found it," I said, reaching for an orange box, and continued to the table to collect the other items.

As soon as I rounded the table, I knelt down opposite my mother. She reached across the man and grabbed the cigarette box and matches. Before I could say anything, she'd stuck one in her mouth and struck a match to light it.

After she moved the cigarette to the corner of her mouth, she spoke to the nurse. "Put the funnel in his mouth."

Only then did I notice the surgeon's face had shifted from a deep vermillion to a blue-tinged white. His body had also stilled, and his breathing was thin and reedy as he tried to suck in air through an obviously closed airway. I watched with rapt attention as my mother blew smoke into the funnel and continued to puff and blow to force the smoke into the man's lungs. Her ease—not a single cough although she had to ingest some of the fumes—suggested previous experience with tobacco. Where had my mother learned a custom so against social conventions for women?

I had no time to consider this new revelation in depth because as I observed Mr. Harvingsham's face, it relaxed, his color and breathing returning to normal. A few seconds later, his eyes fluttered open. After he glanced first at my mother and then the nurse, he must have become conscious of what had occurred because his eyebrows lifted, and he tried to sit up. The nurse pulled the funnel from his mouth and helped him raise his shoulders from the floor.

"Mrs. Harvingsham, you can come in now," Mother called.

The woman rushed in, pushed my mother to one side and knelt next to her husband. "Oh, Richard," she said and broke into another sob.

The surgeon patted his wife's head and glanced at the four of us still surrounding him. "Wha—what happened?"

"You had an allergic reaction," Mother said. "From a bee sting, it appears."

"You need to thank your lucky stars this woman was here," the nurse said, jutting her chin at my mother. "She saved your life. I'd never have known about the cigarettes."

"Asthma cigarettes," Mother said. "So glad you had them. A bit cruder than my herbs, but they did the job this time."

The surgeon checked out the hand patting his wife's head.

"Bees," he said, more to himself than to us. He glanced over his shoulder at the table where I'd found the matches and funnel and at the open window next to it. He spoke louder when he continued. "They flew in the window. Stung me."

"I would suggest you spend the rest of the day in bed," Mother said. She turned to the nurse. "And you should keep a vigil on him. Keep the cigarettes by his bedside."

The woman nodded, and Mrs. Harvingsham raised her head from her husband's chest to address my mother. The woman's eyes were red-rimmed, and her cheeks wet from her tears.

"Thank you, Mrs. Holmes. You saved my husband's life. I don't care what anyone says about you. I know you have only the best intentions now."

Best intentions? What *were* others saying?

My gaze shot to my mother to determine her reaction. Whether the woman's remarks affected her in some way, I was unable to discern. A glance from her in response told me I was to imitate her and not disclose either concern for her reputation or demand for further information.

Following that brief direction to me, she shifted back on her heels and made ready to rise. "Shall we help you to your bed, Mr. Harvingsham?"

The man glanced about himself again, obviously still slightly confused. "Bed? But...but my patients."

"I'm certain your nurse can direct them to Dr. Farnsworth or the apothecary for the day."

Another round of glances to those around him before he nodded and allowed us to help him to his feet. Mrs. Harvingsham called to several of the servants, and they assisted him to navigate the stairs to his room.

When they had gone, the man with the broken hand asked, "What about poor Charlie? Should I take him home in my wagon?"

"I'll get word to the undertaker. He'll come for th— him," the nurse said. "I'll set your fingers. I've helped Mr. Harvingsham enough to do it myself."

She seemed familiar with the process of death, and I wondered how often they had made just such arrangements. The man studied her for a moment and nodded.

Now alone, the nurse studied both of us for a moment and asked, "Which one of you was here for the surgeon?"

"Sherlock," Mother said without hesitation. "But I believe the excitement has resolved the issue."

"Yes," I said, seeking to sound quite chipper. "I'm feeling ever so much better."

The woman glanced back at the table. Charlie, the deceased workman, still lay covered on the table. While I had attended funerals and seen corpses in coffin in their final repose, never had I been in the room when someone died or seen one so recently expired. The motionlessness of the man struck me. No movement of the sheet to indicate breathing. As my curiosity gave way to the realization of the finality of this man's life, my stomach churned enough that I feared it might betray my earlier assertion that I had recovered.

Mother must have sensed the shift in my attitude because she told the nurse, "Please thank Mrs. Harvingsham for her kind attentions earlier and pass on our well-wishes. I believe we should leave you to your tasks."

With that statement, we returned to the carriage and headed home. Mother produced the loaf of bread she'd promised me earlier. After the first bite, I found my appetite had disappeared. The image of the dead man lying on the table and Mr. Harvingsham writhing on the floor made the piece cloy in my mouth, and I found it almost impossible to swallow. The rest of the loaf, I put away.

Mother, however, seemed less affected by all that had passed. A smile remained on her lips, and she giggled at apparently random thoughts of her own. After one such outburst, she said, "I'm sorry, Sherry. I do believe I inhaled more than my share of the smoke. I'm feeling quite giddy. Haven't felt this way in a long time."

I studied her now more closely and saw her pupils were quite large. "Will you be all right?"

"In a bit. Once the effect has dissipated," she said, allowing another giggle to bubble out before sobering slightly. "Thank you for your help, Sherry. You kept your head and were able to find the items I needed. Not always easy to do in a crisis."

Given her elated mood, I decided the time was right to

learn more about her background. "Where did you learn to smoke?"

"How did you know—?" Another chuckle. "I should have guessed you would notice my practiced movements. I was introduced to the *cigarito* in France. It, and cigars, are a filthy practice and quite hard to break." She widened her eyes and met my gaze. "Please, don't tell your father. I'd broken the habit by the time we met. I'd prefer he never knew."

After that, she rested her head on the back of the carriage, and we rode in silence for a bit, until another question occurred to me.

"How did you meet Father?"

Cracking her eyes open, she replied with a rather languid voice. "At a lecture."

She yawned. "I think I should take a nap when we arrive home. Please ask Cook to bring a tray to my room. I'm ravenous. You'd think I was the one faking dyspepsia."

With a final giggle, she leaned back again and a quiet snoring ensued.

Don't tell your father.

Another secret to keep. The relationship between my parents grew more complex by the day. Did my father have similar confidences he withheld from my mother?

Just how much did they truly know about each other? Relationships, especially those between husband and wife, appeared much more difficult than I ever realized.

CHAPTER NINE

Never had I been as hungry and as unable to eat as when we returned home. My stomach cramped from the lack of food, but when I tried to chew or swallow the various items on my plate, I had a reaction similar to that of my attempt to eat the bread in the carriage. I found the taste abhorrent and quite sickening. I was able to drink a bit of beef broth and that eased the hunger spasms enough for me to visit Constance while Mother rested upstairs in her room.

As promised, Uncle Ernest had arranged for a horse, and after I changed into my apprentice costume, I met him and my ride far from the stables and house. Once mounted, I spurred the horse in the direction of the Straton cottage.

Constance appeared to be ready for me. Her hair had been brushed and her face washed as she had done at

Underbyrne. A basket rested at her feet. When I reined in the horse in front of her cottage, she handed the basket to me first and then held out a hand for me to pull her onto the horse. She sat in front of me, and I reached around her to hold onto the reins.

As we headed out of the dirt yard in front of the cottage, she asked over her shoulder, "Did you bring any bread?"

I produced the loaf my mother had carried with us to the surgeon's.

She took a bite and spoke around it. "It's so easy to chew. You can tell it's quality."

As she continued to nibble on the loaf, I was aware of all her little movements: her jaw working as she chewed, the subtle shifts as she adjusted her balance, and the warmth of her body. All in all, it was quite a pleasurable interlude, and we rode for quite a while in silence, her enjoying the bread, and me, her company.

I finally broke the reverie by asking, "What's the basket for?"

"It was my mum's," she said and caressed the woven handle along the top. "She kept her mendin' in it. If you're going to *min* a house, you gots to have a reason. This is mine."

"*Min?*"

"Take something." She turned to face me. "Not as hard as breaking a drum. Then you has to crawl through a window or break a lock to get into a house, but still, you gots to have a plan."

"But you're not going to steal anything. Just see if you can find where he's keeping the ledger. No use taking it until after we have the replacement finished."

"Steal. Replace. No matter. You needs to have a purpose to be there. The more they believe you, the more they'll trust you. The more they trust you, the more time you has to look. Mendin's perfect for getting into the constable's house. She'll have to go find somethin' for me to mend. While I'm alone, I can seek your book."

"And what should I do?"

"She knows you, right?"

"Yes, I'm afraid so. She was at my mother's luncheon a few days ago. I played the violin for them."

She twisted around between my outstretched arms to gain a view of my face and cocked her head slightly as if in thought. "If you can'ts be seen by her, you have to stay away from the house. I *could* use a crow. Someone to keep an eye out so's I don't get caught spying about. Watch for the constable, and if he comes home, you figure out a way to keep him from goin' inside until I leave."

As with the surgeon's home, Constable Gibbons' residence was on the edge of the village. While he had an office in the village proper near the gaol, his job required him to be continuously patrolling the county to check with the watch officers under his supervision. Only those on night watch reported to him at his home. With his duties keeping him out and about, it seemed unlikely he would return prior to the evening meal. While the job didn't seem particularly vital, I was glad to be of service.

After a pause, I said, "That seems possible."

Constance ordered me to stop at a bend in the road about half a mile from the Gibbons' house.

"You can put the horse in the trees here. Let me go first, but follow me to the hedge by the road. You can see both directions from there. If you see the constable comin', run up to the house and rap on the side. I'll meet you here."

While I nodded, my palms became slick at the thought of the impending subterfuge we were committing. I marveled at Constance's apparent calm. The hand grasping the basket handle was still and no perspiration shone on her lip.

"How do you know about all this?"

She paused before responding, as if considering her answer. "When I was in gaol, some of the others talked about how to *min* a house. Like dressin' as a maid and goin' to work in a big house like Lord Devony's. While you dust, you lift some silver. Another trick is to wait for a tradesman to come to the door. While they're talking in the front, you go in the back way to lift a few things. But what we're doing now is the hardest because they see you. I wouldn't do it ceptin' that I'm not really takin' anything. The minute somethin' goes missin', they remember who was about. The constable's house. Lords, would I have a story to tell the others if I'm ever back there again."

My admiration for the girl grew. I might know something of science and maths, but in terms of practical skills and knowledge, she surpassed me in many ways.

After securing the horse inside a stand of trees, she said, "Count to a hundred and then follow me."

Once alone, I forced myself to count at an even, regular pace rather than rushing through the numbers. During the count, I checked the highway for any indication of the constable's return. The moment I reached one hundred, I headed in the direction Constance had taken.

While the thoroughfare had its share of traffic this close to the village, I realized no one paid much attention to me in my current disguise. I was just one more pedestrian in a steady stream of workers, vendors, and people entering and leaving town. Loitering about the constable's house, however, might spark some suspicion, and I determined I needed to stay out of sight once I reached my destination.

I noticed a group of bushes on the other side of the road and chose to hide out there. As Constance had predicted, I had a good vantage point from which to observe all pathways leading to the house and concentrated on spotting the constable's uniformed figure among the approaching horses.

My duties proved both tedious and nerve-wracking. Staying in one place and simply watching offered little mental stimulation, but at the same time, I fretted over the interaction between Constance and Mrs. Gibbons.

Had the woman left her alone long enough for her to find the ledger?

As the minutes dragged by, my concern grew. What

was taking her so long? Had she been caught and was Mrs. Gibbons holding her until the constable returned home?

I battled an increasing desire to either run to the house to check or return to the horse and flee.

This distraught debate almost made me miss Mr. Brown's appearance. True, I had been on the watch for Constable Gibbons, but a cart slowing to turn into the drive should have alerted me sooner. I did, however, catch sight of Mr. Brown before he stopped in front of the constable's house.

Despite the cool day, perspiration blossomed across my face. I had no way to make it to the house without the honey man seeing me. I had to reassure myself that even if he saw and recognized Constance, he would have no reason to suspect her of any wrongdoing. Fighting the urge to extract myself from the hedge and pace beside the road, I focused on my breathing to calm my heart rate. My uncle had shared tales of yogis who could sit in positions for hours, even days, without moving. If they could achieve that, I should be able to hold my place for a few minutes. No sooner had I reached what I considered a calm state than Constance appeared, stepping lively on the path from the constable's house, the basket swinging at her side. Reminding myself to maintain my place, I waited for her to pass and turn in the direction of the hidden horse before finally removing myself from the behind the bushes and following her.

"Lords, you took your time," she said before I could ask her about the results of her mission.

"I didn't want to be seen. I made a terrible mistake. I hid on the other side of the road. I had no way to warn you without being seen."

"You have a ways to go before you're a good *crow*, but most times, you wouldn't *min* a house in daylight, so I'll forgive you."

While her assessment of my skills as a lookout stung, they were true. More pressing matters, however, filled my mind. "Did you find it?"

"No." Her forehead creased, and mine responded in kind. "I searched his office as much as I could, but no red book. Then the honey man came. When I heard him say he was lookin' for the constable, I waited to hear what he wanted. He asked about what the constable found when he searched your house."

"He knew about the search," I said, more to myself than to Constance. "What did Mrs. Gibbons say?"

"She didn't know anything. He'd have to ask her husband, and he should be in his office in town."

Before I could even express an interest in hearing what the constable would tell him, I heard a wagon pass near our hiding spot. I crept forward, staying hidden by the foliage. Mr. Brown lumbered past in the wagon, heading to town.

"Let's follow him. Find out what the constable says."

"To his office? Next to the gaol?" She shook her head. "I won't go there."

I glanced over my shoulder in the direction the wagon had gone. While I had no idea what I would do once I reached the constable's office, I had to make an effort to find out what Mr. Brown was sharing with the constable.

"I don't have time to take you back and then get to town. You can stay with the horse far away from the gaol. I'll find out what the men share on my own."

She crossed her arms over her chest and studied me for a moment. Following a deep sigh, as if she had finally come to a regrettable decision, she said, "Don't muck up being my crow this time. It's one thing to sweet-talk the constable's wife. A whole other thing with the constable."

A smile stretched across my face as relief flooded through me. I was definitely dependent upon her skills at the moment. But with her help, I could develop some of the same finesse she already possessed. The past hour, however, showed me how much I still had to learn.

"Who's that gent heading to the office? If I weren't with you, I'd be talkin' him up as fast as I could cross the street."

I turned my attention from the constable's office across the street to the man Constance had noticed. We'd ridden into the village and left the horse tied to a post on a side street. From our vantage point by an alleyway, we'd been discussing how best to overhear Brown's conversation with the constable. The beekeeper had only just entered his office.

The object of Constance's attention was tall and thin. He wore a well-tailored suit, his beard was more of a goatee, and he carried a valise. A set of spectacles perched on his pointed noise. After my few months at Eton and my years of tutors, I easily recognized the professorial type—only this one's clothing and hand luggage appeared more expensive than any I'd known myself.

"What's so important about him?"

"Look at 'im. The man's gots a silk handkerchief almost hanging out his pocket. I'd have that in my hand before he even had time to turn down my matches."

On the way into town, Constance had regaled me with tales of her abilities to offer matches to "gents" while simultaneously relieving them of certain resaleable items such as silk handkerchiefs, pocket watches, or cigar cases.

"And he's heading to the constable's office. You think someone already robbed him?"

"Not with that lovely hangin' out. Somebody would've already minned it."

I stared at the door where the man had just entered. The valise suggested he'd just arrived in town and his clothes were too well-tailored for a tradesman. He had to be from London. What was he doing here? Given so few crimes requiring any assistance from a Londoner, my stomach's contraction told me his visit wasn't coincidental.

As if to confirm my concern, he reappeared moments

later with Constable Gibbons and Mr. Brown. The constable took his leave of the honey man. Constance and I ducked our heads and slid back into the alley. While the new arrival and the constable headed toward town, Mr. Brown moved to his wagon tied to one side of Gibbons' office. I stepped toward the street, planning to follow the men from the opposite side, but Constance put a hand on my arm.

"Hold on."

"I want to follow them," I said. "Hear what they say. I think it's important."

"Watch out or Brown will see us."

As soon as he drove off, we strolled across the street and caught sight of the two men just as they turned into a building. They had entered the main hotel, which catered to the village's most elite clientele. Knowing their destination, I continued up the street, intent on following them inside. Constance grabbed my elbow and pushed me past the entrance and around the building's side.

"You gots to be more careful when you're in disguise. People like me and you—at least how you're dressed at the moment—can't go into a hotel like that without rousin' people's attentions."

I opened my mouth to protest, but shut it as I realized she had a legitimate point. Dressed as a squire's son, I might have been allowed to enter under the assumption my parents were guests. As an apprentice, however, the only assumption would be I was there for mischief, and I'd be booted out as soon as I stepped inside.

"I have to find out who he is," I said, as much to myself as to my companion.

With a glance at the main street, she chewed her lip before breaking into a grin. "I think I gots a plan. Come on."

She continued along the side of the building to an alleyway and headed to the back of the building. A single door opened onto the alley and the mixed aromas of various cooking meats and vegetables drifted on the air. She passed the opening without even a glance in that direction and turned to creep along the other side.

She signaled me to stay in the alley, and she moved from window to window, peeking into each one. At the third window, she motioned for me to come, but to keep low. When I reached her, she put her finger to her lips and pointed to the window.

"There," she mouthed.

I raised myself enough to peer into the window and spied into the hotel's dining room. I understood why she'd chosen the window she did. Not only did I have a view of the constable and the visitor, it was the only window that didn't have a table beside it. At any other, a guest would have seen someone peering in and probably reported it.

The men were too far away for me to hear their conversation, but I could observe the man no longer had his valise. He'd most likely left it at the front desk, suggesting he was staying as a guest. They leaned into each other, their heads almost touching.

A waiter appeared and placed a bowl of soup before them. My stomach rumbled at the thought of this prelude to their full meal, and I realized my appetite had returned. I would have to seek out something to eat when I returned home.

After a few sips, the constable pulled something from his inside coat pocket. The flash of red in his hand made me draw in my breath. I focused on the men's lips. Could I read what they were saying?

I was able to determine the man's name was Beecher— or was it Bleeker? I hoped the constable would repeat it. Constance pulled on my sleeve.

I waved my hand backwards at her. *Leave me alone.*

She hissed out my name. "Sherlock."

Was the stranger saying "start tomorrow?"

She clapped her hand on my shoulder. I spun about to tell her to let me be and ran into a solid, dark-blue wall. My gaze moved up to a round, flushed face. "What are you doing here, boy?"

Unable to come up with a response, my mouth moved up and down in the imitation of a fish on a hook. I glanced about me, but Constance had disappeared.

His grip tightened on my shoulder. "Let's just see what you have to tell the constable. He's in there now."

Still unable to respond, I allowed him to direct me toward the street. My mind raced as I considered what to tell Constable Gibbons. Would he recognize me in my disguise? Other than some dirt and rough clothes, I hadn't done much to change my appearance.

We had almost reached the street when Constance rushed from behind us. Before I could so much as take a breath, she stomped on the man's foot. He howled and let go of my shoulder. At the same moment, she grabbed my hand and pulled me back toward the alley. We raced around the corner, the man limping behind us. She then pulled me around another corner to the left and soon we were zigzagging through back streets until I stopped to nurse a stitch in my side. Stepping into the doorway of an abandoned store, I gasped for air.

Also breathing heavily, Constance slid into the alcove next to me. We stilled and listened for a moment to see if, thanks to her maneuvers, the police officer had lost us.

After we heard no heavy footfalls coming in our direction, a smile broke across her face. "You should've seen your face when you realized that copper had you by the shoulder. Your eyes were as big as them bowls of soup."

Her jubilance proved infectious, and we both celebrated our escape with a good laugh. "Thank you for stopping him," I said after our mirth subsided.

"It's an old trick my papa taught me. I knew I couldn't let him take you to see the constable."

In that small space, I could feel her breath on me, and I studied her face. Up so close, I noticed the small wrinkles forming about her eyes when she smiled. A thrill ran down my spine, not unlike the one I experienced when viewing the anatomy text. My gaze dropped to her lips, still pulled upward into a smile, and I wondered what it would be like to touch them with my own. I had never considered kissing anyone other than my mother or other older female relatives as required by social convention. This impulse was new to me, and more than a little frightening. My father's etiquette lessons had not included how to address such attraction, and I wasn't certain how to respond. Other than that one embrace I observed when my mother was released from gaol, I'd never seen my parents display any strong affections in public.

With whom could I possibly discuss such sensations?

"You need to tell your brother," she said.

My heart thudded in my chest. She'd read my thoughts?

I swallowed. "Tell him?"

"About the book. That it's not in the constable's office anymore."

"And there's little time. The man said he would start on the code tomorrow. At least that's what I think he said."

"Then we best be crackin'," she said. She stepped back into the side street. "You tell your brother we'll need that new book tonight. I'll tell you about my plan on the way home."

AFTER DROPPING Constance at her cottage to work on the mending Mrs. Gibbons had given her and leaving the horse with Uncle Ernest to return to the stable, I sought out Mycroft. I didn't find him in the library as I expected. Instead, he was in his room. Behind a locked door.

He was wearing a dressing gown when he answered my knock. "Come in. Quickly."

Before he shut the door, he glanced up and down the hallway. When he turned to me, he said, "Sorry. Don't want anyone to see you here. I've been feigning illness all day to work on this ledger in peace. Can't have them thinking I'm well enough for visitors. Even you."

"Do you have much to go to finish?"

"Finish? I've barely started. One must be clever about these things in order to perpetrate a deception. It's not enough to merely write something in the code. What's coded must appear logical as well. I've been adapting some scientific data on plant growth I found in a treatise by a London botanist. Of course, I can't use the exact data, or else it might be recognized as plagiarized from the other piece. Then there's the issue of the writing. Changing ink, etc. to make it appear to have been written on different days and—"

Perhaps the basis for what happened next was my lack of sustenance for almost twenty-four hours. Or the sheer concern over our mother's fate. Whatever the cause, I lost all patience with my brother. While he had been at home, enjoying his meals (albeit a lighter fare due to his feigned illness), I'd almost been arrested—or at least accused of spying on the constable—and chased for blocks by a police officer. I interrupted him with a question tinged with more than a little annoyance. "Just how many pages have you completed?"

My outburst took him by surprise. He drew his chin back. "How dare you take that tone with me, you little twit."

Heat flushed my face, and for the first time, I didn't restrain my anger. "I have spent the day working to unravel the problems in which this family has become embroiled. Thanks to me, I can tell you we have only a few hours to replace that book before some expert from London begins his translation. Then if you think you'll be able to return to Oxford after Mother is tried for whatever crime Constable Gibbons has determined to attribute to her, you are delusional."

The moment I finished, my mood shifted from angry to anxious. I held my breath, waiting for his response. Never had I spoken to my brother in such an impassioned manner. And never from a position of authority. He'd always been the one with more knowledge. For once I had the upper hand, and I wasn't certain how he would react.

When he said nothing at first, I feared he would return my heated outburst in kind and decline any further involvement in the effort. He glared at me without making a sound. When he finally spoke, his response was more reflective than explosive.

"An expert? From London?" He glanced at the papers on his desk, and I released my breath while his back was to me. "That does put a different spin on things. How soon do you need the book?"

"Constance and I have worked out a plan to replace the book tonight. I need it by eight o'clock so that we have time to get to the hotel by nine. Whatever you have by eight will have to be enough."

"You give me only two hours to reproduce the book? And how do you plan to be at the town hotel by nine?" The arrogance I knew so well from him had returned.

"I already checked with Mrs. Simpson. Mother is... indisposed and has requested her evening meal in her room. Father had a tray to be sent up for him as well. Now with you ill as well, I'll offer to take a basket for me and Uncle Ernest to the workshop. He's already agreed to say I'll be helping him in a special experiment to be done after dark, and we would need a cart to carry the apparatus."

He remained silent for a moment before saying, "I'll get you something by eight. I could wait in the workshop, if you wish. In case someone comes searching for either of you."

"Would you? That would be quite helpful."

"She's my mother too, you know." He met my gaze with a pointed one of his own.

The implication I hadn't respected his own feelings for our parents was apparent, but with so much still to do, I decided to apologize later. "See you at the workshop."

"Where are you going?"

"To get what we need for our plan."

By eight o'clock, I had bathed and dressed in proper clothes and eaten a full meal for the first time in a day. As my uncle and I waited for Mycroft to appear, I found myself becoming drowsy after the heavy meal of boiled beef and potatoes. My hunger during the day had appeared to keep my mental faculties sharp, and I decided to experiment with such deprivations in the future.

When Mycroft arrived with the book, his first observation was on the remains of our meal. "Are you going to eat that? I declare, the beef broth Cook sent up barely kept my hand steady enough to write."

"How many pages did you complete?"

"The ledger had thirty-three pages with writing." His mouth turned down. "Without enough time to finish all of them, I considered that the expert might work on the first few pages and then the later entries to determine first the type of code and then whether the pattern was similar in the latest observations. In between is mere gibberish, random symbols that emulate the others."

I took the book and ran my hand over the cover. "Let's hope it will do."

Dropping the book on the floor, I stepped on it and ground it under my boot over the rising protests of my brother, then opened it and ruffled each page.

"See here. After all my work—"

"You know Mother's ledger wasn't new. It has to at least appear similar to the one we are replacing."

"Quite right." He went to the table holding our plates and dipped his finger in the remaining gravy on one. After removing the book from my grasp, he carefully dabbed the cover in three separate places. "The cover held a few stains as well."

When he handed the volume back to me, I picked up a basket I had packed and turned to my uncle. "Let's get to the Straton cottage."

THE MOON WAS bright and full, allowing us to see clearly despite the hour. Uncle Ernest and I rode in silence until after we had left our property and turned toward the Stratons' and town. I found myself yawning, and fearing that I wouldn't remain alert, I decided to engage him in conversation and bring up the subject of the attraction I'd experienced toward Constance in a roundabout way.

"Uncle Ernest, have you ever…?" I paused to consider how to raise the topic and decided on a different track. "How is it that you've never married?"

He glanced from the road to meet my gaze. "I suppose…I've never…found the right woman." He stared at the moonlit road ahead. I knew he was remembering something and waited as I had learned to do with him. Finally, he spoke in a soft tone, one that hung in the air along with the

scents of damp autumn leaves. "That's not correct. I did...
meet one...once. She was...beautiful. Long, dark hair.
Brown eyes that were almost black. Golden skin."

"She was a Hindu?"

He shuddered slightly and cleared his throat. His speech
quickened, as if he wanted to change the subject. "She was
of a royal family in the region. We met at a banquet her
father gave for the troops in the area. He was grateful for the
protection we provided his province."

"Was that allowed? You seeing a Hindu girl?"

"That was the problem. Neither her father nor my
commanding officer would have approved. We met on the
sly. Only three times. But we knew love from our first
moment together."

"Did you...? Did you kiss her?"

"Only once. Mostly we talked. On what was to be our
fourth meeting, she didn't come. I waited almost all night in
case she had been detained. I learned the next day her
father had sent her away. An arranged marriage in another
province. Someone had told him of our meetings." He
blinked several times, and the moonlight glistened in his
eyes. "I never saw her again."

"I'm sorry, Uncle. If I brought up sad memories."

"It's all in the past, my boy," he said and flicked the reins
to encourage the horse along. "But when you have loved so
deeply, anything else pales."

Once again, lethargy settled over me, and I jerked
awake when we pulled into Straton's yard. I had been

kissing a golden girl with long black hair and was glad for the darkness to cover the flush I felt in my face from the dream—as much from guilt for stealing my uncle's story as from kissing a woman, even if it was in a dream. I shook my head to clear the vestiges of the vision from my mind. I was definitely going to experiment with restricting my diet for major events. Perhaps eliminating beef and potatoes as a starter.

Constance opened the door and whispered to me, "You gots the clothes? I'll change and be right out."

"There's a cloak with them for you to cover yourself on the ride in."

She nodded, took the bundle, and stepped back inside. I listened at the door for any indication of the presence of Mr. Straton. The only sound I could detect was the shallow breathing of sleeping children.

When Constance returned, and we were out of earshot of the cottage, she was the first to speak. "The clothes were a bit big, but I was able to tie them up. It made me rather thick about the middle but helps the disguise."

"It's one of my mother's costumes for playacting and the only one I could take without someone noticing. If you put your hair up in the cap, I doubt anyone will recognize you."

Without more to say, we rode in silence until Constance started a tune, humming softly to herself. I found myself intrigued by the melody.

"What's that song?" I asked.

"Somethin' my mother taught us," she said.

Raising her voice, she added the words to the tune.

When she finished, my uncle shared what I had been thinking. "You have a lovely voice."

"Thank you," she said. "I try and practice my singing every chance I get. I saw a lady once, singing on a stage at a village fair. I sneaked under the canvas. She finished just as they caught me and threw me out. They threw flowers at her." She paused and let out a deep sigh. "That's what I wants. People to throw flowers at me instead of chasing me away with a broom or rocks. Someday, I'm going to find a way to be like that woman. So's I can earn my own *push* and not worry that my papa's drunk it all again."

I wasn't sure how to respond. The gap between us had never seemed as wide as at that moment. Our economic differences had been obvious from the start, but the implications lay bare in front of me now. We both had futures set out for us—in very different directions. Constance was the first person with whom I had made a true connection outside of my family. She had demonstrated she was clever, skilled, and independent. Her fate, however, appeared dictated to be similar to her mother's. Marriage, children, and a life of living near the abyss of poverty. I could understand my mother's concerns for the women in the village and the limitations society placed on them.

Perhaps my uncle was thinking something similar, or of the fate of his Indian love, because he responded, "You deserve it, my dear, and I will see how we might help. You are doing a great service for us, and I promise to pay it back in full."

Even in the semi-darkness, I could see the smile break upon her face.

THE PLAN SEEMED SIMPLE ENOUGH. Constance would slip into the hotel through the alley, posing as a chambermaid, and wait on the second-floor landing for me. After inquiring at the front desk about the expert, I would report his room number to Constance. She would tell the expert he had a note and when he went to fetch it, she would replace the ledger. My duty was to keep an eye out for his return.

As soon as Uncle Ernest pulled the cart to a stop in an alley near the hotel, we each went in separate directions, leaving Ernest to wait for us.

Almost immediately I discovered two wrinkles in our plan. The first involved reaching the front desk. Given the hour, guests were arriving from the train station as well as for supper. The reception clerk didn't attend to me for several minutes and by the time he did, I was quite agitated—the second issue.

The round man with the high collar and wide whiskers peered at me over a pair of spectacles. "What is it, boy?"

I held up an envelope. "I have a message for Mr. Beecher."

"Beecher? There's no Beecher registered here."

My stomach squeezed, and I was certain the beef and potatoes were a mistake. I forced myself, however, to appear nonchalant. "Oh? Did I say Beecher? Maybe Constable Gibbons said Bleeker."

"The constable?" The man studied me for a moment, and I blinked at him, hoping I gave off an innocent appearance. He held out his hand. "I'll see that it's delivered."

I pulled back the envelope when he reached in my direction.

"Sorry, I was to deliver it personally." The man's lips thinned to a straight line, but I played my final card. "Constable's orders."

The man gave a *hurrumph* but glanced at a large book on the desk behind him and pointed up the stairs. "Room Twenty-two."

With a tip of my hat, I stepped as sedately as possible to the stairs to find Constance. The hallway stretched to the left and right at the top of the stairs, with several doors opening on to it. A ruby oriental rug ran its length, leading to a set of servant stairs on the left. The gaslights on the sconces located at intervals along the walls flickered slightly, but they illuminated the area with more than enough light to indicate Constance was not waiting as expected. I traversed the entire hallway but found no sign of her. Had she been found out? I considered completing the plan by myself until I remembered that Constance carried the false ledger. No way could I simply take the one in Bleeker's room without casting suspicion on my mother.

Why hadn't we worked on a better system to signal each other?

I had turned toward the stairs, planning to abandon the whole scheme and meet up with my uncle, when she descended from the third floor.

"Where have you been?" I whispered in a tone much harsher than etiquette demanded when speaking to the fairer sex.

"When I got inside, someone handed me a pitcher of water and told me to take it to the man in Room Thirty." She dug in her pocket and held up a coin. "He gave me a penny 'for my troubles.' Do you think I cans get a position here? A penny for just bringing some water. Imagine?"

"We're behind schedule," I said, more than a little frustrated with her skipping subjects at the moment. "The man's in Room Twenty-two. His name's Bleeker."

"You better hide until after he goes downstairs." She took a deep breath and moved up the hallway. Just before the landing where the stairs led to the ground floor, she turned. "I don't wants to go back to gaol. Please, don't lets 'em catch me."

Her plea hit me in the stomach as hard as a fist, and I forced down the rising bile. My concern had focused on keeping my mother out of gaol, but the reality of what we were doing impacted me at that moment. The consequences of getting caught were not evenly distributed. My father might be able to keep me out of gaol, but Constance's fate would most likely be more severe. I owed her more than the bread I'd promised her.

Having stepped into one of the doors' recesses further down the hall, out of sight but not hearing of Room 22, I waited my opportunity to prove a better crow than earlier that day. Constance's knock broke the silence permeating the hallway.

I forced myself to take shallow breaths to follow the ensuing events.

A creak of hinges signaled the door's opening.

"Excuse me, sir," she said, "but you have a message from Constable Gibbons at the front desk."

"At this hour?"

"Yes, sir. I was told it was urgent-like."

A sigh followed. "Can't you just bring it up?"

I gulped. Our plan had assumed he would leave immediately so that Constance could relieve him of his key and use it to enter his room for the search.

"Oh no, sir," she said without any pause. "He wanted it delivered straight to your hands."

Another sigh. "Very well. I'll be down after I dress."

"If you'll be beggin' my pardon, you looks dressed to me."

"Of course, I'm dressed. I mean…" This sigh came out as more of a bluster. "Just tell him I'll be there shortly."

"Yes, sir."

Her voice held none of the panic rising within me.

When her footsteps grew louder, I stepped from the

shadows to stop her. "What are we going to do now?" I whispered.

"Don't worry," she said, the skin about her eyes crinkling in amusement. "Wait for him to leave, and you'll see."

While her attitude offered some reassurance, my heart still drummed at twice its normal speed. She gave my hand a pat and returned to the other side of the hallway and outside of my range of vision.

After what appeared to be an eternity, I heard more footsteps. Only there were too many to be the expert's alone. I peeked around the doorframe just as a couple headed in my direction. When they saw me, they stopped.

"Sorry," I said. "I thought you were my parents. They went to get the key."

They exchanged glances, but before they could ask questions, I added, "I don't know what's taking them so long. I guess I'd better check."

Ducking my head, I stepped into the corridor and moved toward the stairs. The expert, of course, chose that moment to exit his room. He was dressed as he'd been when he arrived, down to the silk handkerchief in his pocket. Keeping my head down, I pushed past him and Constance, who must have been waiting for him on the other side. Once again, I turned to a door, pretending to open another of the rooms.

"Excuse me, sir," she said to the man. "Another man asked for a fresh pitcher of water. I wondered if you'd like one too?"

He paused as if considering the offer. "Yes. Thank you."

"I'll be right up, sir," she said and offered a wide smile. She moved past him and bumped him as she did so. "So sorry."

"Quite all right," he said and tugged on his lapels. He took a few steps toward the stairwell and stopped. "Oh, miss?"

My stomach squeezed again, but once again, Constance's response was calm and matter-of-fact. "Yes, sir?"

"On second thought, I haven't any idea how long I'll be downstairs. I'll request a pitcher at the front desk when I'm finished."

"Very good, sir."

When a set of muffled footfalls descended the stairs, I released my breath, only to draw it in again when I heard a door open and another voice call out, "Miss?" The couple in the hallway must have observed the exchange. "May we have fresh water too?"

"Certainly. I'll bring it up directly."

The door closed, and I heard a quick shuffle of feet in my direction.

"Keep a sharp eye, Sherlock," she whispered as she let herself into the room with only the slightest of creaks.

Stepping to the stairs' balustrades, I watched the expert enter the lobby. In what appeared to be only two breaths, he reached the front desk. The clerk there shook his head at the expert and then pointed up the stairs. He obviously indicated I had taken the note upstairs. I stepped back to be out of Bleeker's vision. That move also put him out of my sight, and only when I heard someone ascending did I realize he had given up and was returning to his room.

My breath quickened. Constance hadn't left the room. What was she doing in there? The man was almost a third of the way from the top. Blood rushed in my ears, making it difficult to hear. My only thought involved keeping my promise not to let her be caught in his room. After a brief consideration of the options, I took a deep breath, rushed around the balustrade, hoped I gave a convincing trip, and dove headfirst down the stairs.

I caught a brief glimpse of the expert's widened eyes and snatches of the stairs' red carpeting and the gaslights flickering near the ceiling as I tumbled down. When I came to a halt on the lobby floor, I heard snatches of several shouts and gasps before everything faded to black.

CHAPTER TEN

My first conscious sensation involved my head. It hurt. A lot. And my limbs felt bruised. I wiggled my fingers. They appeared to be working. Voices floated around me, but I couldn't make out what they were saying. I cracked my eyes open. Darkness enveloped me wherever I was, but a glow to my left suggested a lamp or candle nearby.

"Sherry, dear, can you hear me?"

I turned my head toward the voice. My mother's face came into focus, and I could make out another figure behind her.

With great effort, I managed to ask, "Where...where am I?"

"Underbyrne. Your room," my father said. "Ernest brought you home. After you fell from the tree."

I had so many questions. Where was Constance? Had she found the book? Unfortunately, I could ask none of them in front of my father.

"Can you sit?" Mother asked.

When I pushed myself up onto my elbows, the room tilted slightly. I raised myself a bit more, but the room spun around me. I sank back onto the bed.

"I'm very dizzy."

A line appeared between her eyebrows. "You're suffering a commotion of the brain."

"Should we call the surgeon?" Father asked. "Have him bled?"

"I don't think that's necessary at the moment. The latest scientific evidence from France suggests simple bed rest for a commotion."

Never had I felt more grateful for my mother's medical interest than at that moment. With all that had happened in the past few days, I had no problem with the sight of blood, but the idea of the surgeon using his knife on me made my head swim to the point I feared I would be sick.

I raised myself onto my elbows, but the room stayed still this time—which gave me some level of comfort above that provided by the presence of both my parents. Mother placed her hands on my shoulders and pushed me back into the pillows.

"I want you to rest now. We'll talk about what you were up to in that *tree* later."

Despite my pain and somewhat addled thinking, I

caught her slight emphasis on the word *tree*. At that moment, I knew she was aware of the plot to replace the ledger and was letting me in on the fabrication to explain my fall.

But any additional information required us to talk alone. With no other recourse, I settled back and let her pull the covers to my chin and allowed sleep to draw me back under.

WHEN I NEXT AWOKE, sunlight shone around the edges of the room's drawn curtains. My parents slept in a pair of stuffed chairs, one on each side of me. Mother was the first to realize I was awake.

"Sherry, dear, feeling better?"

I took a brief inventory of my aches and pains. "My head still hurts, but not as much, and my back, too." I raised myself onto my elbows again. "But I don't feel dizzy anymore."

"Excellent news, son. Do you feel up to eating?" Father asked and stretched, sitting up straight in his chair. When I answered in the affirmative, he stood and arched his back. "I'll arrange for a tray for the three of us."

"Nothing too heavy for Sherlock. A bit of broth should sit well. And tea."

While I would have liked to argue that I could manage something a little more substantial—for it seemed that all I had eaten for the past few days had been broth—I knew I was in no position to argue with Mother. I could tell from the set of her jaw she planned to have a private discussion with me as soon as my father vacated the room.

True to my intuition, as soon as he closed the door, Mother turned to me. "You committed a very foolish and dangerous act." As much as I wanted to explain my actions, I waited to learn exactly what she knew. "Your uncle explained everything. He came thundering back in the cart. I would have never thought it could go that fast. He made up some sort of story about an experiment involving you climbing a tree. The branch broke, you fell, and he brought you here. I knew the moment I examined you and found no scratches your fall hadn't included a tree. Ernest confessed all when I confronted him."

"But the book? Did Constance replace it?"

"Don't worry. It's hidden in your uncle's workshop."

I lay my head back on the pillow, knowing we'd been able to save my mother from further scandal and possibly gaol. She placed her hand on my forehead and smiled. "You, Ernest, and Constance did a very brave thing, and I will be in your debt forever. Regardless, it wouldn't have been worth your life."

Unwilling to argue with her, I closed my eyes. I knew it was worth the injury—and more.

The door opened, and a chambermaid entered with a large tray. Father followed a moment later. After the items had been arranged on a table for them and a tray set up on my lap in the bed, Mother removed a cloth covering the plate to reveal a bowl with broth—chicken, if I was not mistaken by the scent—some toast, and a cup of tea. "Eat sparingly," she said. "A commotion of the brain can cause nausea."

I took a sip of the broth, grateful it wasn't beef this time. After a few more spoonfuls and a nibble on a corner of toast, my mother's attentive face relaxed a bit. She observed me a moment more, seemed satisfied I was following her orders, and joined my father for their own repast.

They were almost finished when someone knocked on the door. I had assumed it was the maid coming to remove the trays, but the form filling the doorway didn't belong to a woman.

Uncle Ernest said, "Thought I'd come by and see how my favorite nephew was doing."

"According to Mrs. Holmes, he should make a full recovery. No thanks to you," Father said.

Mother rose from her chair. "Mr. Holmes, we agreed we wouldn't—"

"Quite right. Quite right," he said, raising his hand to still his wife. "I just… It seems to me he should have taken more care—"

My uncle's features took on a strange expression. Hard, but at the same time vulnerable. The poor man accepted my father's admonishment for something that hadn't happened. The whole injustice of his situation compelled me to come to his defense.

"It wasn't Uncle Ernest's fault. I climbed the tree on my

own. And he certainly didn't cause the branch to break. Don't be cross with him."

Father glanced at the three of us, gave a *hurrumph*, but didn't continue his reproach.

"Sherlock is, as you said, going to recuperate," Mother said. "I would suggest that both of us could use a bath and some rest in a real bed." She smiled at my uncle. "That is, if you are willing to sit with him for a bit?"

"My pleasure," he said, stepping toward the bed and the chair Mother had used for her vigil last night.

"I'll send the maid to clean up in here."

She placed a hand on my cheek, turned to my father, and gestured to the door.

My uncle leaned over and snatched a bit of toast to nibble on as my parents left. Only after the door clicked shut did he speak.

"Glad to see you awake."

"Thank you for getting me home. It would have been disastrous if I'd been taken to Harvingsham's. Or worse, if they'd called the constable. How did you find out what happened?"

"Constance came racing up to me, that cap of hers halfway off and her red hair flying behind her, like the devil himself was after her. I thought for sure you'd been caught. I was about to send that poor horse tearing out when she called out you'd fallen down the stairs. I ran to the hotel, said I knew who you were and rushed out with you in my arms before anyone could stop me. How many recognized you, I have no idea, but the most that can happen is that your father finds out the fall was from the stairs and not a tree."

"It's not fair that my father scolded you."

"He's right to be upset. You took quite a tumble. Could've killed yourself. Promise me you won't do anything so foolish again."

I nodded, too filled with emotion to respond through the catch in my throat. Despite Ernest's sometimes odd behavior, I didn't doubt for a second his concern was sincere.

He slapped his knee.

"Tell you what. I'll bring up the chessboard. We'll play a few games."

I barely assented before he dashed off and returned with the board, arranging it on a table by the bed.

"Let's see if that fall has affected your mental abilities."

Over the next hour, I was pleased to find my powers of concentration hadn't been impaired. Of particular interest, I was able to fend off an attack on my queen and turned it around to a checkmate.

"Well done," said Ernest with a chuckle.

His amusement concerned me. Had he let me win?

"Not a chance," he said when I asked. "It's beneath a Parker to allow someone a false victory. But then again, I'm afraid I don't take it quite as seriously as your mother or brother."

As if he knew he'd been mentioned, my brother entered after a rap on the door.

"Sorry. I didn't mean to intrude," he said when his gaze fell on the board.

"Not at all," Ernest said. "Your brother just gave me a good trouncing."

He made a quick study of the remaining pieces, lifted one, and moved it toward my side. "That move would have prevented your loss."

"Quite possibly," he said, scratching his chin. "But too late now. Besides, it's just a game. A rematch is in order, but later. I have some work to do in my workshop. If you'll excuse me."

Mycroft's observation forced my attention to the board, and I replayed the game over in my head. So intense was my concentration, my response to my uncle's exit was simply a wave in his direction. I could feel the heat rising in my face as I convinced myself that Mycroft's suggestion indicated the brain commotion *had* affected my mental abilities. Fear and anger surged through me and pushed out a question to my brother with more force than required.

"What do you want?"

He recoiled slightly at my demand.

"I merely came to see how you were doing. What you did was quite"—I glared at him, anticipating being called foolish, stupid, or worse—"valiant."

All anger drained from me as I realized he'd paid me a compliment. Rarely did he direct anything positive in my direction. I swallowed, unable to think beyond the word coming from his lips. My father's rigorous training in proper behavior, however, took over and provided the appropriate response despite my mental immobility.

"Thank you."

"Mind you, I think it was also quite foolish, but it took courage to do that."

With that pronouncement, he glanced about and shifted on his feet in obvious discomfort at having to admit admiration for his younger brother. A smile twitched on my lips in response to my self-satisfaction. At that moment, the retrieval of Mother's ledger, as important as it was, paled in comparison to the approval he'd expressed. Regardless of his future behavior, I had this exchange to remind me that he didn't always view me as a nuisance.

He was saved from further embarrassment by a knock at the door.

"You have a visitor," Mrs. Simpson said. "Do you feel up to receiving her?"

Mrs. Simpson pushed back the door when I assented, and Constance entered. Her steps, usually so sure and determined, were muted and slow. She dropped her chin and glanced up at me through her lashes.

"It's good to see you, Master Sherlock."

Mycroft coughed and excused himself, leaving the two of us alone.

After the door shut, Constance stared around her, mouth agape. "I thinks this room is bigger than my whole house."

Having seen her house, I couldn't disagree.

"I came to see how you were. Your uncle didn't think it was wise for me to be seen with you, so's he let me out on the road before we's got here."

"I understand. And I think he was right. You shouldn't be connected with me—in case someone recognized me or Uncle Ernest."

"I was just so scared, seeing you lying there on the floor —all still like. All I could think of was getting to your uncle. You turned out to be a right good crow. No one's ever almost got kilt like that...for me."

She turned her head away and raised her hand to her face. When she turned back to me, her features were composed, but a smudge across her cheek showed where she'd wiped the tear.

"You took the greatest risk. Going into the expert's room like that. I...admire you."

A smile stretched across her mouth with those full, red lips, and I realized *admire* fell short in describing what I felt. Her innate cleverness offered a companionship I'd never experienced before. Her cheeks reddened, highlighting her freckles, and she dropped her gaze. That odd feeling returned to me.

"Tweren't that much. But thank you. I...admire you too."

Before we could exchange more, Mother and Father entered.

"Constance," she said, unable to hide her surprise at finding her in my room. She regained her composure in the next instance and said, "How good of you to visit. I'm afraid, however, I need to examine him. Mr. Holmes, if you would be so kind as to open the drapes before escorting Miss Straton downstairs?"

When Father did as instructed, light flooded my room, making us all squint. He then waved an arm toward the door, directing Constance to follow him downstairs.

"See you tomorrow," she said, shutting the door behind her.

After the door shut, Mother placed her hands on the side of my face and moved me into a shaft of light from the window. When the light hit my face full force, I winced, but smiled. "Your pupils contract nicely. I do think the brain commotion wasn't a serious one. Thank goodness. Any nausea?"

I shook my head but stopped as the room spun about me.

"But still dizzy I see. I think you need to remain in bed today." I opened my mouth to protest, but she stopped me with her hand. "Rising too soon can be quite hazardous. We'll reassess you this evening."

Father returned from escorting Constance, and Mother updated him on my progress. He smiled at the news and said, "I see you've been playing with Ernest. Perhaps we could match wits as well."

The prospect of an additional assessment of my mental faculties as well as some time alone with Father appealed to me.

"I'd like that very much."

"Just no physical exertion for the moment," Mother said, wagging a finger at me. "I'll check on you later and bring a book along if you'd like me to read to you. Perhaps the German volume Mycroft loaned me?"

While the thought of grasping economic theories in German seemed tedious in my current state, I relished the idea of some time alone with my mother, just as I did with my father, and agreed to the prospect immediately.

The game with my father progressed nicely with each of us matching the other in moves and countermoves. He even complimented me on my strategic skills. My concerns about my brain dissipated, and I found myself screwing up my courage to ask him a question that'd been on my mind for a while.

"Father, how did you meet Mother?"

He jerked his head up to meet my gaze. After he considered my question for a moment, he said. "At a lecture by an entomologist. He was discussing the lifecycle of the common housefly. You know my fascination with insects. Given the topic, you can imagine the room wasn't overly crowded. Regardless, your mother would have stood out. Here was this young woman, taking notes, no less. And asking very pointed questions. She was interested in their use in wound care."

I could very clearly see how my mother's looks and actions would have drawn attention. Having compared her with other women, I knew her features to be above average, and a younger version would only be more so. At the same time, her direct and inquisitive manner would have drawn attention to her as well.

"And did you speak to her then?"

A smile played on his lips. The memory had to be pleasant. "No. I was much too taken aback by her. Not only quite fetching but intelligent as well. I knew that the moment she asked a question about how much decayed flesh a single maggot could eat in a day. Not at all squeamish. So, I made a few inquiries as to her identity. I had a friend introduce us at a lecture the next week. This time it was on horticulture. Dreadfully boring as far as I was concerned, but again, there she was asking the most insightful questions."

I could also imagine that. My father's interest in plant biology was limited to any agricultural issues, and unless it was related to some crop cultivation, he would be either lost or totally disinterested. "When you finally met, what was Mother's reaction?"

"Polite, but rather aloof. Even furtive." Another smile. "I learned later she had tricked the aunt she was visiting and slipped away to the lectures without permission. She spent a lot of time in France, you know. Apparently, they had allowed her more freedom there to attend medical lectures."

I nodded. We had travelled to Paris to visit that side of her family more than once, and my mother had attended a number of lectures on a variety of subjects during these trips. Whenever possible, she would bring me and Mycroft along, expressing her desire for us to develop our language skills as well as our scientific knowledge.

"I promptly invited her to an evening at that friend's home." He sighed. "She turned me down."

I stared at my father. Social convention would have required acceptance of a supper invitation unless a previous engagement had already been secured. Surely Mother would have followed protocol, unless— "Because she already had plans that evening?"

"That's what she told me at the time, but I learned through other sources, she simply didn't accept any invitations from unmarried men. She had determined not to marry and didn't want to be burdened by the attentions of possible suitors."

"If she didn't want to marry, how did she agree to do so in the end?"

He leaned toward me and touched the side of his nose. "I won her over. If she wouldn't accept any invitations to attend my functions, I would attend hers." He winked. "I was able to persuade her aunt, who was concerned for your mother's spinster future, of my very honorable intentions, and she supplied me with information on her calendar. I didn't attend as many lectures at Oxford as I did in pursuit of your mother."

I moved a piece and announced, "Checkmate."

"Well done," he said and pulled out his pocket watch. "Look at the time. I'm afraid we'll have to pursue our game later. I have to meet with Mr. Simpson to go over the books."

When he stepped from the room, I lay back on my pillow to contemplate what he just shared with me. The image of my father as a young man, slightly older than Mycroft, accompanying my mother to lectures offered a new perspective of both. While I knew they had been young once, I found it difficult to consider that they had not always been together.

I won her over.

My father had shown interest in matters significant to her. Was that truly enough to convince her to drop her conviction of remaining unmarried?

I let sleep overtake me, and was only awakened when the door opened and Mother followed the maid carrying a tray into the room. After the tray had been arranged, and we were alone, Mother again checked my eyes and asked about my general health.

When I assured her I had no headache or dizziness, she smiled. "I think you can get out of bed tomorrow evening, if you wish."

The tray this evening proved more substantial than my last meal. I had actual meat and vegetables. And butter. I smeared a good bit on one of Cook's rolls and bit into it, enjoying the sensation as the butter melted on my tongue and coated my mouth. For the first time, I truly understood Constance's desire for more of Cook's baking.

Mother returned when the maid came to clear my

supper away. As promised, she carried the German volume with her. She took the chair by the chessboard and settled back to read from *Manifest der kommunistischen Partei*. Between her calm voice, the heavy meal, and the complex concepts presented by the authors, my eyelids soon drooped, and I fell into a deep sleep for the night.

The next day passed much like the previous, except I felt stronger and experienced no dizzy spells. With this improvement, Mother approved my joining the family for supper and the discussion in the schoolroom that followed.

Never had I been so glad to wash and dress for a meal. My enforced confinement had grown very tedious, and I couldn't wait to join in the discussion in the schoolroom. Of course, we couldn't speak on the subject at the supper table. Murder was hardly a polite subject and such topics would not be shared in front of the servants. I found myself rushing through what I was served in hopes of moving to the schoolroom sooner.

Of course, the adults seemed in no hurry, and I found myself frustrated with the pace of the meal. After an eternity, Mother rose, and we all stood in response and filed out of the dining room and up the stairs to the classroom. By the time I made it to the schoolroom, Mother had taken a place by the blackboard and reviewed what we'd considered the last time. Following her assessment, she wrote *Rachel Winston* below Mrs. Brown's name, sighed, and turned to us.

"I'm afraid we are no closer to solving what happened to

Emma Brown than when we began," she said. "And now we have Rachel's death as well."

"Pity you weren't able to find out anything from Mr. Harvingsham before his seizure," Mycroft said, his mouth downturned. "Bad break with the bee attack."

"A very bad break," Father said, his mouth mimicking my brother's.

"Not a problem," Mother said. "I learned quite a bit from Mrs. Harvingsham prior to his fit."

"You think Rachel Winston was poisoned too, don't you?" I asked.

The conclusion had been quite apparent when we'd learned of the surgeon's attention to the maid from his wife.

She nodded. "We have two, maybe three victims. But we're missing the connection between them. The common denominator, if you will."

Mycroft stared at the board for a moment and said, "Perhaps if we lay out their connections? For instance, we know Mrs. Straton was friends with Rachel Winston and had seen Mrs. Brown."

Mother drew lines between Mrs. Straton and the other two names. "When we do this, it does appear that she is at the apex of this triangle. Of course, she's dead, but her husband…"

"According to Brown," Father said, "Straton did threaten Mrs. Brown. It seems to me that Gibbons ought to at least bring the man in for questioning. He's been very effective in obtaining confessions in the past."

"Oh, yes," said Mother, her voice taking on a sharp tone. "I've seen the effects of his extraction methods in gaol. Bruises, contusions, and more than one broken bone. Before we resort to the constable, perhaps we should try and find some incontrovertible proof to ensure we have the correct culprit?"

I stared at my mother as the implication of her accusation registered. Mother had certainly been around others accused of crimes and would have first-hand knowledge of why and how others had been arrested, but was she truly accusing the constable of—? Before I could voice my own question, Mycroft asked it for me.

"Are you suggesting Constable Gibbons forces confessions from people?"

"I'm not suggesting it. I'm stating it as fact. I *know* there is more than one innocent person in gaol, sent there by their own words after a rather brutal session with Constable Gibbons or one of his men."

Father shifted in his seat. "Mrs. Holmes, perhaps this is a conversation we should have in private. As a magistrate, I depend on the investigation Gibbons provides in court. If, as you sug—er, *say*…the confessions are suspect, how am I to make judgment on the accused?"

"Facts, Mr. Holmes. Scientific proof. Which is what we have been doing here since I was arrested. Until we have some true evidence beyond what Brown reported about Straton, we shouldn't go to Gibbons. Once Straton falls into the law's hands, the truth may never come out."

He stilled and studied first her, then the board. When he finally spoke, his voice was low and thoughtful. "I suppose another day or two won't make much difference. As long as we can keep Brown from pushing Gibbons to action as he did with you."

"That debacle at the coroner's inquest should have taught him to wait until he has more than just the obvious conclusion," Uncle Ernest said, a smile breaking across his face. "We certainly showed him up that day."

And made an enemy in the process. His seizure of Mother's ledger was no accident.

"Then we are in agreement that until we have some additional information, we will not be going to Constable Gibbons?" Mother asked. With no one voicing another opinion, she continued, "What do we have, then, that would indicate Straton's ability to poison these three women?"

As did the others in the room, I stared at the board with the three names and the lines drawn between them. Something had to be there. Something that we were missing, not seeing. An idea tickled the back of my brain, but I couldn't quite grasp it—

A hard knocking at the door pushed the thought out of my mind. Before anyone could open it, Constable Gibbons burst into the room, followed by a gasping Mrs. Simpson.

"I'm so sorry, Mr. Holmes," the housekeeper said between pants. "He asked me where you were, and I said the schoolroom on the third floor, and he pushed past me before I could stop him."

By this time, we were all on our feet, and Father glared at the intruder. The man pulled on his uniform coat and raised his chin to meet his gaze. He held out a parchment and stepped toward him.

"Excuse the interruption, sir, but I needed your signature on this arrest warrant."

"It couldn't wait until morning?" Father said, taking the paper from him.

While Father skimmed the document, the constable spoke to him in a voice loud enough for all to hear. "I felt it was of the utmost urgency to proceed with the arrest. Before the culprit goes into hiding."

"When did you decide to arrest Joseph Straton?"

My gasp was audible to all those in the room. They turned to me, and my face burned under their scrutiny. What did Gibbons know that we didn't?

The constable ignored my outburst and responded without a glance in my direction. "Today. That beekeeper Brown came by this evening and said you were in agreement that the man was guilty." He glanced at the blackboard and said, "Looks as if you agree that Straton was behind both the midwife's and Rachel Winston's death."

Mother stepped forward. "Actually, we were considering the connections between Mrs. Straton and the other two women."

"But you do agree the man killed Emma Brown."

I glanced at the rest of my family, seeking to determine their agreement with that statement. Given the previous discussion of the constable's tactics and the evidence against Mr. Straton, I wasn't sure of the response. Again, that little nagging thought scratched at the back of my brain, but I couldn't get it to surface.

Father, however, spoke and broke my concentration. "The evidence does suggest that direction."

He stepped to the teacher's desk, picked up a pen and signed the parchment.

With the order now authorized, the man bowed and left, Mrs. Simpson following after him.

"That takes care of that," Father said as soon as the footsteps diminished to silence.

Mother shook her head. "I just hope you haven't sealed the man's death warrant."

"I'll make it clear to the man he's not to force a confession," he said and turned toward the door. "I'll catch him before he leaves."

My father's departure ended our little meeting. Mother ordered me back to bed. I considered arguing, but knew she'd win in the end. Once in my bedroom I took off my jacket and stepped to the wardrobe to hang it up.

Upon opening its door, I yelped and flew backwards about three strides. My pulse quickened and only slowed when Constance leapt from the cabinet and slapped her hand across my mouth.

"Quiet. I don't want no one's to know I'm here."

I pulled her hand from my face and dropped my voice to

just above a whisper. "What are you doing here? How did you get in? Why don't you want to be seen?"

She put her hands on her hips and stared at me a moment. "Did that fall affect your brain after all? Can't you answer these questions yourself? I came to see you. Through that indoor garden of yours. No one ever seems to lock that door. I used to go in with my mother when she'd bring the mending here. She'd pick a bit of parsley or sage when no one was lookin'. And I don't want no ones, especially the constable, to see me and try and use me to find Papa. He says Papa kilt Mrs. Brown, but I knows it wasn't so."

"But he just had my father sign the arrest warrant. How could you already know—?"

"Do you have anything besides questions? He was asking at all the taverns for Papa. One of Papa's friends warned him. So, Papa's runned away to hide." She raised her hand to me, and I froze with my mouth half-open, another question resting on my tongue. "I don't know where, so don't ask."

"I hope you realize all the evidence points in his direction. Mr. Brown even said he threatened him at the tavern. Said Mrs. Brown had given her something that killed her."

"I don't know about him threatening Mr. Brown, but he did carry on about how Mrs. Brown *almost* kilt her. Whatever Mrs. Brown gave her, Papa burnt it."

My stare froze on her face as all the information and conjectures we had assembled in the schoolroom rearranged themselves in my brain. One piece in particular rose to the surface. Rachel Winston's request for pennyroyal for a "friend." Mother had been correct. Mrs. Straton *had* needed more.

"How did your father find out about the medicine in the first place?"

"It was in her mending basket. He was searching for a sock she said she'd mended. It spilt out of the paper she had it in. She said it was somethin' Mrs. Brown had given her 'cause she couldn't be havin' another baby right away. He cursed at her, callin' it Satan's weed. And burnt it in the fireplace."

Perhaps because of the brain commotion, my thoughts raced. I considered the names on the blackboard in the schoolroom, the contents of Mrs. Straton's mending basket, Rachel Winston's efforts to help a friend. I must have stared at Constance for a while because she asked, "Are you all right? You ain't havin' a fit, are you?"

That question let loose a deluge of words that tumbled out of my mouth faster than my thoughts.

"Your father had no reason to kill Mrs. Brown. But still, your mother died from something. If she kept what Mrs. Brown gave her in the mending basket, perhaps she also kept whatever—"

Constance's rounded eyes stopped me before I completed the sentence. I'd been so intent on reconstructing the information, I'd forgotten I'd been referring to her mother—a woman who had only been dead three weeks.

My father's voice reprimanded me for such a terrible breach of etiquette.

"I-I'm sorry. I forgot myself for a moment," I said, and stared down at the rug on my bedroom floor. When I raised my head, she was still staring at me, her mouth open.

"My-my mother was…?"

Her turn to stop herself. She sucked in a breath and spun about. Her ragged breathing made her shoulders jerk up and down in time with her inhalations. I reached out and touched her arm. After a moment, she faced me, her cheeks wet and her eyes red-rimmed.

"I thought she just… Everyone knew she was poorly… How…? Who?"

Unsure of my words and fear of causing her additional pain, I raised my hands in surrender. When her eyes widened again, I feared her emotions had overcome her again and braced myself for an even stronger display. Instead, she grabbed my arm and spoke in a harsh whisper. "Do you think we might find something in her mending basket to show how she … passed? We could check it."

"Now?" I glanced out the window. Only a partial moon shone through the glass. "Shouldn't we wait until morning? Also, I think I should tell Father. As magistrate—"

"Not yet. I want to see what's in that basket. The constable already thinks Papa kilt Mrs. Brown. I don't want him thinkin' he poisoned Mama too. I's gots to see what's in it first. You know more about that kind of thing. You might be able to tell. Come with me."

I paused, knowing my mother had sent me to bed because of my injury. We'd managed to keep the truth from Father about our adventure in town, but if I were caught leaving the house, I was sure to incur the wrath of both parents. Three elements, however, weighed in favor of going with Constance. The first was the girl herself. The soft plea in her eyes pushed me to acquiesce. Also, social convention dictated I accompany her and not let her return to her home alone at this hour. Finally, I considered the worst consequences with respect to my parents. Most likely, it would involve returning to Eton. My father might consider it a reward and refuse my going back. All in all, I was likely safe from any severe consequences.

After a moment more during which Constance chewed her lip, a small gesture that raised my pulse to the point I wondered if it might be bad for my head, I nodded. "Wait for me in the greenhouse. It's best we aren't seen together."

Her shoulders dropped and her lips rose in a smile. She gripped my shoulders and rose to her tiptoes to kiss me on the cheek. "Thank you. I know we'll be able to show Papa's innocent."

After I checked to see if anyone was in the hall, I let her out of my room, and she was gone.

Almost.

I raised a hand to my cheek and fingered the spot where she'd kissed me. Although it had been brief and light, my skin retained the memory of that touch from her lips. Soft, tender, and slightly moist.

I might have continued in that frozen moment had I not remembered the kiss's donor was waiting for me. Pushed into action, I changed into my heavy hunting jacket and boots in a flash. After wrapping a scarf about my neck and pulling my deerstalker hat onto my head, I made to join Constance. My dressing activities must have muffled the noise in the hallway because when I opened the door, I almost ran straight into Mycroft. Only his surprisingly agile jump backwards kept us from crashing into each other.

"Good lord, Sherlock, where do you think you're going? And in such an all-blasted hurry?"

CHAPTER ELEVEN

I raised a finger to my lips and glanced over his shoulder to the back stairs. In a low voice, I said, "I have an...errand to do."

"At this hour?" He studied my clothing, wrinkled his nose, and asked in a lower tone, "You're obviously planning a trip through the woods. To the Straton cottage, I presume?"

"I know Mr. Straton didn't murder Mrs. Brown. Constance told me."

Another wrinkle of the nose. "*Told* you." He glanced behind me and into my bedroom. "Is she in there?"

"No."

He stared at me, and I knew he was assessing me and his next move. I'd seen the same expression when he played

Mother in chess. "You'll have hell to pay if they catch you out of your room."

"I've considered the consequences and find nothing that would be worse than sending an innocent man to gaol." After a weighted pause, I played to his weakness. "I'm doing this for you as much as anyone. Remember, the sooner we resolve these deaths, the sooner you return to Oxford." His brows arched, and I knew I'd convinced him. "I could use some help in keeping everyone from my room until I return."

Another glance into the bedroom. "Sometimes you are truly a twit. Do you think anyone will believe you're in your room when your bed is still made?"

"I was in a hurry, and I—"

He waved a hand at me, as if shooing me toward the servant stairs. "Go. Before Father and Mother decide to retire. I know what to do. I used to sneak out of my bedroom at night in Eton. When I wanted to be alone with my thoughts, I would make my bed to appear I was in it and then go to a storage room in the attic. I made it up into quite a nice sitting area from some discarded pieces. Over time, I even allowed a few of the other boys to join me."

"The Diogenes Society."

"You know about it?"

"It's still there. One of the boys from the upper forms invited me because I was your brother. I can understand its appeal to you. They had a rule about no talking. I found it rather…stifling."

He tucked his chin and studied me for a moment. "I can see that for you. You've always been a rather restless soul. Always running about wanting to do things. Like now. You'd best get going."

"Thanks. For helping me."

"I'm not doing it for you. I'm doing it for me."

He spun on his heel and stepped into my room, shutting the door behind him.

Leaving him to his subterfuge, I headed toward the stairs, listening for any sounds signaling movement on either the main or servants' stairs. Hearing none, I descended to join the girl.

CONSTANCE and I stepped from the greenhouse (She was right. The door was unlocked), and I moved toward my uncle's workshop.

"What are you doing?" she asked in a harsh whisper. "The woods are this way."

"I know, but I want a lantern. It's going to be dark under the trees, and we'll travel more quickly with a light."

At Ernest's workshop, I paused before entering. When I heard no noise, I decided he was either asleep or still in the main house and let myself in. I retrieved a lantern from a bench just inside the door and headed toward the edge of the woods with Constance.

A slight mist blanketed the ground, strips of white

floating about our feet. It grew heavier the further inside we progressed. About ten to fifteen minutes after passing onto the trail, I heard a rustling in the underbrush and jerked my head in the direction of the sound. Chances were the rustling belonged to a deer or similar creature, but even then, some animals would attack if provoked or frightened. Constance, however, continued to trudge ahead, oblivious to the noise. All the same, while I kept pace with her, I found myself listening for any indication of other creatures possibly crossing our path.

As we entered the deepest part of the woods, I found myself clutching the lantern's handle harder as noises seemed to pop up all around me. Despite my heightened vigilance, I might not have heard the sound if we hadn't slowed to climb over a fallen log. Straddling the log, I paused when a low moaning emanated from my right. I turned to Constance to ask if she had heard the same sound, but she stood frozen, her finger to her lips to silence me. We both waited for the noise to come again. Barely breathing, I listened, searching for the groaning until my ears rang.

Then a faint sighing floated on the breeze. I glanced in the direction of the Straton's cottage, feeling the pull to accomplish my mission, and I would have continued on that path had I not caught a word in the next sigh.

"Help."

Constance turned and moved with such speed I could barely keep her within the lantern's glow. I almost ran into her back when she halted at the edge of a small clearing among a stand of yew trees. A dark hump lay almost at her feet. When I raised the light higher to get a better view of the fallen figure, Constance shrieked and dropped to her knees.

"Papa!"

I knelt beside her to help turn him onto his back. Mr. Straton's features twisted in pain, and the only word he muttered was, "Help."

"Papa," she repeated and grabbed his shoulders. "What happened?"

He winced at her movement and groaned, but said no more.

The shadows cast by the lantern made it difficult to make out his injuries. With great effort, I pulled her away from her father, removed my gloves, and ran my hands over the man to see if I could tell where he'd been hurt. When I touched wetness above his abdomen, I pulled my hand back to check it in the light. She cried out again when she saw the red stains on my fingers.

"We have to help him," she said, almost babbling. "Get him to a doctor. He can't die…can't die."

"Constance." I gripped her shoulders and forced her to meet my gaze. "We can't carry him, but he does need help. One of us has to stay. The other must run back to Under-byrne and fetch others."

She glanced back at her father. "He can't die…he can't die."

For the first time since I'd known her, the girl seemed lost, unable to think or respond to the situation. As much as I wanted to shake her, I turned her face to mine and forced myself instead to speak in a low, even tone.

"You have to go get help. Go back to Underbyrne and bring my parents. I'll take care of him while you're gone." I glanced at the man lying still on the ground and said, "I won't let him die."

She focused on me, and for the first time, I could tell she comprehended what I was saying. "Promise?"

I nodded, unwilling to verbalize again what I feared might be an empty vow.

We both rose to our feet, and I accompanied her back to the trail. Before she turned herself in the direction of my home, I pulled a handkerchief from my pocket and tied it to a branch of a bush at the side of the path. "This way you'll know where to turn to find your father. Can you find your way without the lamp? I need it so that I can dress the wound."

"Remember your promise," she said, and rushed away from me.

After she had disappeared into the woods' gloom, I turned to retrace my steps. While the lantern did provide some help in identifying the broken branches and trampled plants Constance and I had created in our search for Mr. Straton, I realized if I marked the whole trail the others would be able to find their way to the injured man faster. I ripped the handkerchief into strips and tied them at various intervals to lead to the yew clearing.

When I reached Constance's father, I sucked in my breath. Even in the yellow light, Mr. Straton's grimy face was pale. How much blood had he lost? A crimson circle covered the right side of his shirt and jacket and soaked the yew needles underneath him. Only the slow rise and fall of his chest let me know he was still breathing.

Kneeling at his side, I now worked quickly to see how I might tend to him until help arrived. I pulled back the shirt and jacket and found the source of the bleeding. It seeped from a slit between two ribs. The image of the dead workman in Mr. Harvingsham's office rose unbidden to my mind, and bile surged into my throat.

I pushed both the image and the rising nausea away, willing myself to return to the job at hand. With shaking fingers, I unwound the scarf from my neck and pressed it against the wound. He moaned, but didn't open his eyes. His skin was cool to the touch. Fearing he might catch a chill, I removed my jacket and covered him as much as possible. Once I completed these tasks, I rested as best I could next to him. All my strength seemed to drain from me. Perhaps I'd pushed myself too far too soon after my fall, or it was the effects of the cool night, but I found my thoughts drifting. I forced myself to keep pressure on Mr. Straton's wound. At some point, my eyelids began to droop.

I must have dozed off but woke with a start when I

heard voices coming toward me. I jerked to attention and shouted in their direction. "Over here."

Father and Benson the gamekeeper were the first to break into the clearing and the lantern light. Mother and Constance followed, with Ernest, Mycroft, and Mr. Simpson the last to arrive. The steward carried a length of canvas attached to two poles. I recognized it as the stretcher Benson used to carry a deer or other animal carcass to the butchering shed.

Everyone held back as Mother knelt next to Mr. Straton. She turned back my coat and, after adjusting the light, checked the wound under the scarf. My makeshift bandage had adhered to the skin, and she had to peel it off. After studying it a moment, she must have recognized it as mine because she passed it to me, and I stuffed it into my trouser pocket without thinking. She pulled a jar of honey out of a small black bag she had brought and quickly applied a thick layer of it to the cut and applied a clean bandage to it.

"That will have to do for the moment," she said, sitting back on her heels. "Once back home, I can determine how deep the cut is. Let's get him there as soon as possible."

The adults exchanged glances, but it was Father who said aloud what I knew the others were thinking. "Mrs. Holmes, you're not suggesting we take him back to Underbyrne? Surely he would be better at the village hospital?"

We had all assumed he would be transported to the low building near the surgeon's home. While Mother and others of our social stature might take care of ill or injured family members at home, the poorer classes would be cared for at the hospital for the surgeon's convenience.

"The trip into town would be dangerous for him. I even fear the travel to our home, but I can care for him better there."

The shadows cast by the lantern light only accentuated the furrows in Father's brow. "As a justice of the peace, I'm not certain we should harbor a fugitive in our home."

"It won't be harboring if we inform the constable where he is. I can tell you now, there is no need to worry he will run off." She glanced at Constance and shifted her tone slightly. "I'll take personal responsibility for him."

"Please, sir," Constance said. "He didn't kilt no one. Master Holmes was going with me to see if we could prove it."

Father shook his head, but said, "He can stay at least until he's healed enough to make his own defense." He turned to me. "You, boy, have no reprieve. We'll discuss your impertinence after the man has been settled in one of the empty servant rooms."

"Yes, sir," I said with a drop of my head.

Over the next half hour, the men loaded the unconscious farmer onto the stretcher, covered him with blankets, and with one on each of the four corners, carried him out of the woods to a waiting wagon. As we tramped behind the men, Mother turned to Constance and me.

"Constance said something about proof her father hadn't killed Mrs. Brown. What did she mean?"

"The constable and Mr. Brown say he killed Mrs. Brown because she poisoned Mrs. Straton. Constance says her mother never took what Mrs. Brown gave her. Her father burned it when he found it in her mending basket. We were going to fetch the basket and see if any was left."

Constance nodded in agreement but glanced down when Mother studied both of us.

"Why didn't you simply tell me? Instead of running off into the woods like this? And you, Sherry, still recovering from a brain commotion."

My shoulders slumped under my mother's rebuke. As much as I wanted to defend my actions, a part of me knew she was right. I also knew that had Constance and I not done so, Mr. Straton would have bled to death in the woods, only ten minutes or so from his home. Mother must have come to the same conclusion because when she spoke next, her voice had lost the tinge of reprimand she'd had earlier.

"We probably *should* consider what might be in the mending basket. Constance, after we settle your father at Underbyrne, I'll send you out with Mr. Simpson to your cottage to collect the basket and your brothers and sisters. We have enough extra beds in the servant's attic for all of you. We'll discuss a more permanent arrangement in the morning."

She lifted her chin to that news. "Thank you, madam. I promise to help in any way I's can."

Despite my relief for Mr. Straton and my previous analysis of the consequences, I still dreaded what awaited me at home. I had not one, but both parents upset about my actions. No head injury in the world would save me a second time from their current disapproval. I did wonder, however, if finding and rescuing Constance's father didn't count for something.

Everyone else remained subdued and in their own thoughts on the ride back. Even poor Mr. Straton remained unconscious. I'd hoped he might be able to tell us who had stabbed him, but the most he did was moan when the wagon wheels hit a rough patch on the road.

Constance stayed at his side throughout, her small hand gripping his. She never glanced away from his face. I wanted to comfort her, assure her he would be all right, but feared to make a hollow assertion. I'd already promised her once and feared repeating it might only raise her hopes. She only let go of his hand when the men took him up the stairs to the servants' rooms. When he was settled in bed, Father remained behind with me and the women.

Mother turned to Constance. "Go downstairs to Mr. Simpson. He'll help you fetch the children along with the mending basket. I'll have Mrs. Simpson prepare a room nearby for all of you."

The girl bit her lip, showing no enthusiasm for leaving her father. At the door, she checked over her shoulder one more time before descending the stairs.

After we could no longer hear her footfalls on the stairs, Mother turned to me. I dipped my head, steadying myself for the reprimand I knew was coming. Instead, she said,

"Go to the kitchen and ask Cook for a kettle of boiling water and a pan. Also more honey. We are going to have to act quickly if we are to avoid infection. Also, have Mycroft and Ernest join us."

As I reached the door, I overheard Father speak in a low tone, "Violette, are you certain you can save him? Perhaps I should call Harvingsham? He does have experience with stitching cuts."

"He would also insist on bleeding him. I think the man has bled enough already, don't you? The stitching will be rather straightforward. I'm more concerned about infection. The honey should help prevent that."

Mr. Straton moaned and twisted on the bed. "Honey."

I turned to check and see if he had awakened, but he had muttered the word without opening his eyes. Mother and Father appeared not to have heard the man, as they continued to speak in low voices as she prepared needle and thread and bandages to minister to the man.

When I returned, Mother had removed the bandage and was cleaning the wound again. "Sherlock, good, put the pan of boiling water on the table and drop the needle and thread in it."

"Won't it make it more difficult to sew if it's wet?"

"Perhaps, but a Hungarian doctor by the name of Semmelweis has found that by washing hands and wounds, the incidence of death decreases." Her hands moved in sure and precise motions as she spoke. "While he didn't specifically note instruments, it seems to me that if washing hands reduces death, wouldn't cleaning all implements touching the body do the same?"

Once the needle was threaded, she paused to examine the cut between the man's ribs one more time. "Rather an odd-shaped incision," she muttered as much to herself as to any of us.

Ernest and Mycroft appeared in the doorway.

"Good, I'll need all four of you to hold the man down. Can't have him twisting about when I try to stitch the injury shut." She turned to her brother. "But before I do, I want you to consider the wound."

Ernest stepped to the bedside and peered at the man's side. "What about it?"

"Consider its shape. It's not the same thickness as a blade would be."

"Yes, I see what you mean. The ends are much thinner than the middle."

"After we finish here, I would like you to work on another pig—"

"Really, Mrs. Holmes," Father said with a sigh. "Another pig? Many more of these little experiments of yours will deplete the swine population to dangerous levels."

"Better swine than people, wouldn't you agree? A killer is stalking our woods. Sherlock and Constance were quite lucky not to have come upon whoever stabbed this man."

Father turned to stare at me for a moment, and I dropped my head. Only at this remark had I realized how close one or both of us might have come to meeting our end. I recalled the rustling in the woods. At the time, I'd only been afraid of animals. Whoever had tried to murder Mr. Straton was definitely the most dangerous creature we could have encountered. I also realized what I had just glimpsed in my Father's eyes. Fear, certainly, but also love. While I'd never doubted my father cared for me, at that moment, I came to understand the depth of his love. The very thought of losing me, when I stood safe and sound in front of him, filled him with dread.

"As I was saying, Ernest," Mother continued, "procure a dead pig and collect all the implements you can to see if you can replicate the wound. Perhaps knowing *what* stabbed the man will tell us *who* stabbed him."

"I'll check the library also," Mycroft said. "I might find the implement among the various books on horticulture and farming."

"An excellent idea," Mother said. "If you do find any, provide them to Ernest so that he can check them."

"But won't Mr. Straton be able to tell us this?" I asked.

She took a quick study of the man from head to toe. "I hope. The next twenty-four hours are very important for him. Now, everyone, I need you to hold him still while I close the wound."

The clock struck two while the four of us struggled to keep the man still. He didn't thrash as much as twist his body when the needle entered his skin. Mother, however, proved to be quite efficient and had the wound closed almost before the chimes' echo died away.

Once the bandage was wrapped over the wound, Mother touched the man's forehead. "Perhaps a little feverish. But then again, he'd been lying on the forest floor. As much as I'd like to give him something for the pain and the fever, he's not conscious, and I fear him choking on a liquid. We'll simply have to wait until something changes. I'll have one of the servants monitor him with orders to come and get me if something changes."

"I'll watch him, madam," Constance said in the doorway.

We all turned in her direction as she entered the room. Her timid step revealed her fear of what she'd find in the bed. Her reach was slow and reluctant as she touched her father's hand resting on the blanket covering his chest.

"Have the children all been put to bed?" Mother asked. Constance nodded. "I would prefer you do so as well, but somehow I think you'd simply return once we left. And you have offered to help. Gentlemen, if you'll excuse us, I'll give some instruction to Constance, and head downstairs shortly."

The moment she referenced sleep, I became aware of how acutely weary I was. All the agitation of finding Mr. Straton, bringing him back to Underbyrne, and treating his wound drained from me, and my extremities became heavy and leaden. With great effort I followed the other men from the room and down the stairs.

Father pulled me aside when we reached the second floor.

"Sherlock, your conduct of late concerns me. This sneaking off when you could have... Your mother convinced me not to confine you to the house this time, but if your behavior doesn't improve, we will have to revisit the freedom you have been afforded." He glanced at his bedroom and sighed. "I'm too tired now to discuss this further, but be forewarned and consider it before future actions."

I nodded and suppressed the grin threatening to appear unbidden despite my fatigue. My logic had paid off in the end. My parents could hardly punish me too severely when my misdeed had saved a man's life.

Once in my chamber, I fought the desire to lie down without taking off my clothes. Only my concern about soiling my linens with the mud from my pants and jacket convinced me to undress. After changing into my night-clothes, I crawled into bed and fell asleep almost immediately.

When I awoke the next morning, the sun was already streaming through the window. I quickly dressed and made my way to Mr. Straton's room. Constance sat by his side, her head resting on the cover near his chest. I hadn't planned to speak to her, but she raised her head when I took a step back to exit.

"What time is it?" she asked.

"Ten o'clock. In the morning. Have you had anything to eat?"

"Mrs. Simpson had someone brings us all somethin' to

eat. I couldn't hardly swallow, but the others finished off what I didn't."

"Any change? In your father, I mean."

She glanced at him and shook her head. "Your mother came in and checked on him. Said he needs to sleep to make more blood, but that he's not been too feverish, and that's good. She'll be in later to change the bandage."

"You know to ask if you need anything. I'm going to get breakfast and find Mother. Do you want to join me?"

She reached out and ran a hand over her father's arm, then shook her head. "I want to be here. In case he wakes up."

In the kitchen, I found Cook already working on dinner, but she offered to fix me a plate to hold me until then.

"If you want, you can also take something to your uncle in his workshop. Your mother's with him. He came in early this morning, asking about my tools that aren't knives. When I showed him some, he took them all and disappeared." She paused as she cut some carrots into round coins. "At least he left the knives."

When I arrived at the workshop with a basket of food enough for three, I found Mother and Ernest standing at a canvas-draped work table. On it lay three sides of pork, their pale-pink skin marked by a number of slits and holes. A jumble of tools, some of which I assumed belonged to Cook, rested near the battered carcasses.

She raised her head when I entered. "Sherry, you're just

the person we needed. You also saw Mr. Straton's wound before I stitched it closed. Do any of these resemble it?"

She handed me a magnifying glass.

I studied the first pig's side. "I don't know for certain, but these cuts appear to be too clean compared to what I saw."

"I agree. You have a keen eye. The blades on these tools appear too sharp and thin." She directed me to the next side. "What about here?"

"These are cruder cuts. That one"—I pointed to one example—"might be similar, but it's not wide enough. The wound was longer."

"Interesting," Ernest said. "That was made by a crowbar."

He picked up a long, iron bar and showed me its flattened, chisel-like end. "But you say it was longer?"

Mother thought for a moment and said, "Perhaps the perpetrator wrenched it about, making the hole bigger?"

"We can see," said Ernest.

He slammed the crowbar's end into the pig's side, then wiggled it back and forth for a moment. When he extracted it, we all peered at the incision created.

"What do you think?" Mother asked.

Both she and my uncle focused on me, and I realized these two adults were actually seeking my advice. I shifted the weight on my feet and studied the gash again.

"It's still not long enough, is it?" I said after a moment.

"And now the middle is all mucked up. The cut was cleaner than that, I think."

Ernest studied the end of the crowbar again. "So the most likely candidate would be something with a wedge-like end, but wider."

"Do you have any instruments that might fit the description?" Mother asked, glancing about the workshop.

"Not that I can think of." He sighed. "I'll go out to the barn and see what I might find out there."

"And check with Mycroft on his research. But let's eat first. While you're collecting the items, I'll see what might be in the mending basket."

I raised my head. I'd forgotten about Mrs. Straton's mending basket. Mother smiled at me when I glanced about to locate the item. While dangling the prospect of the basket might have been to test my patience, the pace at which Mother finished the sandwiches Cook had prepared suggested she was losing that battle herself. In no time, Ernest was off in search of more items to test in the pig carcasses, and Mother and I were gathered at another work table.

As a first step after donning a pair of work gloves, she spread out the contents on the table. The items at the very top were two socks of different colors and an apron with a rip in it. Compared to the assortment of cloth scraps, yarn, and threads in the rest of the basket, I assumed the three pieces were the mending Constance had gathered from Mrs. Gibbons.

Next in the basket was a linen napkin with a rip as well. Mother studied it for a moment. "This appears to be one of ours." She opened it completely. "It is. See the embroidered *H* in the corner? I'll have to ask Mrs. Simpson when she gave it to Mrs. Straton for mending. I don't recall seeing her."

She shook her head and surveyed the items laid out before us.

"Constance said her father destroyed the packet. What do you expect to find?" I asked.

"I'm not certain, but I've observed that when items co-mingle, they often exchange bits of themselves. Like finding horsehairs on your clothes after visiting the stables even when you hadn't touched the animal. Constance said the packet had spilled, so some of it might still be on something in the basket."

"Do you wish me to start on one end while you examine the other?"

"A brilliant idea. What one may miss, the other might see when we cross in the middle."

After retrieving two of my uncle's magnifying glasses and donning my own pair of work gloves, I bent over the first item and examined it from one end to the other and from side to side before going on to the next. I found the glass's display of the weave and various fibers in the cloth or yarn intriguing. When I came across the first bit of foreign matter on a cloth scrap, I called Mother over for her opinion.

She did her own review of the cloth. "It appears to be a bit of fuzz. Perhaps from the yarn or another of the scraps." She straightened and glanced about the place. "Let's make a list of what we find. Perhaps that will help us determine what may be out of the ordinary."

By the time I'd made it almost to the halfway mark, I had an extensive list of bits of fuzz, threads, and...

"Mother"" I asked as I considered my list. "What's the basket made of?"

She turned to it and picked it up. "Willow, I believe."

"Not straw? I've found a few bits of a dried grass or plant."

Her forehead creased. "Something like this?" She pointed to a particular square on her end of the items, but near the center as well. I studied it with my glass. This specimen had a bit of flower still attached to it. I raised my gaze to hers.

"This isn't pennyroyal."

"Very good, dear," she said. Despite my keen observation, her voice carried no joy. "What do you think it is?"

The dried stem had a mottled purple hue along the bottom part. With great care, I crushed a bit using the end of the magnifying glass and sniffed. While not potent, I could still catch the rank odor of...

"It can't be, can it?" I asked aloud, with a similar tone to that of my mother's. "Surely she wouldn't have taken hemlock on her own?"

"How do we know what's in another's heart? I have known others...."

Her face took on the same faraway look Uncle Ernest often showed. When she focused on me again, her eyes shimmered with tears. Who had she known willing to take their own life?

"Do we know for certain that she took it willingly?" I asked. "It's a common enough plant. One can find it everywhere. What if someone else confused it with pennyroyal?"

"All good questions, but I am not certain we can ask anyone in her family. If she did take her life, then they would most likely not admit it. At least now we know what killed the woman. The question is who gave it to her?"

The scent of the hemlock lingered in my nostrils and the itching in the back of my mind returned. Before I could dig down and uncover it, Mrs. Simpson threw back the workshop door, making it slam against the wall with a loud *bang.*

"Mrs. Holmes, I came quick to let you know. The constable's here and is demanding to interrogate Mr. Straton."

In one quick motion, Mother pulled off her gloves and tossed them on the floor at the end of the table by the basket. I followed her example and rushed with the two women back to the main house.

When we stepped into the house through the kitchen, Cook pointed us in the direction of the servant staircase. Constable Gibbons and Father were at the foot. They both turned in our direction when the two women and I rounded the corner into the hallway. From Father's glare at me, I could tell he considered my presence a violation of social conventions regarding conversations among adults. Without a word, I retreated from the hallway, but remained close enough to hear the exchange.

"Ah, Mrs. Holmes, so glad you are here. The constable came to return your ledger."

"How kind of you," Mother said in a voice that betrayed none of the contempt I knew she harbored for the man.

The constable cleared his throat. "It was what you said it was. Notes regarding plant experiments. At least that's what the expert reported."

"You hired an expert? For what purpose?" Father asked. "Who on the village police committee approved such an expense?"

"Because the entries were written in code, I felt the need to confirm its contents. I do have some discretion in my budget. I used that."

"Had you simply believed me in the first place, the expense wouldn't have been necessary, but I am grateful for having my notes back. It represents years of work."

The man gave a *hurrumph* in response and continued. "I thought I might as well bring it with me since I was coming out to interrogate Straton."

"I think you might find that rather difficult, given that the man is unconscious. Or at least he was an hour ago when I checked on him last. His daughter is keeping vigil and has orders to call for me should he awaken."

"How do you know he's not pretending?"

"I suppose he could feign sleep now, but not when I stitched his wound. He also couldn't invent the loss of blood from the stabbing, or the fever that had already attacked him by the time he was found. If you're concerned about him disappearing, I can assure you that even if awake, he would be too weak and ill to flee."

Another *hurrumph.* "I want to see the man. Let me point out you are harboring a criminal. A warrant is out for his arrest."

"Harboring would involve us willfully hiding him. We informed you of his presence the moment he arrived at Underbyrne. As for the warrant, we have it on good authority, sir," Father said, lifting his chest, "that the man was drunk and unable to murder anyone on the night Mrs. Brown died."

"Who says so?"

"The daughter Constance reported it to us——"

"Do you truly think I'd take that girl's word? She's a convicted thief. On the other hand, Mr. Brown will testify the man threatened his wife in a public place. Everyone knows Brown is as close to a saint as they come."

A pause ensued, and while I couldn't see her, I imagined Mother struggling to keep her face and voice civil to the man. When she finally spoke, her words were clipped. "Even a saint can make a mistake about what he heard."

"Perhaps, but I see no reason to think that in this case. The man has been tireless in his pursuit of his wife's murderer. Mr. Holmes was about to take me up to see for myself."

"We'll be down in a moment. Please, follow me, Constable," Father said. After a pause, he added, "I think it best if just the two of us visit the man."

At that remark, I felt for her. Never had I been aware of him shutting my mother out of a matter, especially when it involved someone under her care. The command, mild as its presentation was, clearly set her in her place. Regardless, when she spoke, her tone carried none of the sting I'm sure she felt inside.

"Of course, Mr. Holmes."

After the two men had ascended the servants' staircase, I stepped next to her. Her back was straight and her face set, but I knew she had to be reeling from the backhanded reprimand. As much as I wanted to console her, her posture told me to keep to myself. I opened my mouth to share my concern, but she hushed me by raising her hand. I understood her effort to silence me a moment later.

The narrow corridor leading to all the house's levels made for a perfect sound conduit, and we could hear the men's conversation perfectly.

"I assure you," my father was saying, "should the man regain consciousness and enough strength to become a flight risk, we will gladly turn him over to you. But at the moment, additional movement would probably eliminate him as either a prisoner or a witness."

The constable snorted again. "I have no need of him as a witness."

"An assault was committed against him," Father said. "He is the only one at present who can tell us how he was stabbed and left to die in the woods."

"Probably got into it with one of the others at the tavern. Not the nicest drunk you'd ever meet, I can tell you that. The assault was most likely justified."

The footfalls faded slightly, and I knew they had reached the third floor. A moment later, a single set of footsteps announced someone's descent. Constance emerged from the stairwell. Her eyes were puffy but wide. "Mrs. Holmes, you aren't going to let him take my papa?"

She shook her head. "He's too sick to move. I think the constable will agree to that. Has your father said anything?"

"Nothin' that make no sense," she said, blinking her eyes. "I can hardly make out his words."

"Still feverish?"

A nod.

"Please ask Cook to prepare a kettle of water and give you a pot of honey. I'll check his dressing after the constable leaves."

"I'll help you," I said, and followed Constance to the kitchen.

Along the way, she stopped and grabbed my arm, saying in a harsh whisper, "He said he was arrestin' Papa. What am I going to do if he does?"

"He's not going to arrest him," I placed my hand over hers. As much as I wanted to tell her about how we were working on the identity of her father's attacker, I wasn't certain my mother would want that known. I also found it hard to concentrate on anything but the warmth of her hand on my arm. With great effort, I managed to assure her with, "My parents won't let him. But we do need to make sure he recovers. Come along."

By the time we returned to the servants' stairs, my mother had disappeared—either to hide from the constable or to check on Mr. Straton. After a short discussion, Constance and I decided we would check in the man's room first.

As expected, Mother was there, already seated at his side, the man's shirt raised to expose his bandaged side. When we arranged the water, linen for bandages, and honey on the table next to him, Mother frowned. "Is that all the honey there is?"

"That's what Cook said."

"It's enough for this treatment, but we'll need more." She sighed. "I suppose I could send someone to fetch it for me, but I would prefer to get it myself. That way I can also share what we've learned with Mr. Brown."

Before I could ask if I could join her, Mycroft threw back the door to the room, waving a heavy book over his head. "I found it. I know what stabbed Mr. Straton."

CHAPTER TWELVE

The three of us turned to the door in response to Mycroft's entrance.

He grinned at us, pointing to an image in one of the pages. "A chisel. I'm sure it fits the wound perfectly."

Mother was the first to recover. But before she responded to my brother, she glanced at Constance. I did the same and realized the girl had paled at the news.

"Let's discuss this outside," Mother said and led Constance to a seat next to her father's cot. "I'll be right back. Please keep an eye on him until then."

Once in the hallway, Mother shut the door behind us and indicated Mycroft should move farther down the hallway. When we were out of earshot, she said, "What's this about a chisel?"

Still with a broad grin on his face, Mycroft held out the

book and pointed to a drawing on the page. "See this one? It's flattened on the end, but is thicker in the middle, and the blade"—he raised his chin to stress the next point—"is two inches wide."

Mother took the book to study the image more closely. I also peeked over her arm to examine it as well. When she raised her head, she said, "It does appear to be a good candidate. Who might have access to such a tool?"

"Stone masons?" His grin faded.

"I suppose that would be the next step. Check with Ernest about his own research. See if he has been able to identify any other tools. Perhaps he, too, has tested the chisel? After I finish dressing Mr. Straton, I need to go to see Mr. Brown. We'll review the results after that."

He nodded and headed down the stairs, the book under one arm.

"Do you think that's what stabbed Mr. Straton?" I asked after he had disappeared down the stairs.

She stilled, as if considering different scenarios. "He's right about the size and shape of the wound. I just wish it hinted at someone we knew had contact with Mr. Straton. A stone mason would be new...." She shuddered and turned toward the room again. "First things first. We need to ensure the poor man recovers so that he can tell us himself."

Constance and I assisted Mother in changing the dressing. The honey appeared to be working because the area wasn't as red and swollen as the last time I saw it.

As soon as she'd completed the task, she and I returned

downstairs where she requested a trap be prepared to visit Mr. Brown's farm.

"Why don't you come with me," she said after sending the message to the stable. "I shouldn't visit a gentleman alone at his home. Especially a widower."

The sun had passed its zenith, but the air was still warm. As we approached the Brown farm, a faint humming began and grew louder with each horse's step. By the time we reached the house, the buzzing from thousands of bees fairly roared about us. Despite the incessant droning, Mr. Brown must have heard our cart approach because as we pulled into the yard, a man's figure in a large straw hat with a net that dropped to the shoulders stepped from behind the house where various white wooden houses dotted the land-scape. His heavy-gloved hands held a large, flat tray in one and a smoking pot in the other.

"Mrs. Holmes," Mr. Brown said through the netting, "you've brought news from your brother?"

"Not in relation to your wife, I'm afraid," she said, alighting from the carriage.

I hesitated to follow her. The droning brought to mind the image of Mr. Harvingsham's reaction, and I shuddered at the memory.

"Mr. Straton, however, has been stabbed," she said, step-ping to him. "That's why I'm here. For honey to treat his wound."

"Stabbed, you say? Who? Where?"

"We aren't certain of the perpetrator. The poor man lost

a lot of blood and has remained unconscious since we found him. Or rather, Sherlock here did. Not far from the Straton cottage."

"Master Sherlock found him?" He turned his gaze to me, and I shifted on the trap bench. As proud as I was of the deed itself, I found the man's attention somehow uncomfortable. "Good show, boy."

He then focused on my mother again. "He's at Underbyrne, then? The constable hasn't arrested him?"

"Mr. Holmes arranged a house arrest. After all, he is a justice of the peace. And I can assure you, in his present state, the man isn't going anywhere."

With a rather non-committal *hmm*, he turned and headed in the direction of an outbuilding. Over his shoulder, he said, "You can have the honey, but I don't understand why you want to help my wife's murderer."

"He didn't do it," I said, jumping down from my seat.

The man spun around. Even through the mesh covering his face, I could see the flash in his eyes. He shook the smoking can at me, and I took a step back and hit the carriage's side. "He did do it. Do you hear me? Told me to my face my poor Emma killed his wife, and he would do the same to her. I even have witnesses."

I felt my mother's presence behind me. She placed a hand on each of my shoulders, reassurance in her touch.

"I know how strongly you believe in what occurred in the tavern, Mr. Brown, but you asked us to collect information surrounding your wife's death. We've learned the man was drunk and could not possibly have injured your wife. That was the other purpose of our visit. To share this information with you."

The smoking can dropped to the man's side, and he squinted at us through the webbing. "Your brother sent you to tell me that?"

"Yes. That he is continuing to collect information on Straton's attacker, which might lead us to your wife's assailant. We won't know until he regains consciousness."

"You will let me know if Straton wakes? What he says?"

"Of course," Mother said with a smile. "A great help in his recovery will be the honey we came to fetch."

He stared at us, as if considering additional arguments. After a moment, he appeared to think better of it, picked up the smoking can, and turned toward the outbuilding.

"Right. Follow me to my extracting room." He returned to the path toward the building. As he moved, he continued conversing. "I've been preparing them for the winter. Moving the hives about and such."

The humming grew even louder and several of his subjects flew about us. After the episode with Mr. Harvingsham's reaction the other day, I was acutely aware of the insects and had no desire to determine if I had a similar allergy. I swatted at a particularly persistent one buzzing about my head.

Mother stayed my hand. "You don't want to do that. An aggressive action like that can call more to you."

"That's why I've got the smoke. It quiets them down. Of

course, I've been stung hundreds of times. Not so bad. Unless you're like Mr. Harvingsham."

"You knew he was allergic?" Mother asked.

"Won't ever come out here. Always insisted on Emma visiting him, if she needed to have him consult on a woman. He always had the honey delivered."

We arrived at the outbuilding to the left of his house and in front of the field dotted with the white beehives. He pulled the door open and motioned for us to enter. Once the door closed, the humming dropped to a more tolerable level, and Mr. Brown removed his hat. With the bees securely shut out, I relaxed enough to glance about.

The building consisted of a single room with a rather odd cylindrical device on the left, a long work table on the opposite wall filled with various jars (some with honey, some empty), and beeswax candles stacked in a pyramid in the center. To my right, a series of tools hung from nails pounded into the wall.

"You came at a good time. I was just harvesting what I can before they hibernate. I can give you a very fresh pot."

He held up the tray he was carrying. Now up-close, I could see the tiny wax cells created by the bees and watched a bit of the honey drip to the ground. It was then I noticed the sticky mess on the wooden floorboards. His boots made tiny ripping noises with each step he took as he went about his business.

"Let me get this tray into the separator, and then we'll see to your pot."

He went to the cylindrical machine, pulled off the top, and raised a center rod to which a tray similar to the one in his hand was attached. "This one's already empty," he said and replaced it with the new one. After placing a flat pan underneath the tray, he pulled a long metal tool off his belt. The item had one flat side, and the other side had a sort of hook.

"What's that?" I asked.

"This," he said, holding up the metal bar's hooked end, "is what I use to pull the trays out of the hive. They tend to stick together. I use the other side like this."

He ran the flat end of the tool along the honeycomb's cells to scrape off the beeswax sealing them. Long curls of wax soon gathered in the pan at the bottom of the tray. Once both sides had been cleaned, he lowered the tray into the extractor, and turned a handle on its side.

"You spin the honey out?" I asked. "Ingenious."

"Here, you give it a go."

He stepped back and let me turn the handle. I found it a little stiffer than I expected and the handle itself quite sticky.

While I turned the tray, he went to the work table and picked up a pot. He cut a large piece of cheesecloth from a bolt on the table and carried both back to where I stood. Placing the cheesecloth over the pot and positioning the jar below a spigot at the bottom of the extractor, he let the fresh honey flow through the cloth and into the pot. Soon, he'd filled the small jar.

"That's enough for now," he said when he shut off the honey.

Mother opened her purse to remove some coins. "How much do I owe you?"

One piece fell to the floor.

"I'll get it," I said and knelt to pick it up.

In doing so, I noticed a good number of yew needles stuck about the floor along with the coin. I paused, stopping my efforts to pry the penny free from the honey. The needles appeared fresh compared to the other leaves and debris tracked into the room.

When I rose and handed him the coin, he thanked me but scrutinized me for a moment as if he were sizing me up. I shifted on my feet and turned to Mother.

"We need to be going. I promised to help Father... with...something."

She paused for a moment, then spoke in an even tone. "Of course. I remember you telling me before we left you needed to return shortly. Thank you so much for the honey, Mr. Brown."

She turned to leave and I followed behind her, our footsteps making tearing sounds as we left. Mr. Brown trailed behind us, but I feared to glance back and find out how close he was. My heart gathered speed in response to my growing anxiety to leave the property.

Despite my worries, the man only assisted my mother into the carriage.

"Thank you for the information, Mrs. Holmes," he said

after she seated herself. "I do appreciate your sharing it with me."

"Of course, Mr. Brown. Please have a good day." She clucked at the horse and pulled away.

When we reached the main road, she turned the trap toward Underbyrne. Once we were a good distance from the home, she asked, "What did you see on the floor?"

"Yew needles," I said. "They were stuck in the honey. When I found Mr. Straton, he was in a grove of yew trees. I'm certain Mr. Brown knows I saw them too. But more important was—"

"The tool he used to scrape the wax from the honey comb." A smile parted her face when I turned to her. "I noticed it, too, but was able to better mask it than you."

"How ever did you develop such proficiency in hiding your true thoughts?"

"All part of my training in being a proper lady. I developed the ability to appear interested in the prattle most people consider 'polite conversation' to the point of asking questions to continue the inane discussion while my thoughts were elsewhere. But a more difficult task was learning to ignore the glares men give you when you sit in on a medical lecture."

That brought to mind again Father's description of his first encounter with my mother. As much as I wanted to learn her version of the event, a more pressing matter had to be addressed first.

"Are you going to tell Father? About what we saw at Mr. Brown's?"

"Of course. We have just found our murderer."

THE MOMENT MOTHER entered the house, she called for Father. Barely had "Mr. Holmes," left her lips when he stepped from the library.

"We've just come from Mr. Brown's," she said, holding up the honey pot, "and have come to the conclusion—"

She stopped when Father held up a red ledger. I swallowed past a lump forming in my throat. *Had he found the true one?*

"I believe you recognize this. If you recall Constable Gibbons mentioned he returned it when he came to check on Straton."

That inscrutable face of hers showed no emotion when she said, "Yes. I'd forgotten it. I'll take it back to the greenhouse."

She reached for it, but he jerked his hand high, keeping her from retrieving it. His voice was low, but he ground out his words. "What in God's name have you been up to?"

My heart thrummed against my chest. In the past few weeks, I had seen my father nearly choke a man when my mother was released from jail, bluster at Mycroft for his insistence at returning to school, and stand up to the constable. But never had I seen the eerily quiet rage he seemed intent on containing at the moment. And certainly not directed at his wife.

She opened her mouth to speak, but he raised his other hand. With the book still over his head, he called out. "Mycroft."

My brother stepped from the library, head down. Continuing to stare at the floor, he said, "I'm sorry, Mother. He recognized my handwriting. I told him you weren't involved. That Sherlock and I—"

"He's right," I said. "We were afraid if Constable Gibbons found out what was in it—"

"You see," Father said, still in that low tone. "Your actions have made our sons forgers, thieves. The constable told me of a rather odd incident involving the expert he'd commissioned for the translation. The first night in town, he was called down to the lobby floor to retrieve a message from Gibbons. Only the constable never sent a message. When he was returning to his room, a young boy fell down the stairs. His father, however, came in and took him away before Mr. Harvingsham could arrive."

Father's gaze fell on me. My face burned under his scrutiny. All the same, I had to admire the constable's ability to fit the many pieces of our recent actions together indicated a more logical mind than I had estimated.

"I can explain everything, Siger. Please, if you let me. But I must tell you about Mr. Brown. He's the one who stabbed Straton, and I am certain was involved in the murders of—"

"Enough!"

Father's shout echoed through the front hall. He waved his hands above his head as if he could clear away Mother's words from the air. He pointed his finger at Mother's face, but all three of us flinched in return.

"It stops now, Mrs. Holmes. All of it, including the dispensing of herbs to the village women. Brown told Gibbons how you disrupt nature—a true abomination against God. Not to mention this obsession you have with Emma Brown's death. And that...that *criminal* upstairs. I'll be arranging for Gibbons to take him to gaol. You will damage the reputation of this family and jeopardize my position in the community no more. It all ends now. This minute."

He spun about and stalked into the parlor where he threw the fraudulent ledger into the fire. "I expect to receive the true one upon my return from my visit with Gibbons."

We all remained rooted as he strode to the front door, slamming it behind him with a sound like a cannon blast.

Mother was the first to recover.

"If you'll excuse me, boys," she said, lifting her chin. "I must go to your uncle's workshop to get the true book."

Her movement was odd, almost trance-like, as she headed through the house. Concerned over her state of mind, I followed at some distance. I gestured to Mycroft to do the same, but he shook his head and slid back into the library. When she neared the kitchen, Constance emerged from the servants' stairwell and grabbed my mother's arm.

"Please, madam. You can't let them take my papa. He'll die in gaol. I know he will. And they'll send the babies to an orphanage and me to the workhouse. I don't want——"

The slap was as sharp as a gunshot. Constance's hand flew to her cheek now marked with my mother's handprint, and her eyes filled with tears. Either from shock or fear at my mother's outburst, I found myself frozen in place as she spoke through lips so tight they barely moved.

"Shut up. Can't you see I've no power to help your father? Whatever influence I'd thought I possessed was just an illusion. You, your father—all of us—are at the mercy of Mr. Holmes and the constable."

Constance turned and fled up the stairs while Mother continued out the door and toward Ernest's workshop. I entered a moment after her. My uncle spoke to us from the table still holding the pig carcasses.

"You're both just in time to see. I've tested a few more implements. Mycroft's discovery of the chisel put a whole new light on the search. Come."

Mother and I approached the table together. She waved away his offer of a magnifying glass, stepped to the bench, and with one sweep of her arm, cleared the table, sending pigs and tools clattering to the wooden floor.

"Violette, what in the——?"

She turned to the table with the contents of the mending basket and did the same.

Her back to us, she dropped to her knees and doubled over. The wail that followed sent a chill down my spine.

After that one cry, she made no more noise, but her back shook with silent sobs. My stomach churned, and my knees weakened.

In the past month, I'd seen my mother in the direst situations, including gaol, but never had I seen her display any emotion in such a violent fashion. Staring at the grieving woman, I understood the consequence of husbands and wives keeping secrets. The evidence lay broken at my feet. Their revelation could destroy not only the relationship, but the individuals as well.

The sympathy I felt for my mother was balanced by an antipathy toward my father. The anger roiling in my stomach rushed through me and curled my hands into fists. Had he been standing before me, I would have attacked him, pummeling him with all my might. Fortunately—or unfortunately, depending on one's perspective—he was not. Besides, my mother was the one needing attention. I tiptoed to her side, unsure what I should say. I had no way to undo the pain my father caused, but I could at least make her more comfortable in her anguish.

Placing an arm over her quivering shoulders, I whispered, "Mother, come lie down. Please."

Unable to carry her on my own, I glanced at my uncle to seek his help. He stood immobile near the work table, staring at the debris on the floor—in a shock of his own.

He came out of it, however, when I spoke to him.

"Uncle Ernest, let's help Mother to your cot."

Together, we got her to her feet. Her limbs had no resistance and I doubted could have sustained her weight without our assistance as we led her to the back of the building.

Along the way, Ernest cooed to her. "It's all right, Violette. Don't worry about the mess. I'll clean it up."

A fist knotted in my stomach, and only with great effort did I avoid a display of anger similar to my mother's. I understood her reaction as coming from the realization that the life she had constructed for herself had been a delusion.

Once she lay down, she drew her knees to her chest and remained, curled in a ball, her back to the world.

Ernest stepped behind me and placed a hand on my shoulder.

I turned to him, barely keeping my own anger and sorrow in check. "My father…they had a fight."

"Go on back to the house. I'll take care of her." He sighed as if some memory brought pain to him as well as Mother. "She needs some time to herself. I haven't seen her like this since… I'll let you know if there's any change."

Recognizing my own limitations in comforting her, I considered her brother better equipped for this than I. He had certainly known her longer.

With a pull on my arm, he directed me away from my mother and toward the door. Once outside, I realized evening had fallen. In the distance, I could hear the chirp of insects and the call of night birds. The whole *ordinariness* of the everyday sounds struck a discord within me. How could the world continue its normal course when my world was imploding? I stepped toward the house and stopped, not relishing the idea of facing the tension I knew awaited me there.

If only Mother had been able to convince Father that Mr. Brown had been the culprit in the attack on Mr. Straton. If only we'd been able to show how the tool Brown used to open the honeycombs fit the incision in the man's side....

With a determination I'd lacked a few moments earlier, I headed toward the house in search of my brother.

He was in his room, already in his nightclothes, just sitting in a chair by his window. When I opened his door and called his name, he spoke to the night beyond the glass.

"Whatever you want, I'm not interested. Leave me alone. I want only to get back to Oxford and my life."

"Please, hear me out. I have a plan. Mother and I know who stabbed—"

He jerked his head in my direction and glared at me. "Are you dense? I want nothing to do with anything remotely related to Mrs. Brown."

The set of his jaw and his stare offered no chance of my persuading him to reconsider. I backed out of the room and considered alternatives.

I could think of no one else at the moment who would be willing to help Mother.

Other than I.

And when I proved my mother was right, perhaps this rift between my parents could be mended.

WHETHER BECAUSE I'D used the path a number of times recently or was distracted by my mother's condition, I found myself at Brown's property much faster than I imagined. From the property's treed edge, I studied the buildings for any signs of activity under the full moon. The light proved useful in identifying how I might slip into the extraction building without notice.

As long as no one was about the grounds.

I checked the house. Lights did shine inside, but the noise from any movement was drowned out by the bees. Perhaps the buzzing would cover any sound I might make as well.

Keeping to the woods, I passed the house and moved to the area behind it where the beehives were set out in the clearing. A few bees approached and buzzed about me, but they weren't particularly interested in me. I continued circling the clearing until I came to the other side and the outbuilding.

Finding the door unlocked, I slid inside and shut the door behind me. I immediately regretted not having brought a lamp or lantern with me. The room was almost pitch black without even moonlight to illuminate the interior.

Afraid I might break something and alert Mr. Brown to my presence, I tried to remember the placement of the various items on my previous visit. The extracting machine stood to my left. On my right, various tools hung on nails on the wall. In front of me was a workbench holding various pots, trays, and…beeswax candles. With my arms stretched out in front of me, I took tentative steps toward the bench. The progress dragged on for what seemed like hours as I traversed the room. Once at the bench, I groped for the candles. I found one and wrapped my hand around it. As I did so, I heard another object roll across the tabletop. I fumbled in the dark, trying to catch whatever I'd knocked over. My fingers grazed a honey pot just as it reached the edge of the table. It fell to the floor with a muffled *crack*. It must have been full, given the muted noise, but all the same, it sounded like a gunshot to me in the still room. My ears buzzed in the silence that followed, and I froze, waiting for some indication I'd been heard. When no footsteps approached the building, I exhaled and continued my search for the small jar I'd seen holding some matches. My fingers trembled as I struck one and touched it to the candle's wick. The other honey jars on the table and the machine in the center of the room reflected its soft glow.

I could clearly see the small pot at my feet. After considering for a moment if I should clean it up, I decided that it didn't matter. If all went well, Brown would be in gaol shortly. I was also able to find the scraper on the table where he must have left it after our visit only a few hours earlier—next to the bolt of cheesecloth he'd used to strain the honey he'd extracted earlier in the day.

Now grasping the scraper's handle, I turned to blow out

the candle for a quick escape. Before my lips could pucker, the door banged back against the wall, and Mr. Brown stood in the doorway, a rifle pointed in my direction.

"Don't move, thief."

My hands flew up, the candle in one and the scraper in the other. My heart pounded in my chest, and I feared my knees might not hold me upright.

"Please, don't shoot, Mr. Brown," I said, forcing calm into my voice.

"Master Sherlock? Whatever are you doing in here?" The man squinted at me. "Are you stealing my honey?"

My mind raced as I sought a fabrication that seemed plausible under the circumstances.

"No, sir. I wouldn't do that. Mother…she needed more…for Mr. Straton. I didn't want to…disturb you at this time of night. I planned to…to leave a coin for the pot I took."

The man continued pointing his weapon at me, his back rigid. He jerked the rifle upwards to point at the tool in my hand. "What are you doing with that?"

I'd forgotten I held the scraper. Once again my thoughts spun as I tried to invent an explanation for its presence in my hand.

"When you opened the door, I-I didn't know who you were. It was on the table…by the honey pots, so I-I grabbed it."

Opening my fingers, I let it fall from my still-upraised hand. It landed with a dull *thunk* onto the floorboards.

He studied me a moment more, his weapon still pointing directly at my chest. The urge to urinate became almost overpowering, and I feared I might not be able to resist it. Finally, he jerked his eyes to the right and said, "Go get that rope."

Somehow, my knees and bladder cooperated enough not to give way and let me reach the wall and the loop of stout rope hanging there.

"Bring it here."

Hooking the rifle in the crook of his right arm to free his left, he took the candle from me, set it on the table, and then grasped the rope. In a series of quick movements, he spun me about and tied my hands behind my back. He then forced me into a chair.

"We're going to have a little talk, you and I," he said. "I need to hear what you know and who you told before you have a little accident."

I swallowed before forcing out one word from my dry throat. "Accident?"

"Odd thing about bees. Some people can have any number of stings and nothing happens. I've been stung enough that one doesn't even raise a welt anymore. For other people, like Harvingsham, only one will send them into a deadly fit. One or many, though, everyone will fall into a fit at some point. We're going to determine how many stings are required for you."

Twisting my hands, I tested the rope. The bindings, however, held fast and cut into my wrists. I reminded myself

I'd have to keep my wits about me if I was to make it out alive. "What exactly do you want to know? Because if you are worried about Mr. Straton, he still hasn't awakened."

"But you know, don't you? You know I was the one who fought with Straton. What was it?"

"The yew needles on the floor over there," I pointed to the area with my chin. "Mr. Straton was lying on yew needles when I found him. That and the tool you use for scraping the wax from the hives."

He picked the device up from the floor and waved it near my face, turning it under my nose. "You mean this? How did you know that?"

"The shape of the wound in Mr. Straton's side. It had a similar point on each end. You needn't worry, no one believed us anyway." I dropped my head. "Not even my father. He's arranging now for the constable to take Mr. Straton to gaol."

"*Us?* Someone else knows?" He paused before hanging the tool back onto his belt. "Your mother? That is a problem."

"I told you. No one believes us. Mr. Straton will be tried for the murder of your wife."

"As he should be. I've got the constable convinced of it."

"But we know he had no reason to murder her. He burned the pennyroyal she gave his wife."

His head jerked toward me, and his features grew hard. "What do you know about the pennyroyal?"

My heart skipped a beat. I'd hit upon something. Some

bit of information I had misinterpreted or overlooked until this moment. I had to discover more. Something that would prolong the time before he went to get the bees. This was one experiment in which I had absolutely no desire in learning the results.

"I know your wife gave pennyroyal to women. Mrs. Straton for certain."

"The Straton molly was one. But not the only one. Emma even took it herself. The devil's work. An abomination against nature. She deserved her fate."

In the time I drew in a gasp, I saw everything clearly. The woman deserving her fate was his wife. He killed Emma Brown because of her use of pennyroyal.

"Pennyroyal, if used wrong, can be fatal," I said, studying him. "But hemlock is poisonous for sure. We found hemlock among Mrs. Straton's things."

"Easy enough to switch one for the other. Emma never knew I'd done it."

"And Rachel Winston? You gave it to her?"

"Another of Satan's disciples," he said, his mouth turning down. He spat as if the thought put a bad taste in his mouth. "Came to me weeping and carrying on. Begging me to check and see if Emma had left some pennyroyal. So, I obliged her. Wicked women all—including your mother. That's why I laid Emma's body in the garden. Would've cleansed the town of two vipers at once. But thanks to that meddling uncle of yours and the spectacle at the inquest, I had to find another to blame the murder on."

"You've done well. Even the constable thinks Mr. Straton killed her."

"And I'm going to keep it that way."

In two strides, he was at my side, the rifle under my chin. I feared he might not wait for the bees, but instead, he pulled me from the chair and forced me forward, out of the building, the rifle barrel in my back. The moonlight still illuminated the open field, making the white beehives glow against the dark earth and casting shadows along the ground. With my arms bound and the uneven ground, I found myself stumbling.

When not concentrating on the terrain, I thought about the fate awaiting me. Would one sting be sufficient, as it almost had been for Mr. Harvingsham? The image of the poor man twitching about sent a frisson of panic along my spine. I had to get him to redirect his interest from eliminating me toward taking me someplace else. But for what purpose? To retrieve something—something that would point to him as his wife's murderer.

"I know I told you how no one believes us about Mr. Straton not killing your wife, but they will when my uncle shows them the cheesecloth you left when you took her body to our garden," I said, keeping my gaze straight ahead.

His footfalls ceased, but the rifle barrel poked my back.

"What do you say? Face me, boy."

As I turned slowly about, the rifle glinted dully in the moonlight, keeping me aware of its close proximity.

"I didn't realize it until tonight. Something about the

way the candlelight played on the bolt. I found a small square of it in our garden. You wrapped her body in it to carry to Underbyrne, didn't you?"

Brown's voice was almost a growl. "Liar. You're inventing this."

"I gave the piece to my uncle for safekeeping. It's in his workshop. No one but you would have need for it. It points directly to you as the one who put your wife in our garden."

The man pulled the trigger back, and I froze, certain these were my last minutes on this earth. At least Brown wouldn't be able to blame my death by gunshot on another, and I would have the satisfaction of knowing justice would be served—even though I wouldn't be there to observe it. After a moment, he appeared to have reached a decision and released the trigger. My knees wobbled as the tension subsided.

"You know where the cloth is?"

I nodded, hoping that Ernest and my mother would still be in the workshop. Between the three of us, he could be overpowered. He straightened his back as if a plan had been hatched. I held my breath, hoping my words had the effect I desired. He placed a heavy hand on my shoulder and shoved me in front of him, back toward his house.

"We're going to your uncle's workshop, and you're going to give me that piece of cloth."

When he pushed me forward, I tripped and fell face-first onto the ground. I moaned into the dirt.

He flipped me over onto my back and growled at me again. "Get up, you oaf."

"It's my hands," I said, wiggling slightly on my back. My fists closed about the soft dirt, and I grasped two handfuls. "I can't walk with them like this. I have no balance."

Another moment passed as he made some sort of decision. With a sigh, he turned me over and undid the ropes binding my arms. "Now get up, and remember, I still have my rifle."

I rose to my knees but swayed slightly. "I hit my head two days ago. I think I aggravated my brain commotion."

He grabbed my coat at the shoulder and pulled me to my feet. "Get up."

As he set me upright, facing him, the rifle dropped to his side. I threw the two fistfuls of dirt into his face, spun about and ran past him. The most direct course away, however, was straight toward the beehives. I had no idea how good a shot he was, so I dodged behind the first hive and checked his progress. He staggered forward, obviously still having some problems with his eyes. Either he forgot about the rifle or couldn't see well enough because he still had it at his side. With the small advantage I had of unhampered sight, I decided to risk making for the woods, and slow his pursuit in the process.

I hit the hive protecting me with all my might. A swarm of disturbed bees emerged from the fallen hive and while some chased me as I headed toward the next hive along my way to the woods, more attacked the object following me.

Mr. Brown roared as the bees flew about him. I continued to knock over hives, and the buzzing drowned out almost all sounds except Brown's howling.

I was, however, not immune to the insects' fury. Minute points of extreme pain hit my cheeks and neck, but I didn't slow. Reaching the woods' edge, I glanced back to determine how close my pursuer was. While he persisted, he did so at a slower pace as he fought through a large cloud of angry bees.

Once in the woods, my vision diminished considerably. At first I thought it was the loss of the moonlight, but when I swiped at my eyes, I found them swollen. My hands, too, were puffing. Ahead, I heard rushing water. I plunged toward it, stumbling on roots and rocks I could no longer discern, and practically fell into the stream leading to the Devony estate. How had I gotten so turned around?

The almost frigid waters made me gasp, but at the same time brought relief to my burning face and hands. Over the noise of the speeding water, I made out a crashing in the woods, warning me Brown had not given up his hunt.

Forcing myself to my feet, I lurched over the rocks in the creek and pulled myself up the bank onto the other side. I stopped for a moment to orient myself. Following the water would surely lead me to Hanover Manor. I was no longer certain where or how far Underbyrne or the road lay. Even with my limited sight, the surest path involved following the stream to the Devony estate.

I pressed on through bushes and branches that caught

my wet, heavy, clothing and scratched my face and hands. My shoes, also soaked, squished with each step, and the wool socks rubbed against my heels. I couldn't hear anything beyond my own efforts and the rush of water and had no idea if the honey man still trailed me. I longed to lie down and rest, but knew death would certainly come either by gunshot or exposure.

After what seemed an eternity, I broke free and staggered into a field on the far side of the Devony estate. I drove through the fallow rows, the moist earth giving off a pungent, fresh scent. Making it to the back of the estate, I pounded on the kitchen door—the same one where I'd learned of Rachel Winston's death. When it opened, I fell at the feet of a man in a robe and nightcap.

"Please," I said through bloated lips, "I-I'm Sh-sherlock H-holmes. G-get me t-to Uh-underbyrne."

MY RECOLLECTION of the events that followed was shadowy. I recalled being lifted and carried, but to where I couldn't tell. Voices reached my brain, but I was unable to decipher any meaning or any identity—even whether male or female. A bitter liquid was forced into my mouth, and I gagged some down.

After that came the dreams.

I was at Underbyrne in the yard. A giant bee with Mr. Brown's head chased me through our back garden. Seeking refuge, I ran into the greenhouse. There, I turned about and grabbed pots from the tables and heaved them at my attacker. The bee simply dodged them and decreased the distance between us. Becoming desperate, I selected a larger one and prepared to take better aim. When the pot was at eye-level, I stopped. A fingerprint glowed red on its side. Only then did I realize I held a hemlock plant in my hands. A loud buzzing pulled my attention from the plant, and I flung the container toward the monster insect. The projectile hit Mr. Brown square in the face, and he exploded with a massive shower of blood.

I must have thrashed about then, because I remember hands holding me down. More bitter liquid followed, and I drifted back into oblivion.

In the next one, Mrs. Brown and Mrs. Straton danced together at the foot of my bed. They pulled their hair and wailed in unison.

"Avenge us!"

This time, my own screams awoke me.

A pair of cool hands grasped my face, and I focused on my mother's studied squint.

"Deep breaths," she said. "It was only a dream."

Once I had calmed, she sat back into an armchair set by my bedside. Judging from her rumpled appearance, she had maintained a vigil next to me for some time.

My tongue ran over my dry, cracked lips. "You're... you're all right?"

"Better," she said, lifting one side of her mouth. "Your

father has had…something…of a change of heart since we brought you home. But things are still…strained between us. I also apologized to Constance. I may not have been forgiven, but she did hear me out. Perhaps time will heal the rift."

She turned her face from mine, and I knew she was trying to compose herself. I reached across the space between us and placed a hand on her arm. I noticed a number of red welts covering the back of my hand. At least I now knew the answer to Mr. Brown's experiment. I was not allergic, and it took more than the stings I suffered to cause a fit.

She placed a hand over mine and turned back to me. "I know what you were trying to do. Mycroft alerted us when you went missing."

With a start, I sat up. "Mr. Brown. He—"

"Has disappeared." In response to my frown, she continued. "You were able to tell the Devonys' butler that he was chasing you. They sent for the constable, but by the time he arrived with his men, they were unable to locate him. His horse is gone. They suspect he has fled the county."

"How did I get back here?"

"When they sent for the constable, they also sent someone to Underbyrne and for the surgeon. He got there first and gave you laudanum. You were unconscious. We transported you back to Underbyrne, and you have been here ever since. Are you hungry? You haven't eaten since they brought you back."

After a quick inventory of my condition, I nodded. "Some soup would be quite nice. I had the most profound dreams."

"Laudanum has been known to do that. You became quite agitated a few times, calling out and reaching for things."

"Yes. There was one with Mrs. Straton and Mrs. Brown. And another—" I shuddered, thinking about the giant bee.

But there was something else besides the bee…

CHAPTER THIRTEEN

I drew in my breath and stared at my mother. "We need to go to the greenhouse."

I made to rise, but she restrained me, placing her hands on my shoulders. "It's the middle of the night. And wholly unhealthy for you."

"I *have* to check something. It's terribly important. It's about the hemlock we found in Mrs. Straton's basket."

The creases in her forehead turned to arches, but she shook her head. "I promised your father—"

"But that was *before* Mr. Brown tried to kill me. If I'm wrong, no one will know. If I'm right, I'll say Mr. Brown told me. If you don't let me go, I'll slip out when you're asleep. You know I will."

"We certainly haven't done a good job of keeping you

home," she said and sighed. "Fine. To the greenhouse and back. Only. And you must wear your robe and slippers."

Mother's slow, deliberate movements as she selected a robe and retrieved my slippers had me fairly bouncing on the bed. At the same time, I was grateful for her insistence because my sudden exertion after the laudanum brought on a cold sweat. Without the robe, I would have caught a chill on the way there.

Once in the conservatory, I said, "I'd forgotten about this until the dream tonight. I kept thinking there was something, but it would slip away when I thought about it too hard."

She followed me down the far aisle, and I stopped at the pot holding the hemlock. Lifting it, I turned it to the side with the smudge. "I think this is from Mr. Brown. I noticed the other day when he brought you honey his gloves are covered in it. At first I thought it was yours but it's too big."

"Why would he take hemlock?"

"To replace Mrs. Brown's pennyroyal. Before I was able to get free from him, he told me he'd learned that Mrs. Brown was dispensing pennyroyal and using it herself— when Mr. Straton told him at the tavern his wife had gotten it from her. He said he put Mrs. Brown's body in the garden to have you arrested for her murder. He called you both vipers."

"I've been called worse," she said, one side of her mouth lifting, then dropping.

"He also knew about Harvingsham's allergy to bees."

"But Harvingsham doesn't dispense pennyroyal." She drew in her breath. "But he did see Rachel Winston. Brown must have given Rachel some of the hemlock as well. Good lord. I was the one who told him we were going to consult Harvingsham about her death. He was probably afraid the man knew she'd been poisoned."

"He must have slipped a few in the window and—"

"Aren't you the clever boy?" a man asked at the far end of the greenhouse.

We both pivoted to see Mr. Brown standing in the doorway to the outside and pointing his rifle at us. The beekeeper had certainly passed a rough time since my escape. His face was still marked with bright red spots I assumed were bee stings. His clothes were torn and dirty, and his hair wild and tangled about his face.

"I came back just to finish off you two meddlers. You ruined my plans to cleanse this village of godless women like my wife, but I can finish at least with you, Mrs. Holmes, before I vanish forever."

"Do you truly believe you won't be apprehended? After all, you poisoned all three women. It will come back to you in the end."

"I have the constable on my side. And once I get rid of all to the contrary, I'll keep it that way." He pointed the rifle at me and then at the pot in my hand. "Throw it on the ground."

I swiveled my head toward my mother as if I needed her permission. She nodded. "Go ahead, dear."

The crash echoed among the rows of plants. I hoped the sound roused someone and caused them to investigate. His next words, however, dashed that wish.

"Now for that piece of cloth you told me about, Sherlock. Take me to it. Once I have that, there'll be nothing left to prove I did it."

It occurred to me he hadn't realized our deaths would certainly be linked to him, but I decided it wasn't prudent to argue with him when he held the rifle. Not to mention that my previous encounter with him suggested he wasn't logical in all his actions.

When I hesitated, he shouted at me. "Where is it?"

"M-m-my uncle's workshop," I managed to answer.

He pointed his weapon at us and waved the end slightly to indicate we should move toward him. "Move along outside."

Mother and I exchanged glances. While I thought I might be able to get away from the man as I had before, I was certain Mother's skirt would hinder her ability to run. The risk was too great. I was going to have to catch him off guard in another manner.

He took a step to the side of the doorway and indicated with his weapon we were to continue outside. The night air was crisp and quite chilly. I shivered as it penetrated my robe. My slippers, too, failed to keep out the ground's dampness. Overhead, the stars sparkled like so many jewels tossed onto a bit of black velvet. Perhaps it was the lingering effect of the laudanum, but I believed I had never seen them with such clarity or brilliance. Would this be the last time I would ever savor such a sight? The thought made me shiver all the more.

I forced my thoughts back to the matter at hand, and attempted to convey the bit of a plan I had to my mother.

"What are you going to do with the scrap when you find it?" I asked, glancing over my shoulder for a second. The man still carried the rifle pointed at our backs.

"Burn it, just as Straton did the packet my Emma gave his wife. Pity about the man. I should be grateful to him. He's the one who let me in on Emma's secret. She'd always said she was barren. Now I know she was treating herself same as she did the other women. It was simple enough to change the pennyroyal to hemlock. You don't live with a midwife without learning something about plants and poisons."

"But why Rachel Winston?" Mother asked. "What did she ever do?"

"Came to me after my Emma died. Said she needed pennyroyal, like the Straton woman. Another sinner." I could almost hear his shrug behind me. "If you hadn't gotten away, I'd be able to stay here and slowly rid the village of all such hypocrites. I've got righteousness on my side. The day Straton told me in the tavern about finding the pennyroyal, I knew my life's work was to purify the village from abominators."

At the workshop, Mother knocked on the door.

"What do you think you're doing?" Brown asked in a sharp whisper.

He shoved the weapon into my mother's back. She gave a little gasp but replied in a calm voice.

"My brother sometimes works late at night. He is not one to surprise. Besides, I assume you wish to ensure he is not in the building at the moment." After a pause, she said, "Given he has not provided a response, we can assume we are alone."

"Where's this cloth?" he asked, his voice a deep grumble, after we entered.

"I need to see," I said. "Let me light a lantern."

During the pause where he considered my request, I held my breath. After a moment, he asked, "Can you feel this, Mrs. Holmes?"

Another slight gasp, followed by, "Yes, I do, Mr. Brown."

He continued in the same harsh tone. "Any tricks, and she dies."

I swallowed. "Understood."

In movements so deliberate I felt as if I had slowed time, I located and lit the lantern. When I turned and saw my mother and our captor, I had to force down a scream. The man held the rifle under my mother's chin. Her neck was stretched and bent backwards, but her rounded eyes sent tremors down my spine. The intensity of her gaze telegraphed a silent caution to keep the man placated.

At the edge of the lantern's light, I saw my uncle's crossbow lying on a workbench to my right. Even from this distance, I could see it held a *hira shuriken*. But only the one. The others were nowhere in sight. My hands ached to grab the weapon and point it at the beekeeper, but as long as my mother was in his grasp, I couldn't risk his harming her.

He pushed the rifle under my mother's chin farther up until the full length of her white neck was exposed. I could barely see her eyes, her face was so turned upwards. "Stop your dawdling. Get me that cloth."

My head bobbed once. "Yes, sir."

The last time I had seen the cloth, Ernest had put it in a workbench drawer. I stepped to the bench, praying the handkerchief was still there. My heart pounded in my chest and my hands shook so violently, I fumbled trying to open the drawer.

"Hurry up, boy," the man said with a growl.

A gasp followed, and I knew the man had used the rifle to threaten my mother more. Afraid of what I might see, I didn't turn around, but focused on the task at hand. When the drawer gave to my pulling, my knees went weak. The handkerchief wasn't there.

My head spun, and I feared I might faint. What would happen to mother, if I did?

Think.

My gaze fell on another object in the drawer.

Mother's red ledger.

Drawing in a breath to steady myself, I grasped the volume and turned about.

"It's in here. Between pages twenty and twenty-one."

"Bring it here," he said.

I approached him with movements that seemed at half-pace. When I was within arm's length, I extended my hand with the book. He had to release my mother's arm to reach around her for the book. The moment his fingers touched its spine, I let go, and the book fell to the ground.

With a howl, he lurched forward to catch it. At the same moment, I kicked the rifle away from my mother and shouted to her, "Run!"

The rifle went off with a *boom!* that made my ears ring, and smoke from the exploded gunpowder burned my nostrils. When the man scrambled for the book, I spun about and dashed for the workbench and the crossbow.

By the time I had reached it and whirled around to shoot at him, Mother was crawling on her hands and knees toward the door, her boots peeking out from among her white under-garments. Mr. Brown scrambled after her, grasping at her feet. The rifle lay abandoned between me and him.

The *hira shuriken* flew from the bow's end and hit him between the shoulder blades.

He screamed and grabbed for the object imbedded in his back, twisting this way and that, trying to reach it.

With her assailant distracted, Mother clambered faster toward the door. He must have realized she was getting away because he quit squirming and reached for her again. Catching a bit of her hem, he pulled her toward him. I ran forward, the bow still in my hand, and using it as a club, struck at the man's head.

The sound his head made when the wood hit his skull reminded me of a gourd hitting the floor. With a growl, he whirled around to face me. I raised the bow over my head, but the heavy instrument threw me off balance, and before I could bring it down again, he yanked my leg. I fell backwards, landing on my back with a *thud*. The bow flew out of my hands, and I heard it hit somewhere behind my head.

He raised himself up on his knees, both fists clasped together over his head. With no other weapons, I raised my arms to fend off his first blow.

A loud *boom* echoed through the building. Something wet sprayed across my face, and Brown fell forward, landing on my chest. I struggled under his weight, trying to push him away. My uncle, father, and brother all rushed toward me and lifted the dead man from on top of me. Only when my mother also knelt beside me, grabbed my face, and called my name did I realize I was screaming.

After that, a numbness settled over me. In a sort of sleepwalk, I allowed her to lead me from the workshop and up the stairs to my bedroom. I recall vaguely being undressed, my face and hands washed, and put to bed. I was too stunned to even protest when more bitter liquid was forced down my throat, and I fell into another deep sleep.

"IT'S ALL RIGHT," a male voice said to me. Hands put pressure on my shoulders and held me down as I twisted in my bed. "You're fine."

I cracked my eyes open. Father's face came into focus.

"Bad dream?" he asked.

I scrunched my face as I tried to piece together the events leading to my being in my bedroom. The thoughts came slowly, as if they had to slog through heavy mud to reach my consciousness. I had been in my uncle's workshop, and—

I bolted upright, and I checked my hands. My last complete memory was of blood. *His* blood. Spraying my face, splattering my hands.

They were clean, but all the same I rubbed them, as if the friction would erase the recollection along with the nonexistent spots. After a moment, Father's wide hands covered mine and calmed their frantic movements. I lifted my gaze and saw the creases in his forehead.

With a great deal of effort, I forced my grip to relax. Father did the same, and he sat back in the armchair Mother had brought to my bedside when watching over me only hours ago.

"Where's—?" My voice cracked, and I coughed before trying to finish my question. "Where's Mother?"

He glanced over his shoulder in the direction of their bedroom before answering. "She's resting. Mr. Harvingsham wanted to give her laudanum as well, but she refused. She wanted to stay with you. The only way I could convince her to rest herself was if I promised to stay instead and let her know when you awakened."

"I'm sorry, sir. I'll be all right. You don't have to stay with me."

"But I wanted to, son." Another glance over his shoulder. "I wanted to tell you myself how...*proud* I am of you. And how...*sorry* I am about how I treated you and your mother. When I realized how close I was to losing both of you, I almost—"

He turned away from me, but I could hear his labored breathing as he tried to regain his composure. My hands clutched at the bedclothes, uncertain how to respond. After a moment, he turned and continued.

"Your mother told me how calm you were. And clever. How you lured Brown to the workshop and saved her life. First getting him to drop the rifle and then shooting him with the crossbow."

"But you were the one who ki—shot him."

The image of my father with the smoking hunting rifle in his arms the moment after he hit Brown popped uninvited into my mind. With a shudder, I forced the image down.

But not before my father caught the involuntary response. He pulled the covers up about me. Awkwardly, but with great care. "Warm enough, Sherlock?"

Unwilling to explain the true cause of my discomfort, I said, "Yes, sir." I raised my gaze. "What brought you to the workshop?"

"We heard the shot. From Brown's rifle. We didn't know you and your mother were out there until—"

In a move so swift I had no time to react, Father reached across and pressed me into his chest in an embrace so tight, I could barely breathe.

"Son," he whispered in my ear.

A moment later, he stiffened and released his hold on me. His hand passed over my hair. "When we pulled you out from under that man—all covered in blood—I feared I had hit you as well. It wasn't until after we had cleaned you up, I could assure myself you were all right. I don't know what I would have done if I'd lost you."

Another strong embrace followed.

When he released me, he cleared his throat and sat back in the chair.

"Uncle Ernest? And Mycroft? Are they all right?"

"Yes," he said and cleared his throat. "Although I'm afraid the events upset your uncle terribly. Seems to have brought back memories of the war. Mr. Harvingsham insisted on giving him laudanum as well."

"What's going to happen now? Do I have to talk to the constable?"

"He's come and gone. While you were sleeping. Since I was the one who shot the man, the constable declared it justifiable. And that's the end of it."

"Has he released Mr. Straton?"

"He...he doesn't have him."

I sat up in my bed, my stomach contracting to a small

knot. "He...he *died?* Is that why he's not here? What's happened to Constance? And the others? Have you shipped them to the orphanage already?"

"He's here. He's here," Father said, pushing me back onto my pillow. "Constance too. We persuaded the vicar and his wife to take the younger ones for the time being."

I lay back at his insistence, but continued to stare at him, waiting for an explanation.

"I hadn't had time to send for the constable before we discovered you were gone, and then when you came back after your ordeal with Brown, I couldn't worry about Straton. He's awake, by the way. Came to shortly after I...after the struggle in your uncle's work room."

"I want to see Mother."

"She wants to see you too."

He helped me out of bed. I found myself even weaker than I had been on our visit to the greenhouse and leaned heavily on my father for the short walk down the hall. When he opened the door, we found Mother seated in her bed, a book open on her lap.

"Violette, dear, whatever are you doing awake at this hour?" He crossed the room, leaving me near the door and leaned over to kiss Mother on her cheek. "You promised you would rest if I didn't insist on the laudanum."

The tender way he scolded her and how she smiled at his kiss told me they had somehow reconciled after the confrontation with Mr. Brown.

"You know me, Mr. Holmes. I rarely need more than a

few hours' sleep. I was catching up on some reading. Besides, I wasn't able to sleep well alone." Father's face flushed, and I glanced away when I recognized his discomfort over her reference to their sharing a bed. "Would you mind, dear, seeing about some broth for Sherlock and tea for me? The poor boy hasn't had any nourishment and I fear he has weakened himself."

Father studied her and then me and nodded. We both understood Mother was dismissing him for a private conversation with me.

Once we were alone, Mother patted the bed beside her and said, "Come. Sit." When I perched myself on the bed, she took my face in her hands and stared at me. After a long pause, she said, "Your bee stings are healing nicely. Your pupils appear rather wide, but I assume that is from the laudanum. In a day or two, you'll be fully recovered."

My stomach contracted, and I glanced away when she let go of my face. Father would surely insist I return to Eton once I was well. Could I convince her I wasn't fully healed, regardless of my true state?

She placed a hand on my far cheek and turned my face back to hers. "What is it, Sherry?"

"I…I don't want to go back to Eton. Ever."

"Darling, as much as I understand your loathing of the school, you have a social obligation to meet. I, too, found much of the education my parents insisted I follow lacking in substance. In your case, it will, however, create the path you'll need to be self-sufficient. As the second-born, your prospects are not the same as Mycroft's, and the contacts you make at school can help you as you make your way in the world."

While her logic made sense in theory, I wasn't convinced Charles Fitzsimmons would ever prove a useful contact. I resigned myself to resuming my studies with a sigh.

"That being said," she continued. "I think you would benefit from some additional recuperation here at Underbyrne, given how much of your studies you already missed."

I jerked my head upward and met her gaze. That all-knowing smirk of hers graced her lips. Only my father's etiquette lessons kept me from leaping off the bed with a shout of joy. I promised myself to do so later, in private. An additional thought, however, sobered me.

"Are you sorry?"

She blinked. "About you not returning to Eton immediately?"

"About marrying Father. Having me and Mycroft. All this talk of babies and burdens. And marriage and freedom. It seems to me that it's not necessarily as neat a package as I thought it was."

The right corner of her mouth lifted, and she placed a hand on my cheek. "You forgot one important aspect. Love. I married your father because I loved him. And he forgave my deceptions—and they were deceptions in that I never told him the full account of my activities—because he loved me. And we both love you and Mycroft. For me, you and your brother are two of my most brilliant achievements, and

I'm quite proud of both of you. Your father, too. These past weeks have shown us both skills and maturity neither of us knew you two possessed—especially you, Sherry."

I grew quiet and considered her last statement. My mother and father were proud of me. I'd always considered myself falling short compared to my brother's and mother's intelligence and my father's strict observance of social convention, leaving little for them to consider worthy. Perhaps mother's reference to love explained their acceptance despite the shortfalls I exhibited? Before I could ask more, Father appeared with a chambermaid carrying a tray with the requested repast.

"My love," Father said as he stepped to the bed, "I must insist both of you try to get some rest tonight. I would like you both to be involved in our discussions with Straton tomorrow."

I stopped halfway to the table where the maid was setting my meal and turned to face my parents. "But you said you convinced the constable Mr. Straton was innocent. What is there to discuss?"

"The future, darling," Mother said. "The Chinese have a saying that if you save a man's life, you are responsible for it. We saved Mr. Straton twice—once from his wound and then from the gallows—and now we have an obligation to ensure his life is a good one."

I studied the two. Mother's reference to a "good life" had to mean they had a plan, and not just for him, but for Constance and her brothers and sisters as well. Did it involve moving them from the village? What if it meant I would never see Constance again?

Father put his arm over my shoulder. "Don't fret, my boy. Of course, it all hinges on Straton's acceptance of our proposition, but if he knows what's good for him, he will."

SHORTLY AFTER BREAKFAST, at which the whole family (including Ernest) gathered for the first time in several days, Father, Mother, and I ascended the stairs to Mr. Straton's room.

Although staring was against social convention, I couldn't help doing so given his transformation. He had been bathed, shaved, and provided with fresh clothes. The scent of soap hung in the air. His features were still gaunt, given his long period of unconsciousness, but his eyes were bright and clear. Had I not known better, I would have never guessed he'd been at death's door only three days before.

Constance, too, had been given some attention. Copper tints shone in her cleaned and brushed hair. She also wore a starched apron over a clean dress. When I entered the room, our gazes met, and a hint of pink colored her cheeks. A moment later, my face burned as well, and I was glad I was behind my parents so they didn't observe my reaction to her.

Straton made a move to stand, but Father raised his hand to stay the man.

"No need to rise. Save your strength," he said and turned to Constance. "I would appreciate it if you would give us a moment, child. We have some things to discuss with your father."

She glanced at each of us. When she got to me, I tried to reassure her with a smile, but she only nodded and left, head down, without a word.

After she closed the door, Father said, "Straton, my whole family has worked very hard to keep you and your family united, and with your understanding, this whole ordeal might lead to a new life for you. If you are willing to accept certain conditions."

He studied my father through his eyes' narrowed slits. "What exactly would these conditions be?"

Father pulled on his vest before beginning. "First, I need your word you will become a better father than you have been. Of utmost importance, no liquor. You did not always have this problem, and we'll not stand by and allow you to drink yourself to death. If you continue on the path you're on, your children will be taken to an orphanage or the poor house with you. Either way, you'll have lost your family."

"I-I don't know about no drink. I can't abide those teetotalers."

Mother spoke up. "You have survived the last few days without alcohol. You simply have to keep it up."

"As long as you remain sober," Father said, "I have a proposition for you."

He glanced at Mother who nodded for him to continue. "I'll pay off your debts, and you will come and work for me. Our steward, Simpson, is getting on in years. He could use another hand to help out. Once your debt is paid off, we'll increase your salary."

His eyes shifted as he studied first my mother and then Father. "Why would you do this for me?"

Mother spoke in a low voice. "Remember, we asked you to keep an open mind. Mr. Brown took something from my greenhouse. A plant. Hemlock. And gave it to his wife, Rachel Winston, and... Mrs. Straton. In a way, I feel responsible."

He stared at her, obviously weighing the information they had just presented. After a long silence, he said, "You're no more responsible than if he'd gotten it elsewhere."

"You must honor her memory by caring for your family."

"Family. Right." He paused and then asked, "You ain't going to make me sign one of them pledges, are you?"

"Only if you feel it necessary."

He screwed up his face as if he were about to be shot and nodded. "All right. No drink. For my family."

He held out his hand, and Father took it.

CHAPTER FOURTEEN

My parents and I stood on the village platform with Mycroft, awaiting the train's arrival. He bounced on the balls of his feet, stretching to see if the train had appeared. As much as he looked forward to leaving, I anticipated staying. I already had arranged a meeting with Constance in the schoolroom to begin her music lessons.

"I suppose it won't be long until we see you again," Mother said. "After all, Christmas is right around the corner."

"Hmm?" asked Mycroft, checking the tracks one more time. "Yes. Christmas. I'll be back then I suppose."

Father pulled back his chin. "Where else would you go?"

"Nowhere, I guess. It's just...I do have friends, you

know. And they have been hinting at inviting me to visit. Some even live in London."

Mycroft's statement about friends pulled my attention in his direction. Given the rather isolated life of the country squire, I assumed he had remained as reticent at school as he did at home. He had created the Diogenes Society at Eton to mimic the solitude of our father's library. But then, he had done this in concert with other students. Perhaps he had done a better job at making friends than I?

My postponed return to Eton might actually offer me an opportunity to work on doing just that. I considered Constance my friend, and I could learn a lot about being one from continuing our acquaintance over the next few months. If nothing else, Constance would be honest enough to let me know what I needed to do to be a friend.

A far-off whistle announced the train's approach to the station, and Mycroft craned his neck one more time to confirm it. The others waiting on the platform with us moved about, gathering valises and other items in preparation for boarding, and my brother followed suit.

Shortly after, he turned to step into the train's compartment after shaking Father's and my hands and accepting a chaste kiss on the cheek from Mother. She placed a hand on his arm to detain him for a final word. He faced us, but his gaze darted toward the train.

"Mycroft, dear," she said, "I wanted to thank you again. I realize it was difficult for you to tear yourself from your studies, but your presence—and support—proved invaluable. I trust you won't find yourself too far behind."

He shifted on his feet, from eagerness to be on the train or embarrassment at Mother's public declaration, I couldn't be sure. Then he stilled and said, "I'm glad I could be of service. I have to say, it was quite stimulating to apply my knowledge to real situations. I'll write. Keep you informed of my progress."

With that, he jumped onto the train and leaned out the window after closing the door to wave at us as the locomotive pulled away from the station.

In the carriage on the way home, both my parents grew quiet, and Mother dabbed her eyes more than once.

MRS. SIMPSON WAS WAITING for us when we arrived. She pointed to the parlor.

"They're waiting in there for you."

Mr. Straton and Constance stood when we entered. Straton pulled the cap off his head and ducked it slightly before addressing my father.

"I came like you asked. To sign the contract."

Father cleared his throat and studied him for a moment. "Right. Come into my office. I have the papers ready."

After the two men left, Mother turned to Constance. "Are you starting your music lessons today?"

"Yes, Mrs. Holmes." A broad smile split my friend's face. "He promised to teach me to read music, too."

"You have a good teacher. He is quite accomplished at the violin. Perhaps in the future, all three of us can work on some pieces together. I play the pianoforte, you know."

"I'd like that very much."

"We'll be in the schoolroom," I said, taking our leave of my mother. "Follow me, Constance."

When we left the parlor, we fairly ran into my father and Mr. Straton in the hallway.

"You'll find Simpson in the barn. Have him get the wagon ready to bring over the hives. I've been reading up on how to transport them, and I think if we're careful, we can do it without mishap."

My eyes widened at the last word. "Are you bringing the bees here?"

I knew my father had decided to take over Brown's apiculture efforts. He'd noted a few days ago the village still needed someone to raise bees. Not only did they supply honey, they also served a major function in the spring in the fruit orchards. And he considered it an extension of his life-long study of insects. Until this moment, I hadn't given this announcement much thought. The realization that he meant to keep the bees on our property, which was both the sensible and logical choice, sent a shiver down my spine. The bee stings I'd suffered in my escape from Mr. Brown were still visible. I might not be allergic like Mr. Harvingsham, but I still had no desire to spend any time among them.

He chuckled and patted my back. "Don't worry, son. They'll be in the back field for the winter, and we'll be loaning the hives to the neighbors in the spring. Besides, we *do* have protective gear to keep us safe."

While I nodded in agreement, I wasn't completely convinced. At the same time, I relished the idea of working with my father, and so I thought perhaps a few bee stings were worth it.

"I'm going to change into work clothes," he told Straton. "I'll meet you at the wagon. After the bees are settled, the vicar has asked you pass by for your children. I understand his wife will be returning with you to meet with Mrs. Holmes. Something about seeking her advice regarding..." He glanced at Constance and me and cleared his throat. "She wants to consult with my wife."

I smiled, knowing Vicar and Mrs. Evans had obviously determined a large family wasn't necessarily the blessing he had always preached.

Father turned toward the stairs, but when I went to follow him, Straton placed a hand on my arm.

"I never truly thanked you for saving my life that night. I still don't remember anything after leaving the tavern, but I do recall lying there in the cold and thinking I couldn't die and leave my children with no parents. Thank you." He thrust out his hand, and I took it. After shaking it, his grip tightened and his gaze met mine. "I know about the music lessons, and that you've been seeing a lot of my Constance. If your intentions turn out not to be honorable, no amount of skill on your mother's part will be enough to save you."

I swallowed and nodded. "Understood, sir."

He turned on his heel and went toward the back of the house to arrange for the wagon.

In the schoolroom, I pointed to the blackboard, which had lost the information Mother had entered on the victims and now contained five parallel lines. "I thought we'd start with the treble clef. Each line represents a note on the scale, E. G. B. D. F."

"What's that? Eegeebee?"

"Names of notes. Like the letters."

"I don't know my letters."

"Didn't you go to school?"

She shook her head. "My mama needed me to help with the children."

I paused. How could I teach her to read music if she couldn't read at all?

After a moment, I walked to the bookcase and pulled out a book and handed it to her.

"For me?" she asked.

"We'll work on your letters too. And writing."

She opened to the first page with a drawing on it and sighed. "Ooo, I can't wait to find out what this house is all about."

In a move so quick and unexpected, I had no time to react, she pulled me forward into a strong embrace, the opened book forming a barrier between us. "Thank you, Sherlock," she whispered into my ear, "for everything. For my father…for me."

She planted a kiss on my cheek.

Her lips were as soft as I remembered, and a warm rush flooded my body. I stiffened in defense of this sensation, and she must have felt the change because she pulled away, her own cheeks deepening in color.

"Tell me about the letters."

I took the book from her and turned to a drawing of an elephant. "This is the *e*."

As she studied the page and traced the letter with her finger, I raised my hand to the spot on my cheek where her lips had touched, re-experiencing the same rush of affection.

Somehow, I knew she was more than just a friend.

I also knew that despite the gruesome aspects of the three village women's deaths, the whole ordeal had brought my family together in ways I couldn't have imagined. As evil as it sounded, I truly hoped for another mystery to keep us close.

ACKNOWLEDGMENTS

I began this project more than seven years ago, and had a great deal of help along the way. Many eyes viewed earlier versions of this manuscript, and I am grateful to all their comments, remarks, and corrections. I would like to especially thank the following: Nancy Alvey, Vicki Batman, Karilyn Bentley, Diane Kelly, Chris Keniston, Liz Lipperman, Steve Mason, Sandy Rice, Richard Schmidt, and Lori Weber. A special shout-out goes to Brenda Hutchinson's eagle eye for details. In addition, I received comments from numerous anonymous reviewers in contests where I entered the manuscript as well as from agents and editors who shared their views on earlier drafts. Finally, a special thanks to Alicia at iProofread and More for her final polish. Any errors that remain are my own.

ABOUT THE AUTHOR

Liese Sherwood-Fabre knew she was destined to write when she got an A+ in the second grade for her story about Dick, Jane, and Sally's ruined picnic. After obtaining her PhD from Indiana University, she joined the federal government and had the opportunity to work and live internationally for more than fifteen years. After returning to the states, she seriously pursued her writing career. She is currently a member of The Crew of the Barque Lone Star and the Studious Scarlets Society scions and contributes regularly to Sherlockian newsletters across the world.

You can follow her upcoming releases and other events by joining her newsletter at
www.liesesherwoodfabre.com

THE ADVENTURE OF THE DECEASED SCHOLAR

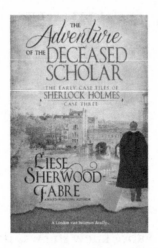

Before Sherlock Holmes became the world's greatest consulting detective...

The discovery of two bodies disrupted the 1868 Oxford-Cambridge boat race.

When Mycroft Holmes identifies the body of a drowning victim, the Holmes family is drawn into a scandal that could destroy not only the deceased's name, but their reputation as well. Sherlock and his family have only a few days before the coroner's inquest to explain Lord Phillips' demise. If it is ruled a suicide, the Phillips family assets will be returned to the Crown, leaving them destitute. Should that happen, Miss Phillips, the victim's sister, has threatened to drag Mycroft's good name through the mire as well. Will Sherlock be able determine what happened before more than one family is destroyed?

THE LIFE AND TIMES OF SHERLOCK HOLMES,
VOLUME THREE

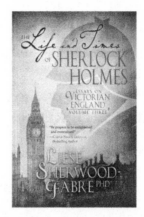

*"[P]repare to delve into a charming set of illustrated
guidebooks to Holmes and his 1895 London."*
- Carole Nelson Douglas, Bestselling Author

This third collection of essays provides additional
insights into English life of the late 1800s. During this
era, gas and electric lights appeared, the telephone made
its debut (although Holmes seemed to prefer the
telegram), and the gramophone recorded Sherlock
playing his own Stradivarius violin. Holmes enjoyed
attending the opera at Covent Garden, reviewing the
agony columns, and keeping his own scrapbooks.
Medical issues included yellow fever and diabetes. And
murderers included jellyfish, snakes, and the Italian-
American import of the Carbonari. In all, twenty-four
articles address aspects of everyday Victorian life from
the mundane (cardboard) to the singular (the Crown
Jewels)—a little something for everyone.

As an added bonus, Volume Three includes a reprint of
Dr. Sherwood-Fabre's Baker Street Journal article on
"Evil Women: The Villainesses of the Canon."

EXCERPT FROM "THE ADVENTURE OF THE MURDERED GYPSY"

Mother pivoted, swung her foot, and hit her opponent squarely on the jaw. The man landed on his back against the wooden floorboards with enough force to send tremors through the soles of my feet.

Mr. Moto raised himself onto one elbow and rubbed the side of his face with his other hand. "Very good."

Mother extended her hand to our *baritsu* instructor, but he waved it away. "I'm quite amazed," she said, "at the freedom of movement these Turkish trousers allow."

I couldn't argue with her statement. The blousy coverings permitted full use of her legs—something her skirts had never done. At the same time, I found them rather unsettling. Until she had introduced the garment for our lessons, I had not seen her lower extremities, and certainly not in motion. I also couldn't help but wonder what our instructor thought of her visible, albeit covered, limbs.

On the other hand, both he and I bared most of our legs. The traditional *baritsu* costume, or *gi*, consisted of a loose, long-sleeved white tunic that all but covered a pair of very short pants.

When he rose to his feet, I was struck again by our instructor's diminutive size. He matched my mother closely in height and weight, but I had learned at our first lesson his stature did not indicate his strength when it came to defending himself.

Of course, my mother was rather tall compared to many women in our village. Slim and dark-haired, I was told repeatedly how much I resembled her.

"Your turn, Master Sherlock."

By this time, I'd gotten used to his accent and enjoyed how he pronounced my name, roughening the *l* almost into an *r*.

I took the traditional opening stance, but before I could bow, Trevor entered, leaving my uncle's workshop open to the winter air. My seven-year-old cousin stood just inside, almost as if he were afraid to enter. The cold air rushed in, causing goose bumps to break out on my legs.

"I was told to come and get you. Cousin Mycroft is here."

"How wonderful," my mother said. "I know he'll want

to freshen up from his trip, so we'll be there shortly. Sherlock was about to have a go at this new move. If you wish to stay and watch, you may. But please shut the door."

Once we were no longer exposed to the elements, I bowed to our trainer and prepared to imitate the kick my mother had just executed.

Trevor spoke up behind my back. "But Mother said you were to come directly and bring Uncle Ernest with you because a friend of his has come too."

I turned my back to Mr. Moto to ask my cousin to repeat the statement. In all my years, I couldn't recall a single time my quite, private uncle had received a visitor. Before I could voice this observation, my instructor swept his leg behind mine, flipping my feet out from under me and the rest of me toward the floor. The air rushed out of my lungs with a *whoosh*. I wasn't sure which hurt more, my back or my pride, when I heard Trevor giggle.

My instructor's face hovered over mine. "Are you all right, Master Sherlock?"

I nodded and accepted his hand to pull myself up.

Once righted, he pointed a finger at me. "Never turn your back on an opponent."

My cheeks burned from his reproach. While he might have overplayed his point, he was correct in demonstrating I had given him the advantage. I had no time to note this because Mother spoke again.

"A friend of Ernest's? That does put a different wrinkle on things." She tilted her head to one side, as if weighing this new information, and turned to Moto. "I'm afraid, then, we'll have to cut our lesson short today. Let's continue tomorrow, shall we?" She glanced at me. "Sherry, dear, please collect your uncle from the barn and join us in the parlor. We'll see you at dinner, Mr. Moto."

The man bowed low. "Until then."

Retrieving my pants from a nearby workbench, I pulled them on over my *gi*.

When I turned to go, Trevor asked, "Might I go with you?"

I hesitated in my response, seeking a socially acceptable excuse to avoid including him. To be honest, I found the boy annoying. I was, after all, six—about to be seven—years his senior, yet he insisted on following me everywhere. Since he'd arrived two days ago, whenever I turned around, I found him staring at me with wide eyes and a slight smile on his face.

Mother solved my quandary, although not in the fashion I'd hoped. "An excellent idea. Trevor's been asking to see the horses. This will give him an opportunity to do so."

With a sigh, I bowed once again to Moto and moved to the door, where I jammed my feet into my boots and wrapped a scarf about my neck. "Come on, then I need to change before dinner."

The boy's delight was obvious. He bounced next to me and kept up a running commentary as we made our way to the stables. He noted how cold it was, how we could see our breath, and didn't he resemble a dragon when he blew out through his nostrils, and how quiet it was here in the country. I considered pointing out the last was difficult to note with his persistent jabbering, but instead, let my mind wander, providing various grunts and other noncommittal noises while he nattered on. My ill humor was only partly related to his constant tagging along. Another portion reflected the humiliation I'd just experienced at the hands, or rather the feet, of Mr. Moto.

The majority, however, involved Mycroft's arrival. While he'd been away at university, I'd been able to relax in a way I found difficult when he was at home. His criticisms of my violin practicing; constant corrections to my French, German, and Latin pronunciations; and complaints about any noise I made that disturbed his thinking always kept me on guard. With his return, I would have to, once again, increase my caution. Not that I didn't like my brother. We had certainly developed a greater appreciation for each other when our family had solved a murder and freed my mother from gaol a bare three months ago. He simply wasn't the easiest person to get along with.

As we neared the barn, I stopped and turned to Trevor. "Can you repeat what you just said?"

"I said the woman visitor was very pretty."

Thankfully, I was no longer in the middle of a *baritsu* lesson because Moto would have kicked me onto my back for a second time as I stared dumbfounded at my cousin. Uncle Ernest's friend a woman? And pretty? I didn't recall

Ernest ever mentioning a woman, other than once, and she had been the daughter of an Indian royal.

"Is she an Englishwoman?"

When he nodded, I quickened my pace. I had to get my uncle back to the house to see his female friend for myself.

Made in United States
Orlando, FL
10 December 2021

11471266R00211